8/22

HOW WE RICOCHET

FAITH GARDNER

HARPER TEEN
An Imprint of HarperCollinsPublishers

Also by
FAITH GARDNER

Girl on the Line
The Second Life of Ava Rivers
Perdita

HarperTeen is an imprint of HarperCollins Publishers.

How We Ricochet
Copyright © 2022 by Faith Gardner
All rights reserved. Printed in the United States of America.
No part of this book may be used or reproduced in any manner
whatsoever without written permission except in the case of
brief quotations embodied in critical articles and reviews. For
information address HarperCollins Children's Books, a division of
HarperCollins Publishers, 195 Broadway, New York, NY 10007.
www.epicreads.com

ISBN 978-0-06-302235-5

Typography by Torborg Davern
22 23 24 25 26   PC/LSCH   10 9 8 7 6 5 4 3 2 1
❖
First Edition

For Roxanna Tulip and Zora Firelily

PART ONE

ONE

BREAKING: 1 DEAD, 4 INJURED IN RETAIL STORE SHOOTING

In the hospital, everything is clean, eggshell white, and the TV is stuck on local news. Onscreen, police in midnight-blue uniforms swarm the front of a fashion store. I Glam, the store's sign reads. Yellow tape embraces the store's broken front window display, where bald mannequins strike poses in the latest styles, innocent and oblivious to the shattered glass and emergency vehicles around them. Meanwhile, onlookers point and capture it all on phones. The news ticker reads: *MAN DEAD AFTER MASS SHOOTING IN EMERYVILLE MALL.*

Takes a moment for it to sink in: the gunman is the dead man, the injured are the women I heard him shoot, the retail store is the last place I visited.

I was there.

Holy shit, look at the news footage: I *am* there. I am standing next to my mother and sister, crying. It's as if, for a moment, I'm the audience of my own life.

There's no one in this room but me and my sister and a machine hooked up to her, emitting metronomic beeps. She's in a gown and a pair of no-slip socks, dozed off and breathing heavy. Her name is written on a whiteboard, *Joy Maple Lavelle.* I don't know what time it is, exactly, but the windows, curtainless, are pitch black. The whole gruesome scene floods back to me, and I sit for a moment in disbelief. This cannot be. *1 DEAD, 4 INJURED IN RETAIL STORE SHOOTING.*

Yes, those are facts. But right now they seem like lies to me, because they are nothing close to the whole story.

TWO

The day is a backward eternity away. I worked my internship at Retrofit. My mother picked me up. Joy was already in the car. I climbed into the back seat of the battered Prius, shut the door, and asked Mom to turn down the music. It was Elvis. It was always Elvis. The CD's been stuck in her car for months and her radio is broken.

"Appreciate the ride, but if I have to hear this album again, I *will* lose it," I said.

In the rearview mirror, Mom gave me a long stare through her oversized sunglasses and turned up the volume.

"You are such a troll," I told her.

She burst out laughing and turned the music off.

"Betty," she said, "you're too easy to torment."

Without Elvis crooning about Kentucky rain, we could hear the tinny faraway sound of electronic drums and screaming wafting from Joy's headphones. Joy sat shotgun, sunglasses on. Her face didn't flicker in the side mirror. No signs of life.

"Hi, Joy," I said.

Silence.

"Great to see you, too," I said.

My sister is a badass. She rides a motorcycle. She plays bass guitar. She gave herself a poke-and-stick tattoo of a black heart on her wrist. She supersedes me by almost three years and an infinity of coolness.

Mom was pulled up in the loading zone of a bus stop with her hazards on, and at that moment, a car pulled next to us and honked.

"Excuse me, I don't like to be hurried!" Mom yelled.

She peeled away from the curb in her usual way. Heads probably turned. I long ago had to stop caring if anyone stared when my mother was around, or I'd have been caring all the damn time. My mother is beautiful—and loud.

"Want to go to the mall?" Mom asked then. "I need new blouses. Apparently my business casual is too much casual, not enough business."

"They told you that?"

"They sent out a memo about jeans today. I'm the only person on the floor who dares to wear jeans."

After working for years in the office of my old middle school, Mom started a new job working as an executive assistant at a finance company this week. It pays better, so maybe her days of broken CD players and rent-controlled apartments are numbered.

"Does it have to be the mall?" I asked.

"Where else am I going to get clothes at 5:11 p.m. on a Thursday?" Mom said. After I responded with silence, she added, "I'll buy you both dinner after."

"Deal."

At rush hour in the Bay Area, traffic was at its usual standstill. So much merging. So much honking. On one side, beyond, there were the lush green hills; on the other, the glimmering bay with its silver bridge, silhouettes of skyscrapers. We made it to Emeryville a little before six. We parked on the third floor in the garage at Bay Street, the outdoor mall that is a long, narrow lane composed of chain stores with apartments above. We took the elevator. Joy complained about the mall, and I joined in, and Mom threatened to not buy us dinner if we didn't stop because she hates the mall too and she'd just "driven through vehicular Hades."

Small details I remember now that everything is different:

We went into I Glam first. Mom walked around squinting at labels on pants with her reading glasses on, murmuring words like *bootcut* like she was learning a new language. Joy went riffling through black lace underwear. Nothing seemed off. Teenagers trying on bras over their clothes and giggling; a woman talking on her phone on speaker; some zombie-eyed employees folding leggings. I told Joy and Mom that I was going next door to the cupcake shop. I took my time. I sat and unwrapped a vanilla cupcake with salted caramel frosting and scrolled on my phone at a confetti-patterned plastic table. I took a bite and closed my eyes, the salt and sugar together a drug. I could hear the music from I Glam next door, an earworm about living in the moment, and the sound of the girl behind the register humming along.

And then popping. Snapping. Like fireworks—two, three, four. I opened my eyes. The girl behind the counter had stopped humming.

"Shit, that sound like a gun to you?" she asked.

THREE

Mom joins me in the hospital room after her exam. She's fine, in a way, and in another way, she'll probably never be fine again. She's pale from shock, mascara smudged. She gets angry that the news is on, and when I tell her, gently, there is no remote, she rips the cord out of the wall. Then she collapses in my arms and cries, and I cry too, even though I don't feel I have the same right to cry as she does. I wasn't in the store when it happened. I didn't see anyone get shot in front of me. I didn't hide in the middle of a clothes rack and whisper prayers into my hands for five minutes that stretched into a nightmarish eternity.

When Mom and I pull apart, both our shoulders are wet and stained black from each other's makeup and tears.

"I can't believe this happened," she keeps saying.

I nod.

"We were just *shopping,*" she goes on. "I was buying *pants* for *work.*"

I nod.

"And then he just—he just—came in and started shooting. He kept doing it and he didn't stop. How did we not get shot?"

"Did I get shot?" Joy asks from the bed.

Mom and I gasp, because Joy's awake. We rush to her side. Joy's gaze is glassy and thick, her eyes smaller than usual. She pulls her blankets off her legs, looking for wounds.

"No, no, no," Mom tells her. "You whacked your head trying to hide under a counter."

Joy touches her head.

"You fell down," Mom says. "You played dead."

"But I didn't get shot?" she asks.

"You don't even have a concussion," Mom says. "They sedated you because you were hysterical when the paramedics arrived."

Joy knits her dark brows. "Right."

We give her a moment of silence, leaving her with her thoughts. Her eyes flash. She starts breathing quickly. I put my hand on her arm, but she shakes it off.

"Joy," Mom says.

"He killed himself, I remember that part," Joy says, her voice climbing. "He was only about ten feet away from me. I tried to keep my eyes shut. I lay on the floor and I heard it happen. I opened my eyes for just a second and there was so much blood and . . . and . . . other stuff . . . and I was so happy. So happy when I saw him lying there. Because it was over."

She puts her face in her hands, and Mom wraps her arms

around her and they cry, one being, one traumatized being, and I am inept, watching them. I can't understand what they went through because I was steps—just steps—outside of it. I dig my fingers in my palms to feel anything other than this useless ache.

"How's your head feel?" Mom asks, pulling back and running her fingers through Joy's black bangs.

"Who died, Mom?" Joy asks, ignoring her question, wiping her eyes. "Other than the shooter? Did everyone in there but us die?"

"I'm not sure," Mom says. "They shuttled everyone to the hospital. I remember stretchers . . . so many stretchers . . . I don't know."

"On the news it said one dead and four injured," I tell them. "Just the gunman. The gunman is the one."

Both Joy and my mother look back at me, amazed.

"No one else died?" Mom asks. "Are you serious?"

"As far as I know," I say.

"We're fucking lucky," Joy says. "There were so many bullets. We should have died."

"I'm so glad you're okay," Mom says, holding Joy's head to her chest. Joy closes her eyes and her lips turn downward as she fights tears. It's not a fight she wins.

"I'm so glad you're *both* okay," I say.

I feel dumb crying, but I guess I always feel dumb crying. I grab a box of tissues and little cups of water for them, and we sit in silence for a few minutes, sipping, blowing noses, taking deep breaths until the weeping turns to sniffing turns to sighing turns to quiet again. A shared quiet. I go look out the window. The city has never looked more exquisite—tall buildings lit with eyes of yellow light, a dark park scattered with oak trees—because we are alive.

"Knock, knock," a nurse says, opening the door.

Mom and I wipe our eyes and sit on the chairs.

The nurse walks in with squeaky shoes. She tells us her name is Candelaria. She's got long hair in a braid down her back, cartoon characters on her scrubs, a tattoo of a cross on her strong forearm.

"How you doing?" she asks Joy with concern.

"I'm fine. How are all the others?" Joy asks.

Candelaria doesn't answer. She studies the beeping machine, seems satisfied, pulls a monitor off my sister's fingertip.

"The other people in the shooting," Mom reiterates.

"I really don't know details about all the patients admitted here," Candelaria says, switching the machine off and wheeling it a few feet away into a corner. "It's been hella hectic. But I have a police officer in the hall who wants to check in with you—just wanted to make sure you're awake and up for it."

"Sure," says Joy.

"I'll let him know."

"I feel weird," Joy says. "Like I'm not even here. This isn't even real."

"They gave you something to calm you down; it made you sleepy." Candelaria pats Joy's blanket-covered foot. "You're going to be okay."

She's right, of course she is, but it seems a weak thing to say.

I leave the room so Joy and my mom can talk to the police. I already talked to the police on the scene and told them what I saw: nothing. I just heard the shots.

I go into the waiting room, which is bright and busy. Seems like everyone's murmuring about the shooting. The TVs in the upper corners of this room are also stuck on Channel 3, and we're all mesmerized by it. There's some of the same footage as before, interspersed with other scenes that look to have been filmed outside this very hospital. The words 1 DEAD, 3 INJURED IN MALL SHOOTING, 1 IN CRITICAL CONDITION sit at the bottom of the screen. Critical condition— that doesn't sound good.

Then there's a man's picture with the words GUNMAN IDENTIFIED.

I gasp. There he is—the gunman—only he looks more like a boy here, and there's no gun; he's flashing a smile in an official-looking picture, a senior portrait, maybe. He has acne. He has long eyelashes.

I've seen him before.

FOUR

It's been only three months since I graduated high school, only three weeks since I turned eighteen, but it seems longer. Gone are the days divided up into six periods, the heavy backpacks, the cafeteria lunches, the seas of familiar but not necessarily friendly faces. I walked by my high school recently when I was in downtown Berkeley, and the place looked different, like it had a fresh coat of paint, and the kids standing on the corner still had baby fat on their cheeks. I thought, was it only months ago? Was it only last year? It seems a summer can contain a lifetime.

Joshua Lee went to my high school. He was in Joy's class, two years ahead of me. I never knew him or spoke to him that I can think of, but we were in so many places at the same time, and I can see him now, trudging through the halls: his greasy hair a little longer than his ears, his scowl, his acne scars, his ROTC uniform. I knew nothing about him except he was the guy who started a fire in a trash can at lunch and got suspended. Some rumor floated around about him sexually harassing a teacher. Suffice to say he emanated a *steer clear* vibe, as some do, and I obliged. His little brother, Michael, was in my grade and was someone I'd existed beside since freshman year—an English class, a bio class. But we hardly interacted. Michael struck me as sweet, but shy as hell. Joshua, though, was off. You could see it on his face.

Or maybe I'm just saying that now that I know he tried to kill a bunch of people.

The truth is I shared a school with him for two years, passed him by probably hundreds of times, stood behind him in line waiting for burritos, sat steps away from his brother in multiple classes, and I've only ever really stopped to think about him right now, when I see his face flashing across a news segment on a waiting room TV with the words *GUNMAN IDENTIFIED* plastered below.

How incredibly fucked up is that?

FIVE

Joy gets discharged from the hospital. We take a Lyft ride back to where my mom's car sits in the nearly empty mall parking lot. We say nothing, but hold hands, squeezing tight as we hurry toward the Prius. When we get in the car and shut the doors, something about the car feels so safe and familiar, we exhale in harmony.

It takes my mother three tries to get the car started. Mom turns on the stereo and her CD player lights up, Elvis crooning about suspicious minds. Joy and I both yell in unison.

"Mom," I say.

"Mother," Joy says.

Mom turns it off and drives. We don't say anything as she leaves the mall complex. It's barely even ten o'clock. I can't believe not even five hours ago we were heading here. It feels like three a.m. We pull out onto the dark streets. None of us look backward, behind us, where the mall is, where the shooting happened. We look ahead, at the road that flows before us like a black river. The traffic lights so bright, they have halos around them. The holy glow of megastore signs. Even the moon up there, a jaundiced blue, almost full.

Everything is different.

We drive by chic warehouses and brick buildings and coffee shops with shuttered windows. *Welcome to Oakland*, a sign says, and just as soon as you see that one you see another that says *Welcome to Berkeley*. The sound of those gunshots and that picture of Joshua Lee's face on TV. Imagine hiding in a rack of clothes or lying on the floor pretending to be dead. It makes me sick, though not in my stomach, not in the way you think; my heart is nauseated.

None of us are saying anything. It's not like us, such quiet. I wait for them to talk, because I don't know what to say anymore.

"Drive-through?" Mom asks.

"Sure," Joy says.

"Sounds good," I say.

We eat hamburgers and fries in silence in the parking lot. I taste nothing. Even though the earth is still spinning and my sister and my mother are alive and well. Even though the smell of the dumpster coming in through the open passenger window and the man pushing a shopping cart full of bootleg DVDs down the sidewalk and the woman on a bike drunkenly yelling into the drive-through speaker are a miracle.

Now I know how precious, how delicate, how dangerous the world really is.

It's a wonder any of us survive.

SIX

I don't know what I was thinking, grabbing my purse and fleeing the cupcake store as the popping continued. Running full speed *toward* the sound. Actually, I do. I was a zombie seized by panic, and I had only two things on my mind: my mother, my sister.

Outside, on the pavement in front of the store, the popping sounds grew louder. I was still counting. Seven, eight, nine. I didn't know what to do, where to go. I stood frozen under the just-lit streetlamps, a few other people also frozen around me with shopping bags in hand, all of us looking at each other for an answer. Where was it coming from? Was this real life? Were we in danger? People started screaming from inside I Glam, and I was instantly ill. I was standing next to the window, but all I saw were mannequins through the glass. A couple people around me broke into a run in the opposite direction up the street, someone called the police and started shouting, and I dropped to the ground. I lay there even as I heard a window shatter. I lost count of the pops. I closed my eyes. All I could think was *My sister, my mother, my sister, my mother—*

My sister, my mother, and I, we're all going to die.

I heard sirens. The popping got faster for a minute and then it stopped altogether. I lay there with my eyes shut like a kid in a nightmare, because I *was* a kid in a nightmare. The police and the fire engines pulled up and someone asked me if I was okay. I didn't want to open my eyes. I didn't want to witness a world where someone would shoot my family dead. But when I opened them, a firefighter was escorting my mom and sister out the front door, stepping over broken glass. Then I sobbed.

SEVEN

We open the front door, flip the switch. The living room's gold lamplight seems so bright. Our books (our mother's books) with the rainbow spines in the built-in bookcases, the sagging couch with the cheerful throw, the birdcage in the corner with a candle in it—our home feels unfamiliar at first. Joy goes straight to the bathroom and I hear the shower running. I follow Mom into the kitchen. She puts her purse down and starts going through the mail like it's any other day, only it's yesterday's mail, and it's already opened. She puts it down and goes to the window and pulls the curtain aside. The window looks onto our side yard. It looks onto our neighbor's trash cans. It's nighttime and you can't even see anything anyway.

"Mom," I ask, standing behind her. "What are you looking at?"

She doesn't answer me.

"Mom," I try again.

I hate how I sound, like I'm four, like I need her reassurance.

"Are you going to be okay?" I ask.

"Yes, Bets."

"Are you sure?"

She turns to me. The emotion has evaporated the day's makeup off her face and visibly exhausted her. My mom is inches shorter than me. I don't often notice, because she's a creature constantly in motion, and she is commanding. But I notice it now. Her eyes fill, but don't rain.

"I'm angry," she says. "I'm so fucking angry right now."

"Really?" I ask, surprised.

I don't know why I'm so surprised. I expected her to be upset—but with fear. Sadness. Not rage.

"I've never been so angry in my life," she says. "That . . ." She searches for the word. "*Piece of shit* almost killed me and my daughter today. And why? Why us, *why*? We didn't do anything to him."

I open my mouth, but she keeps talking.

"You know, I've lived through so much—I've worked so hard—to have that taken from me? In a stupid I Glam store when I'm buying some"—(air quotes)—"'business casual' clothes for a stupid job I hardly even want to work in the first place?"

I am tempted to take a step back from my mom's rage like it's a blazing fire. But I don't. My mom's a force. She has

19

opinions. She has a slight temper sometimes—might snip at us if she's in a mood. This, here? Is entirely something else.

"We went to high school with him," I tell her.

"You—with the *shooter*?"

"Yeah."

She cocks her head. "How do you know that?"

"I saw his picture on TV in the hospital waiting room when you were talking to the cops."

"I didn't know that," she says. "That seems . . . like it should matter."

"Did Joy say anything to the cop, like she recognized him?"

"No. No, she did not," Mom says.

"It's not like we knew him," I say. "He was just a kid at our high school."

Mom opens the fridge and peers inside with a confused look on her face, then closes it again.

"Shit," she says. "Your father. I have to try to call your father again."

"Good luck with that," I tell her. "You might be better off with telepathy."

My dad is somewhere in Spain right now leading one of his "digital detox" retreats. People pay him a ridiculous amount of money to hand over their devices and drink green smoothies and do weird breathing exercises and get high for ten days. My dad is a guru. He has a website with his smiling picture on it, trim beard and glowing eyes as he sits in easy pose. His website features blurbs from people who speak wonders about the enlightenment he delivers. Right now, I miss him. But there is nothing unfamiliar about missing him.

I head back to my room, hearing the beginning of her phone call.

"Hello, is this Sequoia? Hi, I got your phone number from the Namaste House people. I'm trying to reach Kyle. Yes, Teacher Kyle. Yes, I know he's currently 'unplugged. . . .'"

I close my door behind me. I change into my pajamas and check my phone. I have two messages—one from Adrian, one from Zoe—both people who don't have any idea that my sister and mother almost died today. Who knows if the news in Seattle and New York City even picked up the story. I don't open their messages. It's late. What would I say? I log on to social media, and people—mostly fellow classmates from my high school—are sharing a local news article about the shooting. The story's picture features I Glam swarmed with police, yellow tape, broken glass, gurneys, crying faces.

I click.

4 INJURED, 1 DEAD IN EMERYVILLE MALL SHOOTING

Alameda County, Ca.—A man armed with an assault rifle opened fire in an I Glam store in Emeryville's Bay Street mall, shooting four. An additional victim was later treated for minor injuries. The gunman died by suicide at the scene of the crime.

The shooting started around 5:45 p.m. on Thursday evening and lasted fewer than ten minutes. The weapon and bullets found on scene match an AR15 assault weapon. The sheriff's office reports the assault weapon experienced a technical malfunction, after which the shooter used an additional handgun he carried to shoot himself. He was pronounced dead when police arrived.

The mall is one of the most frequented shopping sites in the East Bay area.

The injured victims were taken to Kaiser in Oakland. Sgt. Cecilia Garcia says the shooting victims were "shaken and in serious condition," with one victim in critical condition and requiring emergency surgery.

The shooting started in the center of the store near the dressing rooms. I Glam is an all-women's apparel store.

"It is horrific that the gunman opened fire in a public place like this, among families, women, teens, and children. Mall employees, witnesses, and the larger community are understandably shaken to their core by this," Garcia said.

The sheriff's office said there were dozens of witnesses both inside and outside the building.

"My guardian angel was nearby today," I Glam manager Desiree Johnson said. "The bullets whizzed right past my face. I heard it in my ear, like a wasp buzzing."

A man who asked not to be identified said he could see the active shooting from outside the window and ran.

"I couldn't believe it—like, for real?" the man said. "Then I heard the sound—peeked through the window and saw that dude walking around just spraying bullets like he thought he was Scarface."

One woman, twenty-five-year-old Emma Farooqi, broadcast the shooting live on social media from her smartphone. She was locked in an I Glam dressing room.

"I don't know why I did it," she said. "I thought maybe someone would see it and call for help. I just wanted a record of it, for my family to know what happened, in case I didn't make it."

The shooter has been identified as twenty-one-year-old local Joshua Lee. The motive is yet unclear.

My heart races as I come to the end of the article. The very act of reading it feels like something I shouldn't be doing, some violation, but why? I was there. This is a news article, meant for public consumption. It's weird to see my sister described as an "additional victim." It's weird to be retold the details that comprise the worst day of my life in such an objective, calm tone, as if this kind of thing happens every day.

Which, I suppose, it does.

EIGHT

Right now it's late morning in Spain. They're nine hours ahead. My dad is probably drinking herbal tea or doing sun salutations. "Be here now" is what I imagine he'd say if he were here now. This is a thing he says often. In fact, he has it tattooed on his left wrist in cursive. I think of that tattoo often, though not probably in the way he means it.

I spent the last ten years since their divorce wishing he were around—wishing Joy and I could be as compelling as an Indian pilgrimage or ayahuasca retreats in the Peruvian jungle. It wasn't until I graduated that something clicked. I looked at the crowded bleachers where my mother sat in a giant red sunhat you could probably spot from outer space, Joy a black-clad, bad-postured figure beside her. He's not coming back, I realized. Not ever. And even if he did, it's too late now. He's someone I know from email, from video chats, from an occasional belated and shockingly misspelled birthday card. I haven't seen him in person since I was eight years old. I grew up without his nearness. My mother, my sister—they're all I have. And they are enough.

That's what I told myself, anyway.

Maybe that wasn't true though, because now I want him, even if he's in a screen or on a phone. Even if he just tells me what Joy calls *stupid dollar-store self-help crap* like "be here now" or "watch your thoughts like leaves carried by a stream" or "concentrate on the drum of your heartbeat."

I press my palm to my chest. I am not comforted.

(*Pop. Pop-pop.* The gut-drop at those *pop-pop-pop*s.)

I can't sleep yet. I go out to the living room. Mom and Joy share the sofa in their bathrobes—Mom's pink and fuzzy, Joy's leopard print. Joy is talking intensely, in a low voice, and neither of them stop to acknowledge my presence in the room at first as I sit in the armchair next to them.

"I think it was *his* blood," Joy is saying, her voice tight.

"Well, it's off you now," Mom says.

Joy turns to me. "I scrubbed his blood off my neck."

"Gross," I say before I can stop myself. "Sorry," I recover quickly. "I mean, I'm sorry."

Joy looks so different now than she usually does—no dark makeup, her hair pulled back, her freckles apparent. She wipes her nose, her eyes. She seems to be permanently leaking.

"It was Joshua Lee," she says, looking at me.

"I know."

"That guy from our high school."

"I know."

"Mom said you said—I didn't realize."

"Yeah, it's what the news said."

She said, she said, the news said. What a strange carousel we've hitched a ride on.

"He came in—he just came in and said, 'Which bitch wants it first?' and started shooting," Joy says.

"I heard the shots from the cupcake store next door," I say.

"I didn't hear him yell that," Mom says. "I heard the gunshots, and one of the women who worked there, I saw her go down, and that's when I hid."

"I was thinking, 'Really? I'm going to die while I'm shopping for *underwear*?'" Joy says.

"I was thinking, 'I never should have taken that dumb job,'" Mom says. "'Because if it wasn't for that stupid dress code . . .'"

"You *thought* that?" I ask.

"It flashed through my mind, along with many other things," Mom says. "Mostly 'please don't kill us, please don't let this be the end.'"

"I thought, 'All these years I've seen these stories on the news, and here I am, it's happening to me,'" Joy says.

What would I have been thinking if I'd been there, feet away from a violent man with an AR15? What would have flashed through me? Instead I was feet outside, with my eyes shut, filled with nothing but fear and the thought of my mother and sister.

They don't mention thinking of me.

How selfish am I, to even think such a thing?

"I heard the gunshots and I didn't know whether to run in," I say. "I ducked, froze. I kept my eyes closed."

"Joshua Lee," Joy says. "From high school? Who *was* he, even?"

"Remember that guy who got suspended for starting a fire in a trash can?" I remind her.

"Maybe," she says.

I can tell she doesn't remember.

"But . . . why him?" Mom asks. "Do you think he had some reason to target you, Joy?"

"I never even interacted with him. I didn't recognize him or anything," she says.

"He said 'you bitches' like he had some reason to target someone," Mom says.

"Right? Like he was angry at us," Joy says.

"I don't think we're going to answer 'why' tonight," I say.

"Of course not," Mom says. "Doesn't stop us from trying."

My mom gets up and puts on a record, Blossom Dearie, an old bespectacled white lady jazz singer with a funny little voice. Mom sits next to Joy and I on the sofa, brings out a crystal decanter of bourbon and three glasses. She has never brought out bourbon, or three glasses. She rarely drinks, except when there's something to celebrate—a promotion, a graduation, us winning a case against our landlord last fall.

And never has she poured for us. She sets the glasses down on the coffee table, three clicks. Raises one eyebrow, three glugs. We bring our glasses up high in the air and don't say anything for a moment.

"To life," Mom finally says.

"To life," we repeat.

We clink. We drink. It burns. Thank goodness, the burn.

NINE

The next morning, I awaken sitting up, mid-gasp, sweat-drenched. My alarm is beeping. The room is bright with day. I put my glasses on, blink, and the room comes into focus. The reality settles in a sickening panic. The blood, the police lights—it's hard to describe the sheer terror of remembering so many awful details at once. Gunshots. Broken glass. News headlines. His face on TV.

Joshua Lee from our high school, I think.

My clothes are laid out from the night before. They look deflated, person-shaped.

(When I first saw the gurneys and the people on them I thought they were corpses.)

The alarm is still beeping.

(Sirens. So many sirens.)

I turn off the alarm and stare at my phone. There is a picture of a vintage doll I took in a thrift store, black vacant eyes and a Victorian dress. My wallpaper.

(Mannequins, standing chic in the middle of the broken-glass disaster.)

I can't do this today. I can't.

What would be worse than calling in sick to my amazing internship? Losing my shit at my amazing internship.

I call my boss, a perpetually upbeat woman named Tammy.

"Tammy speaking," she says, picking up.

I squeeze my eyes shut. "Tammy, I have to call in sick today."

"Oh no."

"Did you see the news about the I Glam shooting?"

"I did, and I *so* understand your concern. But I assure you—and this is something leadership is working up a response on *as we speak*—we take building security here *very seriously*."

"Oh." I hadn't even thought of this yet, to be honest—that because of what happened yesterday, all of us in the industry of women's clothing and retailers would be afraid of going to work now. "No."

"Oh *yes*. I'm one thousand percent serious. We're going to be getting a keypad installed *today*. And our retail store is getting metal detectors this week as well. Not that you have to worry about that, since you're in the office, but, you know, in case you *were* worried."

I'm imagining poor Tammy up all last night trying to figure out solutions to a problem no one should ever have to deal with in the first place. Tammy, guardian of interns and copywriters, who is always sending encouraging messages with disco balls and dancing pickle emojis whenever anyone does a halfway decent job, who worries about our self-care routines and if there are gluten-free snacks stocked in the break room for the one person who eats gluten-free snacks.

"I was actually at the shooting," I tell her.

It's weird to say it out loud. It's still so surreal, the truth leaves an aftertaste like a lie.

"No!" she says.

"Yeah, I'm fine."

"You weren't—you weren't *shot*, right?"

"Well, I wasn't in the store," I say. "I was outside. I heard the shots, and then I came running. . . . The glass broke." The words get stuck in my throat with the emotion. "My sister and mom were in there."

"They were? Are they . . . ?"

"They're fine."

"Oh, goodness gracious," Tammy says, her relief an audible exhale. "Oh, y'all must be shaken."

My nose burns and I beg myself not to start crying on a call with my boss. Of all the times to cry, not now. "We are."

"You take as much time as you need," Tammy says.

"I was supposed to be at that meeting about the spring line—"

"Oh, honey, it's fine. We'll take notes."

It's not that. It's that it was going to be the first early-look meeting I was allowed to attend. Early-look meetings are the first peek at the next year's big designs. It means I was going to have a shot at brainstorming with the copyeditors, a chance to maybe show people I can write and I have good ideas. A first step at maybe eventually getting hired with a real wage and benefits included.

"Thanks," I tell her. "I'll hopefully be back Monday."

TEN

I'm not stupid. I am aware the world is dangerous, that even on sunny days on the open freeway with the wind in your hair, there are car crashes; that even in the expensive neighborhoods, there are muggings and broken windows. Berkeley is a wonderland of funky houses and head shops and yoga studios, but it's got grit, too. Drug addicts nod off in People's Park, a fight erupts on a street corner, the curb glitters with broken car-window glass. Every time I ride BART past West Oakland station, I'm well aware, as the windows blacken, that we are now in the Transbay Tube, 132 feet below sea level flying at eighty miles per hour and if an earthquake hit us—

I've always been an optimist, though. Because while I have been momentarily aware of life's delicate nature, of the sadnesses down certain alleys, I keep my head up high, my breath steady, and focus on the better parts. I'm trying to do that today. I'm trying to think of how lucky we are to have survived. Instead of calculating the odds that a shooting would have happened to us in the first place, I'm trying to calculate the odds of the AR15 jamming up at that exact moment in time.

"Lucky? Fuck you, Betty," Joy tells me when I try to explain this to her.

I'm standing in her doorway. She's sitting on her bed in her robe, the light dim. Her laundry—all black—sits in a pile near her feet. Her bass guitar is in one corner, an inexplicable witch hat sits on her desk, and the only splash of color in the room is a weird painting of eyeballs floating in outer space done by her ex-boyfriend Lex.

Most people might startle at a "fuck you" from their sister, but "fuck you" is as casual a part of Joy's lexicon as "good morning" is to a normal human being. "Fuck you" is versatile; it can mean "you're annoying," "no way," or, in this case, "I disagree with your sentiment."

"How are we *lucky*?" she asks. "I watched some dude blow his brains out ten feet away from me."

"Yeah," I say.

Because, I mean, she's right.

It seems I can never say the correct thing with my sister. When she starts to cry, I come to give her a hug and she yells at me to leave her alone.

I back out, my hand on the doorknob.

"Shut it!" she says.

I stand in the hallway for a minute, listening to her cry and hating myself for never being enough for anyone. It's weird how it feels good, almost warm, a comfort, to turn this all on myself.

"She did the same thing to me," Mom tells me from her bedroom.

Our hall leading to our three bedrooms is short. If our doors are open and we're all in our rooms, we can hold a conversation in our regular voices. Mom's door is open. I glance over. She's lying on her bed, laptop open, the morning sunlight coming in and highlighting the honey-glow of her hair.

"Come in here," she says.

I oblige, sitting on the foot of her bed. She's had the same comforter since our dad left ten years ago. She traded the queen for a twin and a comforter with unicorns on it, like something a little girl would sleep in. She said she did it to prevent herself from ever making the mistake of bringing another man home into this house; so far, it's worked.

"Just leave her alone," Mom says. "You know how she is. Remember when she broke her wrist and she didn't want to talk for two days? This is how she handles her pain."

"How do you handle yours?" I ask.

"I'm in problem-solving mode." She flips her laptop around so I can see her screen. **EAST BAY TRAUMA RECOVERY GROUPS**, the webpage says. My mom clicks on a tab and shows me a spreadsheet she's working on titled **SHOOTING RESOURCES**.

"Of course you have a spreadsheet," I say.

"It soothes me," she says, showing off the table she's created.

This, right here—a spreadsheet with alphabetized trauma resources banged out fewer than forty-eight hours after she almost died—is all you need to know about my mother to fully understand her.

"What's 'MAGS'?'" I ask, pointing to an entry.

"Mothers Aligned for Gun Safety," she says. "It's some kind of local gun control organization. I don't know. They have regular meetings. Could be something."

"You really want to go talk about guns?"

"I want to do whatever I can to make sure this sort of thing never happens again."

I admire my mother, I do, but I want to move on. I want to go back to work next week and think about nothing but adorable clothes. I want to forget guns entirely, forever.

My dad doesn't call. He's still digitally detoxing, I guess, and Sequoia in Spain has been no help at all. Saturday, I do the calculations: he's seven days deep into his ten-day retreat. I don't know what I expect he's going to say or do to make this any different, but when I think about him, I get an invisible kick to the gut. The gulf between now and three days from now feels enormous, too big to make it across. We need him now.

Oddly, I mostly digitally detoxed too over the weekend. I'm sure people are probably still marking themselves "safe," sharing articles, and talking about their near misses. ("I was at I Glam just the week before!" Barf.) Part of me is sick with curiosity over who's saying what. But also not. I know soon I go back to work and into the world, but for now, I can lie around in my bathrobe eating bowls of cereal and flipping through *Vogue* and watching *Too Cute* and bedazzling my Mary Janes. I can do the opposite of my mother, who I hear on the phone with our health-care provider half the afternoon, then leaving voicemails with potential therapists' offices.

Joy posted on social media about surviving the shooting, and now I have an avalanche of messages in my own inbox. Some of them are my friends from high school, some are Joy's friends, some are frantic messages from Lex—the love of her life, or at least her life from age fourteen to age nineteen—who is on tour with his band Electric Wheelchair right now. Lex Loser, I've always called him. But privately. In my own head. And it doesn't matter anymore anyway, whether her ex-boyfriend is a loser or not. (He is.) Because everything—every heartbreak, every rift—has been diminished in proportion to the massiveness of yesterday's shooting.

I write a message to Adrian before going to bed about how fine I am, and then copy-paste it to Zoe. I know it's a cheap and crappy thing to do, but it feels like small talk. Hi. How are you. How's the weather. We almost died in a shooting the other day. Talk soon.

I send a quick response email to my cubicle neighbor

and intern bestie, Antonio, who also saw the social media news that I was a witness to the shooting.

Hi, appreciate you reaching out. Yeah, it's hard to describe. . . . It's been unreal. See you Monday, I hope! Thanks again.

I will myself to go to sleep. I listen to the sound of rain on my phone and push the horrible thoughts from my head. Amazingly, it works.

Though I wake up the next morning freshly gross as reality sets in.

I can't help myself. I look up—and up and up—the news. And that's how I spend my Sunday morning. There are more articles online now, this time not just in Berkeleyside, but the *Chronicle* and even the *LA Times*. They repeat the same info as the articles I saw last night, but with a few more details. Turns out Joshua Lee had met a woman on a dating app who was an employee who worked at I Glam, though she didn't happen to be there the day of the shooting, and Joshua Lee's social media history showed he was active in men's rights groups and Second Amendment groups.

I stare at all these facts, reading them like they are in a foreign language, unsure of what they mean, what they add up to.

I stare at his face there, staring back—three feature photos from top news articles. In one, he wears a green military-looking cap, smiling like some normal human being, not the strange monster who almost killed my mom and sister. My skin prickles. The next is a senior photo from our high school. He's in a tuxedo. He has dead eyes, I think. I would look into those eyes and know they belonged to a killer.

But of course, that's a lie, because I saw those eyes over two years' time and never once did such a thought even flicker.

I knock on Joy's door.

"Joshua Lee had gone on a date with a woman who worked at the store," I tell her. "That's why he targeted I Glam. It had nothing to do with you."

Joy sits cross-legged on her bed, her hand splayed on her unopened astronomy textbook while she paints her finger-nails midnight blue. "Who said it had anything to do with me?"

I seem to remember either her or my mom saying it at some point, but maybe I'm wrong.

"I don't know," I say finally.

"You come in here sounding so excited he targeted some poor I Glam girl," Joy says. "Like, so goddamn *elated*."

"Just thought you'd want to know," I say.

"Wrong."

"Lex is trying to get ahold of you."

"I know. We texted," she says softly.

If you want to tenderize my sister—to the point of near breakage—Lex is how you do it.

"Also, the *LA Times* and the *Chronicle* wrote up what happened—"

She closes her eyes, exasperated. "Can we talk about anything besides the shooting, or is this the only topic of conversation allowed in this house anymore?"

I shut the door quickly. I leave her on her bed with her eyes still shut. I have had enough Joy for the time being.

My sister has an incredible gift for making me feel dumb, although maybe I make it easy for her, I don't know. But then there are the good times—the times we watch horror movies in the dark in her room and make fun of the special effects, the time she dyed my hair magenta last year, or last week when I ran into her in front of Berkeley City College and she yelled, in front of all her punk-looking friends, "That's my baby sister!" and threw her arms around me.

I can't help it. I know I'm going to keep googling. I would like to read the articles again, make sense of all this information. I would like to look up Joshua Lee's profile on social media. I know Joy would hate it if she found out I did.

ELEVEN

I am a friendly person. I smile, even at those who frown. I ask lots of questions when I end up on a bus bench with a stranger.

"You sound like an interviewer sometimes," Mom told me once.

I can't help it. I have a curiosity about human beings, about what's inside of them. That curiosity is like a string that pulls me forward in the world. It's where my mind goes as I watch the tableau of life from windows. So many people, so many minds, so many experiences that are mostly unknowable and endlessly deep and fascinating.

I have a lot of friends; silver, gold ones, like that song goes. Ones from childhood, like Zoe, who might go their own way but remain in my circle forever. I'm friends with all my exes—all three of them. Adrian, Molly, and Hassan.

Hassan was my ninth-grade boyfriend, lopsided smile and wire-rimmed glasses and business-casual attire. I liked the way he held my hand but hated his tongue in my mouth.

I loved playing video games with him but hated when he wrote me poems about my soft lips. We're still friends. We message sometimes, and right before he left for MIT, he and I spent a whole afternoon playing pinball at the pinball museum in Alameda.

Molly was my next. Nobody has ever made me laugh as hard as Molly, to the point of pain, gasping for air. Molly is short, round, with explosive hair, a theater nerd who turns the room when she enters. She and I were on and off throughout sophomore and well into junior year. I adored her, but it never seemed enough. I didn't crave her like she seemed to crave me. I was always so happy to spend time with her, but if she left for a week, I didn't miss her. She broke up with me finally, officially, for reals at the end of our junior year because she and Casey Bluth fell in love after kissing in *Twelfth Night*, and I told her, "I'm happy for you," because I was, and Molly just stared at me and said, "That is so mean." Molly, literal winner of the Best Actress award three years in a row in our high school, volcanic, talented beyond belief, is not an easy girl to date unscathed. Every one of her exes are nemeses at this point. But me? We FaceTimed her first week when she got to LA. I sent a care package to her dorm. I cannot stand the thought of losing someone I shared so much of myself with, no matter what went wrong or never went right.

Then there's Adrian Roca, the most pensive, artistic, complex human being I've ever met. Adrian of long hand-sewn skirts and bell-bottoms permanent-markered with poems.

Adrian the flute player, the painter, with the flawless features and unwavering stare of a Roman statue. Our relationship never even hit the point where we called it a relationship earlier this year, but we cuddled and said *I love you*s and fell asleep FaceTiming every night. I fell for Adrian hard, in a way that didn't feel good at times, because Adrian never wanted to fully commit. When I let myself love them, I never felt entirely secure. I wondered if that was how Molly felt. Then Adrian left for school and that was that; I had to accept they now lived in Seattle. Somehow the distance was a relief. I felt like I could start over. Now I could love them freely, without the burden of possibility.

I am a friendly person. I check on Joy, who I haven't seen outside her room since she made me feel dumb this morning. It's nearing dinnertime. I bring her snacks and try to cheer her up. She's been organizing everything. There are brown bags of old clothes in a tower outside her closet. I list off all the people reaching out to me online to ask about her. She tells me she doesn't need a secretary. I'm not her secretary, I say. I'm her sister. I'm her friend. She can talk to me. She knows she can talk to me, right?

"But can I *not* talk to you?" she asks. "What about that?"

I stand there not responding. My mom keeps saying that maybe Joy just needs space. What is it about people needing space that makes me want to give them exactly the opposite?

Later, I'm eating a bowl of cereal for dinner—my comfort food, if you can't tell—and I hear a shriek. Mom's in her room in a kimono. She comes into the hallway, where I can see her from my room and probably Joy can see her from hers, and holds up her phone. Her eyes are wild behind her reading glasses.

"I was contacted by NBC," she says. "Should I talk to them?"

"Why?" Joy calls back.

"They want to interview me about the shooting, I guess," Mom says, clearly astonished. "What should I say? They're asking if I can come down to their Berkeley studio now. . . . Something that's airing in the morning."

"That's . . . unexpected," I say.

"Do you think it's going to end up on TV?" she asks. "I never expected to be on TV."

"Do you *want* to be on TV?" I ask.

"I've never really thought about it before," she says. "It could be a good opportunity to . . . I don't know, talk about what happened. Isn't talking about a problem the first step toward fixing it?"

I hear Joy get up and close her door.

"Well, maybe," I say. "Although it's over. He's dead. So . . . the problem kind of fixed itself."

"This is a much bigger thing," Mom says. "Don't you think? I was reading online this morning that mass shootings have tripled in the last eight years. That is *mind-blowing*."

I really don't want to talk about this right now. I feel some kind of political rant coming on, so I just say, "Mmm-hmm. You should call them back."

"I should," she repeats, as if she's trying out the words.

I nod. She goes into her room and shuts the door.

And that's how my mom ends up going viral.

TWELVE

I head to my internship the next morning, Monday morning, even though I'm still stunned—or an extra step beyond stunned that I can still be stunned now when four days have passed. Stunned to be stunned.

On the BART ride, I imagine a man storming in and shooting a gun at all us commuters staring lovingly at devices or books. I have to push the image out of my mind. On the elevator up to the office, I wonder if the other four passengers are carrying weapons. My internship is on the thirteenth floor of a very tall building at Oakland City Center, and now we have a new keypad. . . . I have to look up my code on my phone and work the new door once, twice, thrice before I get in. Safety measures, I thank you, but you are a pain.

Seventeen people, plus a rotation of doe-eyed interns, work at this location: a sprawling open office painted in candy colors surrounded by executive offices. *RETROFIT*, the stenciled letters say. It's fancy as hell, much fancier than the sandwich shop I worked at before this, that's for certain. The windows overlook Oakland: a metropolitan mess of brick buildings, glimmering streets, and Lake Merritt a mirror splash before the hills. The color of the trees, the apartments, the human beings all blend into something like a violet noise twinkling in the sunshine. I gape at its novelty still, while most of the other staff members breeze by it like another forgettable wall.

Sometimes I get the sense I'm out of my league with these twentysomething, thirtysomething people, like I'm posing as an adult but I'm still just a kid inside. Maybe that's how all grown-ups really feel.

"Betty," whispers Antonio behind me. I know it's Antonio because no one else speaks to me this intimately here, and also he's one of only two males who work here. I turn around. Antonio is adorable. He wears bow ties and gels his hair back like a fifties-movie boy. He clearly had some skin issues at some point that have healed over and he hides with a well-trimmed beard. He's one of three interns and has fast become one of my work besties. "How are you, BB?"

"I'm okay. Thanks for your email."

"I'm, like, in shock."

"You think *you* are?"

"*Clearly,* girl," he says. "Clearly."

"I'm just trying to not think about it."

"I get it," he says.

There's a silence.

"I don't, actually," he goes on. "I'm so awkward right now. I'm so bad at this. Like, what do I say to you?"

"How about hi, how was your weekend?"

"How *was* your weekend?"

"It was weird, not going to lie."

"Do you want to talk about . . . *it*?"

"Honestly, not here. Not now. Maybe we can get lunch later. But for now I'm trying desperately to hang on to my mascara."

"Request heard and respected."

We walk back to the intern cubicle area, past soundproof booths usually hogged by the sales team (blabbers, phone-talkers), past the quiet IT team at their shared community table.

Antonio and I plop into our ergonomic chairs, our backs facing each other. We boot up our laptops.

"My weekend was weird too," he says. "Not like yours, of course. But I went on this date with a guy."

"Go on."

Antonio's dating life is more entertaining than reality TV.

"Well, he seemed chill at first. And he wasn't great-looking, but you know, he wasn't bad-looking. He was like if Jeff Goldblum had a grandson who had gotten progressively less hot with every generation."

"Okay."

"Also, he works in tech. Some video streaming company.

He's an engineer. So, you know, he's rich. One of the gentri-
fiers."

"Ohhhh."

"Right? Which we hate, until we go to his house and
realize he has a hot tub and a pool table and view of the city.
And then we're like, okay, maybe for a minute."

I'm rapt as I straighten my keyboard and my boxed
tissues and my yellow legal pad I hardly ever use because it's
the twenty-first century.

"Girl," Antonio says. "He gave me the grand tour."

"Is that a sexy euphemism?"

"No; like he was a realtor showing off his square footage.
And guess what he shows me?"

"His penis?"

"You are so crass," he gasps. "*HR! HR!*" he pretends to
yell. "But seriously, no. He showed me his baby room."

"Oh, he had a baby," I say, thinking this is the punch line.

Antonio is a storyteller, and he's good with the twists.

I open the window of my email program, our intranet,
our work chat program. The logos all dance in various places
on my screen as they find themselves.

"No, he didn't have a baby," Antonio whispers. "He had
like *a hundred* babies."

I turn around slowly in my swivel chair. Antonio is
waiting for me, turned away from his desk, toward me, eyes
wide.

"You know those realistic-looking dolls? The super-creepy ones?" he whispers. "He collects those, and his entire second bedroom was *bursting* with them. Shelves upon *shelves.*"

"What did you say?"

"I pretended to get a headache and went home. I mean, how can we recover from that?"

"How do you find these people?" I ask him.

"It really says something about me, doesn't it?" he asks sadly. "That the app keeps matching me with them?"

I shake my head. Stories like this are why I would never join a dating app.

It's weird that I'm old enough now to join a dating app.

It's even weirder to think about how, according to that article I read, the whole reason Joshua Lee shot up I Glam last week might have been all because he met a girl on a dating app.

"I'm boring you," Antonio says. "With my verbal vomit. I'm nervous, can you tell? That shooting, I keep thinking about it. Are you really okay, BB?"

I could melt down right now, if I gave myself permission. But I do not. I will my face to be a mask, steady my breath. I toughen myself up.

That thing shining in his eyes—pity, I suppose—I'd like to never see that shining thing again.

"Better than *you*, sounds like," I reply, mock-sassy.

I swivel a 360 in my chair.

"She's pretty . . . pretty *fierce*," he says.

He's saying this about me, yes, but it's also an inside joke. It's a very cheesy tagline for our company repeated in all our fall-line videos.

"I'm okay," I tell Antonio.

He gives a single nod. "Okay."

"Okay, then."

"Okay!"

We giggle and turn around and finally start getting our tasks done.

That's when I see the email screaming **YOUR MOM!!!!!!!** from 6:11 a.m. this morning, sent by Zoe. I freeze for a moment, afraid to click. I'm afraid something bad happened—although, how could it? I heard her return home last night, the front door latching shut. She's fine. Joy's probably still sleeping. Nobody has been shot. Everything's fine.

I never used to have to say these things to myself, over and over, mantras to try to rebuild, brick by brick, that illusion of safety up again.

THIRTEEN

From: Zoe Hayashi
To: Betty Lavelle
Subject: YOUR MOM!!!!

Hey hi hey

Listen, I know you're still reeling from the I Glam shooting. Been thinking of you and your fam nonstop. Can you believe the guy who did it went to our high school?? He was in my PE class freshman year and all I remember is he never changed his gym clothes. Anyway I figured an email is the least intrusive thing I could do, but Betty I HAVE to reach out after this morning. . . .

So I woke up today to a text from my mom, who, as you know, is a TV-forevermore-on, Twitter-ever-open news junkie. She sent me a clip from NBC this morning and it was YOUR MOM!! And she was hella eloquent!!! I literally screamed in the hallway of my dorm room. And did you see how many views the video had? It was posted last night and it has almost five thousand!

What she was saying was so RIGHT ON, and even though the I Glam shooting was so, so tragic, it's refreshing to hear someone call it out like it is. Tell your mom I love her. Love you. Hope you'll call me later.

I read this, with its hyperlink and embedded video at the end, my mother's face frozen in some NBC news screenshot. I close my eyes. Blood seems to slow in my veins. I get sick from the shooting all over again, the popping right there in my ears, the fear fresh and alive within me. But it's not like I can *not* watch it after reading that email. My mom is in a video on *NBC*.

I get up with my phone and go to the bathroom and lock the door and press the little triangle that means play on my phone.

An anchorwoman with blonde helmet hair and teeth so white, they're fluorescent shuffles some (blank, I'm sure) papers at her desk. Behind her, a photo of I Glam in disarray.

"I'm Tiff Brenner reporting," she says. Anchorpeople. What's with that voice they use? The climbs and melodramatic drops in pitch, the unblinking eye contact. Who *talks* like that? "Two nights ago, a shooting at a retail store rocked a community in the Bay Area of California. As authorities piece together the question of why it happened, the victims—who have all survived—have questions. And they're *not* keeping quiet with them."

On the bottom of the screen, the words **LOCAL ACTIVIST SPEAKS OUT AFTER I GLAM SHOOTING** shine in white.

Then my mom appears. She sits, gussied up like she's headed to a job interview, in her black blazer and favorite earrings, silver lightning bolts that catch the light. Her lips are bright pink. Hey, now. Apparently my mother is striking on camera. But that's beside the point. "BEVERLY LAVELLE, LOCAL ACTIVIST"? Since when did my mom become "LOCAL ACTIVIST"?

Since right now, I guess.

"Our shooting wasn't extraordinary," Mom says. "Not at all. In fact, there was another shooting that day on a college campus in Texas with two casualties. It was a bigger deal. I should be grateful."

I turn the volume up on my phone. I can't help it. The emotion is there, just below the quiver in her voice, just below the glassy dance in her gaze.

"I should be *grateful*," she repeats. "We were almost shot while shopping. And . . . here I am, thinking . . . how grateful I should be? That's where we are right now in this country. What have we become? How did this become so mundane? We live in a nation where guns are so idolized and fetishized, we see people blasted away on shows without blinking, heartbeats unfazed; where my kids and their classmates hide under desks and in closets for drills in case a shooter ever holds them captive—and these drills become something so ordinary that they *joke* about them."

I cringe. She's talking about me. I didn't take shooter drills that seriously. I joked that I hoped they'd happen, saving me from pop quizzes and assignments. I never thought much about them; they were like any perfunctory, annoying part of school—running the mile in PE, standardized tests.

My mom goes on from my phone, her speech gaining passion. "Toddlers are shot in accidents caused by careless gun owners daily. *Daily.* People talk about gun safety. Gun owners promise that they care so much about safety. Oh, the NRA, that's what they're there for, right? Well, did you know the NRA spends less than ten percent of its budget on safety and education? Mass shootings scream from headlines every morning—so common we don't even click the links. Statistics that tell us that our country has the highest murder rate by firearm in *the developed world*. Who have we become? What has become of us that a man walks into an I Glam store, opens fire, shoots four women and then himself, and it's not even national news? I almost *died*. My daughter almost *died*. We're not special, and that's disgusting."

End of the clip. The comments are a storm of everything from preach sister to shut up betch. Typical internet. But when it's about my mom, it spikes my blood pressure and I have to stop reading. Zoe was wrong. The video doesn't have five thousand views.

It has *twenty* thousand.

FOURTEEN

I throw myself into my internship today. I post to our social media accounts and work two hours updating a PowerPoint presentation. In the back of my mind, I'm bothered. My mother, on TV. With loud opinions. She's always been that way—not afraid to speak the truth, even if it's embarrassing. Freshman year, she came to school to speak with my English teacher and informed him his syllabus was racist and sexist. "I've calculated the authors of the works on this list," she told him. "A total of eighty-eight percent of them are white men." She made a pie graph to illustrate her point. Last election, she made me knock on doors with her while she talked about some woman running for state assembly. It was bortifying, a word I just made up to describe something simultaneously boring and mortifying. Plus, how could my mom act like it was so offensive when church people came to proselytize, yet knocking on doors and telling people they had to vote for Willa Wu was somehow acceptable? One man tried to argue all politicians are lizard people. Another man barked

"NEOLIB! NEOLIB! NEOLIB!" until we left his doorstep. Every time mom wears her *YES WE WILLA!* shirt, worn thin and soft as a vintage T, I get flashbacks from those uncomfortable conversations.

And now my mom's preaching on TV, with over twenty thousand views. I should text and congratulate her. Everything she said was true, as far as I could tell. She wants the world to be a better place, less guns, no terrorists shooting in malls. She has every right to talk about it on TV.

Why, then, does it feel like *this*?

I don't like being the center of attention. Never have. I'm a clothes geek, sixties mod–inspired vintage, specifically. My walls are covered in supermodel collages, but not because I have any interest in modeling. I just love the art of it. I want to be a beauty editor or work at a magazine. In high school, I was drawn to the wild theater kids, the black box plays, but I painted sets. I appreciate loudness, but I am not the loud one.

Someone's car backfires on the street outside and I have a moment of complete panic at the *bang*, gasping.

"You okay?" Antonio asks.

"Fine," I answer, almost too fast.

Throughout the day, my mom's words reverberate, mental Ping-Pong balls bouncing. *We're not special, and that's disgusting.* I'm honestly uncertain what's worse—that she's so loud, or that she's right.

I find myself sad clocking out and taking the elevator down to the BART station. It was the safest I'd felt since the shooting—there, surrounded by cubicle walls, behind a padlocked front door with secure personal codes, floors up in a secure building. I did my job and I did it well. I knew just what to say. I knew just what to do.

This seems like the only place that's true.

FIFTEEN

When I get home, I'm surprised Joy is still there in her pajamas in her room—exactly the same as when I left her there this morning. Her room looks cleaner than I've seen it in years, though. Her hardwood floor has been swept, her books arranged on her shelf by color, her desk cleared. But her curtains remain drawn and the lights dim. Her backpack and textbooks sit next to the door, along with her leather jacket, like they're patiently waiting for her return to normal life.

"No school today?" I ask from the doorway.

"Not yet," Joy says.

"Can I come in?"

"Sure."

I know I just turned eighteen last month in August, and she turns twenty-one next month, but I still get an elated flutter when she invites me into her room. I sit next to her on her bed. She puts down her phone and gives me a half smile. She looks improved since yesterday.

"You see Mom's video?" I ask.

"Yeah," she says. "What the hell?"

"She made good points, I thought."

"Me too, but it's still bizarre seeing Mom on NBC."

"Agreed."

"How was work?"

"Spreadsheety. PowerPointy. How was your day?"

"I went to a psychiatrist this morning."

"Yeah?"

"I had a panic attack outside the hospital. I honestly thought I was going to die."

"Joy!" I say, putting my hand on her arm.

"Yeah," she says. "It sucked."

"You went alone?"

"I thought I could handle it. Mom had her own appointment. We were in the same building."

"I could have gone with you," I offer.

"I don't need a baby-sister chaperone," she says.

She blinks at me, as if deciding whether to dig into me further or not. Her eyes are a muddy color—I can never decide if the green or the brown in them wins.

"Anyway, at least the panic attack happened *before* the appointment," she says. "I got some medication for anxiety. It helped a lot." She reaches into her pocket and pulls out a pill bottle and shakes it.

I take the orange bottle and read the label.

LAVELLE, JOY.

CLONAZEPAM, 0.5 MG

Generic for: Klonopin

Take 1–2 tablets by mouth as needed and at bedtime if needed for insomnia.

May cause drowsiness and dizziness. Alcohol and marijuana may intensify this effect. Use care when operating a vehicle, vessel (e.g., boat), or machinery.

Call your doctor immediately if you have mental/mood changes like confusion, new/worsening feelings of sadness/fear, thoughts of suicide, or unusual behavior.

"Looks serious," I say, handing them back.

"Well, so far, they've worked."

She says it like she's had this bottle longer than, what—a few hours?

"How many have you taken?" I ask.

"Just two. 'One to two by mouth, as needed.'"

She returns the pills to her pocket.

I suppose if ever there is a time for antianxiety meds, it's in the days after you've almost been killed in a mass shooting. I'm tempted to ask for one, but I wouldn't. I don't need nor deserve one.

We hear the front door slam and both Joy and I sit, spines straight, listening for our mother.

"Because it's *convenient*, Kyle. It's oh-too-convenient," Mom says loudly.

Kyle. My dad's name. The sound of it, one syllable, fires up my pulse. I hear the *thump-thump* of Mom kicking off her shoes.

"Yes, how lovely for you to have your spirit cleansed." Mom's sarcasm is so strong it could be detected from space. "And you do realize your daughter and I were involved in a mass shooting? And what that means?"

Mom appears in Joy's doorway, showing us the video screen and saying "Your father," as if we didn't already know. Joy and I have both sprung up to talk to him, but I quickly realize Joy has dibs on this conversation, considering how close she was to death the other day. Mom hands off the phone to Joy, and I get up to vacate the premises. Joy closes her door shut behind me. I try not to let it bother me.

"Congratulations," I tell my mom as she opens the freezer and pulls out a frozen pizza. "I saw the NBC clip."

"Yeah, what the hell was that?" Mom asks me, wide eyed, tearing the plastic off the pizza.

"Um, I don't know. You were the one there, saying those things."

"No, but I mean . . . it got so much attention. Your *dad* had seen it, and he's in Spain at his hippie spa."

"Really?"

"That was what prompted him to call, apparently," she says. "Not my dozens of messages, which apparently Sequoia never delivered. God, Sequoia is such an airhead."

We don't actually know Sequoia. I think that's why it's so easy to hate her. She's just a breathy voice on the end of a phone line with an unidentifiable European accent.

"How's dad?" I ask as Mom shoves the pizza in the oven.

"Oh, he's, you know. The usual. Self-righteous and pontificating." I've probably learned more fancy vocab words from my mom disparaging my dad over the years than I did in all my high school English classes.

"And how are you?" I ask.

Mom leans against the counter, takes down her bun, and shakes her hair out.

"Fine," she says breezily, as if she wasn't almost shot to death four days ago. "But Joy had a panic attack."

"I heard."

"We've got to keep an eye on her," she says, combing her fingers through her hair. "I worry."

"But you both went to therapy?"

"We did," Mom says.

"And . . . it's covered by insurance?"

"For now," Mom says. "One session a week, through Kaiser. They gave us eight sessions each."

"And that's enough?" I ask.

My mother is a single mom. We rely on rent control, shop at thrift stores, save coupons. We are poor people in the Bay Area, one of the most expensive places to live in the country. These are the kinds of considerations we constantly make.

"For now," she says. "If it's not, we'll figure something out."

"I can pitch in," I say.

"Bets," she says, leaning over and cupping my chin.

"What? I can."

She lets go of my chin. "You work an unpaid internship. How are you going to help?"

"I could get a job."

"The whole point of you taking this year off to work at Retrofit is so you can get your foot in the door and get a real career started at a fashion company. I'm not about to make you sacrifice that to get some crappy job and pay for your sister's therapy."

I don't tell her how relieved I am to hear this, because I love my internship, and I so want it to turn into a real job. But I also wish I were actually making money. I would never be able to work an unpaid internship if it weren't for free rent and food thanks to my mother. And Joy would never be able to attend city college full-time these past two years if it weren't for my mother paying for it and letting her stay here too. My friends all got sent to out-of-state schools on their parents' dime. Their tuition was probably more than what my mom makes in a year. My friends and I all lived in the same city, but entirely different worlds.

Through the wall, I can hear Joy laughing. My dad can tease the laughter out of my sister like no one else in this world. It aches to hear it, though I'm smiling. I want to know the joke. I want in.

"Zoe emailed me the clip," I tell my mom. "She was super inspired by what you said."

"Oh, tell Zoe I say hi. How's New York treating her?"

"Wonderfully," I say, even though I have no idea if this is true.

My mom burns the pizza, just a little, and when Joy comes out, she has a rosiness to her cheeks and is smiling to herself. She hands me the phone. There he is, my dad, my pocket-sized Dad on a screen. In my hand. Separated by an ocean and a continent and a million complexities, but, hey, hi. I leave my pizza and go into my room, shut the door, plop on my bed.

"There you are," he says.

"I'm always here," I tell him.

He nods. My dad has this way of not blinking or answering you, conveying entire messages without ever opening his mouth. I guess that's why he's some kind of guru. My mom has many complaints about the exact same attributes that make people want to go to his retreats. What some see as stonewalling, others see as sainthood. My dad has the sun-kissed skin of afternoon hikes, just-graying hair that touches his shoulders, and bright, clear, weak-coffee eyes— the same color as mine, the same wide shape and long lashes as Joy.

"Tell me about it," he says.

I know what he means when he says *it*.

"It was bananas," I say. "The guy who shot everyone went to our high school."

"Horrifying. Let me just say, I can't believe Sequoia didn't interrupt my session."

"Yeah, what was up with that?"

"She misunderstood what your mother was telling her."

"What was there to misunderstand? 'There was a shooting.'"

"Sequoia has some hearing issues. She refuses to wear hearing aids. That's her choice."

I could argue, *But hiring her to answer phones at Namaste House? That's* your *choice.* But I don't argue. I have a spoon on hand with my father, but I never stir the pot.

"How do you feel?" he asks.

"I'm okay," I say. "I wasn't in there."

"No."

"Just outside."

"Well, I'm thousands of miles away and I'm feeling the ripples, so I can't even imagine what you're going through."

I tell him about what happened. It's a story now, one I memorized—not only my part, but the parts offscreen to me. My sister's and my mother's parts, and how the women who were shot survived but one is still in critical condition, and how Mom is now a capital-*A Activist* on TV. Dad says he wishes he could be here with us, and he wishes he could protect us, but he knows he can't. It's so disappointing to hear him admit that. Even if it's an illusion, it's the natural order: Dads are supposed to think they can protect their daughters.

Dad, instead, tells me a story. He has a way of annunciating every syllable, elongating his words so theatrically and mesmerizingly. And he has this accent, impossible to pinpoint, from his years of traveling the world.

"Lizzy," he says. (My dad's always insisted on calling me Lizzy.) "A few years ago, I found myself in a troublesome spot. Nothing like what you're going through, but—I experienced some loss and displacement. So I did what any normal person would do."

I raise my eyebrows at him.

"I bought a one-way train ticket to Thailand, shaved my head, and decided to become a monk."

"Of course you did."

He grins for a moment, almost mischievously, a break from his usual collected expression. "I lived in a wat next to a river with Siamese crocodiles."

I laugh, because it's always a surprise with him.

His grin relaxes. "The wat was a strange place, tropical fauna just *exploding* around this long, rectangular path that wrapped around the premises. There were gold Buddha statues everywhere, peeking from behind the palms. A lot of fellow expats there. I got to know some of them. One was this guy named Kaleb. Young guy, early thirties. So cheerful, so . . . *Zen*. I ended up sharing my pain with him, which was all financial, worldy distractions. A business opportunity had failed, woe is me. He shared his story with me and, man, did I feel like a dolt for even opening my *mouth*. He had been this high-paid executive at a pharmaceutical company in the States, and some completely unhinged ex-boyfriend murdered his fiancée just days before their wedding. My God. I didn't know what to say. What do you say to a story like that?"

"I don't know."

"I didn't know either! Speechless, I was. He left the next day, but his story stuck with me. Later, I spoke to one of the monks about it—asking him, how can you explain cruelty like that? How do we go on living and accepting our fellow human beings after such random acts of violence? He answered me with a verse from the Buddha.

"If you surveyed the entire world
You'd find no one more dear to yourself.
Since each person is most dear to themselves,
May those who love themselves not bring harm to anyone."

I let the words sink in a moment. I know the end is what he was going for, but it's the beginning that trips me up. Isn't that such a lonely idea—that I'm the one most dear to myself? That I'm all I ultimately have? I refuse to accept that. Also, what kind of a person remembers passages like that and spits them back to you on a FaceTime call? I can barely even remember my PIN.

When I was only twelve, my dad, who has had a lifelong fear of open water, an avid traveler who only ever took trains and cars, crossed the Atlantic for the first time. It was apparently such a traumatic event, he had to be restrained by the stewardesses during a panic attack. Once he landed in Paris, he vowed to never do it again. I've never asked him to come to us, though I've wished I could. I've been too afraid to hear him tell me no—rejection all over again.

"I miss you," he tells me. "Namaste House is always here if you want to come visit and explore Spain."

"Someday," I say, smiling. I do appreciate the offer. He's offered before. But how would I pay for it? My imaginary money from my unpaid internship? Worse, if I did say I wanted to go, Mom would probably take a second job to get me there, even though she can't stand my dad. That would kill me—she works hard enough without having to worry about sending me to Spain. And I could ask my dad, I guess, but I know nothing about his financial situation except credit collectors still call our house for him on occasion.

We don't ever say goodbye. He always says "till our souls meet again." I know he says it because he thinks it sounds hopeful, but I think it sounds morbid. It sounds like one of us might die and not see each other again. I've never had a reason for this, but now, since the shooting, I do.

SIXTEEN

It's been a week. I'm trying, but I wish it were a dream and I could wake up. I do my best to move forward and forget about the shooting. Joy doesn't go to school this whole week. She doesn't work her two afternoon shifts at the thrift store, either. Instead, she trims her own hair, sews patches on her pants, deep-cleans and organizes. She exists solely in her room.

"I'm making my space feel right," she tells me.

She's wearing purple lipstick and a funereal Victorian dress like she's going somewhere, but she's only FaceTiming with Lex in a few minutes. Her room has an antiseptic smell. Despite the fact I worry about her, despite her pale complexion, her eyes dance.

"I wish you'd go out on a walk with me or something," I say.

She needs to leave the house. Not that I'd say this, because you'd be safer lighting yourself on fire than telling Joy Maple Lavelle what to do.

"I wish you'd let me do my thing," she says. "And not scrunch your face up like that."

"Is my face scrunched?"

"Semipermanently." Her phone rings and she says, "Hi, baby!" and closes the door.

Well, *hi, baby* is good, I guess, even if it's directed at Lex.

"Her friends have come over," Mom informs me as she blends foundation on her face, looking in the bathroom mirror. "Mouse. That girl from work, Tamika. That other one . . . the one she almost started a band with—Brie."

"Well, that's good," I say.

"Don't worry about her," Mom says.

"What about you? Can I worry about you?"

"About us," she finishes, putting the cap back on her foundation.

I use my fingers to blend her jawline. She closes her eyes and lets me help her.

"Please stop worrying," she says.

"Hard not to."

This is something fresh I have noticed in myself. I always thought of myself as someone who didn't think too hard about things. If my mind ever started to go someplace I didn't like, I would distract myself with a magazine, pick up my phone and scroll, text someone. I would think of dresses I'd like to wear or how shimmering-pretty the trees looked when they shook. But since the shooting, I hear a distant river of disquiet, of unease, run rampant and loud in the world.

A dangerous hum beneath the peace I've been keeping.

"You want to do something?" Mom asks. "Come to the MAGS meeting with me next week."

At her MAGS meeting a couple nights ago, she was basically a celebrity. They immediately adopted her as a spokesperson and now she even has some official title—all because of that internet video. Tomorrow she has another news interview on a major network about gun safety. She said that MAGS told her to call it "gun safety" and not "gun control" because the phrase polls better.

"Turn your worry into action," she continues. "I think you'd really like the meetings. Everyone is so dedicated, so interesting. There are some cute guys there, students your age. Girls, too."

Mom always adds that in, that clause. She's trying to be inclusive and see me, which I appreciate. But it's so awkward the way she does it. Like it's an afterthought. Anyway, I'm not about to go to a *gun safety* meeting and sit around talking about how horrible the world is and how many guns people have. That will worsen the worry situation. I'm trying to think *less* about the horrible problems in this world, not more. Also, even if I were—not about to be on the dating prowl in such a place.

"Maybe next time," I tell her.

I wish there wasn't a next time.

No one died at that shooting, other than Joshua Lee.

Still, somehow, I'm mourning.

SEVENTEEN

When I talk to Adrian on the phone, they ask how I've been and I give them the rundown. How I'm shaken, but okay. How my sister has retreated into temporary hermitage in our apartment, how bizarro it is to see my mom go viral. I'm about to ask what Adrian's been sewing and wearing and what Seattle is like, but they steer the conversation straight to Joshua Lee. There's something relieving about getting to go there—to finally gossip about the murderer who has been circling my mind since the shooting.

"I can't believe we went to high school with him," Adrian says. "I keep staring at his picture and I have no memory of ever seeing him."

Let me pause and add that I'm not at all surprised. Adrian Roca spent four high school years solely in AP courses, art classes, the theater building, and the band room. They never attended a dance, never ate lunch in the cafeteria or quad, and boycotted sports events because of "toxic competitive culture." Adrian has a laser focus on the activities or people who interest them; everything beyond that is noise. The fact Adrian ever noticed I existed in the first place, let alone had romantic feelings for me, has always felt like a generous stroke of luck from the universe.

I remind Adrian that Joshua Lee was a senior when we were freshmen, and of the trash can fire and rumor that he harassed a teacher. Doesn't ring any bells for them.

"Sounds like he was emanating psychopath vibes from early on," Adrian says. "Did you know something like four percent of Americans are psychopaths?"

"That's terrifying."

"What else do you remember about him? Did Joy know him?"

"No, she didn't. She must have seen him around, but I'm not going to pry about it. He killed himself right in front of her. She had to wash his blood off her body."

"Fuck."

The silence has a sound, a hum of 800 miles between us.

"I remember his brother more than I remember him," I say.

"Who was his brother?"

"Michael Lee, same grade as us. He was in my bio class."

"Wait . . . Michael Lee? Like sweet-pea shaggy-haired Michael Lee? Glasses? Always wore a hoodie?"

"Yeah, sounds like him."

"He was in band with me. Drum line. Wow. I *never* would have pegged those two as brothers."

The two brothers did seem different, just in terms of how they dressed and their attitudes, and there wasn't an obvious family resemblance beyond their dark brown hair. And with a last name like Lee, it wasn't an easy dot to connect. How did I even know they were brothers in the first place? For a moment I have no idea, maybe I jumped to some conclusion, but then the memory floats back: sitting in class the first day of bio and my teacher Mr. Yang doing roll call. When he got to Michael Lee, he shot him a look and asked, "Any relation to Joshua Lee?"

"My brother," Michael mumbled, doodling in his notebook.

"Let's hope you follow directions better than him."

A few people laughed. Mr. Yang said, deadpan, "He's the reason we have legal waivers now to dissect squids. That's not a joke." Then more people laughed.

I didn't think about all that until right now.

"You still there?" Adrian asks, snapping me back to the present moment.

"Yeah, sorry. Anyway, how's Seattle?"

They say they've had no time for sewing, and no room for a machine in their dorm room, but that they went to a queer art show on campus and someone sculpted a whole exhibit out of drag queens' shoes.

"That sounds amazing!" I say.

I'm all for practicality. I love pointed toes and zany prints, but they have to be flats, because I walk everywhere. But I sure appreciate stilettos and platforms when someone else is wearing them.

"I'll send you some pics," Adrian says. "I've been meaning to. Just been so busy."

I picture Adrian there, exploring a new city, attending queer art shows, bonding with their roomies, sitting in front of class and raising their hand every time a professor asks a question. (Classic Adrian.) And here I am, sitting in my bedroom—the same bedroom I've lived in since I was in middle school.

"I miss you," I tell them.

"Miss you too, boo," they say.

After ending the call, I get on my laptop. I tell myself I'm just going to check up on social media, but really, I know what I'm doing. I can't help but suddenly think of Joshua Lee as a psychopath. Or a person in need of mental help. Maybe he was a person suffering. Like my dad said last week—what was it he said? That Buddhist verse about loving yourself? A person who was in a good state of mind, a person who loved themselves, would not have done what Joshua Lee did.

Joshua Lee and I have two mutual friends from high school. Not real friends—more like acquaintances.

It looks like every other page, white background, blue Helvetica. There is nothing here that alerts you that you're looking at an attempted murderer's page, or a dead man's page. On his banner photo he has a snake on a yellow flag that says *Don't tread on me.* On his small personal photo, it's him in a snow jacket, sunglasses, smiling.

I click on the photo of Joshua.

Tahoe? someone named Alison asks.

You know it!! Joshua responds.

Lookin good! Michael L says.

Its called a haircut, HIPPIE!! Get one! Joshua responds.

I can't tell if he's joking or not. Michael L must be his brother.

Joshua doesn't have that many photos. Five back and it's two years ago. He's in high school, clearly, in a prom picture from our school, his arm around a petite girl with curly hair and glasses whose name I don't know but whose face I recognize. I stop and linger on that one a while. I can see something in him here, something pre-monster, pre-man. A happiness, a hope in his eyes. A him I never saw in high school, a self-doubting slouch in his shoulders under a too-big tuxedo. I go back one photo and see Joshua lying on a sofa, embracing a large Labrador, mugging at the camera with innocence and a wide, crooked grin. He looks different than the other pictures, and different than the scowling guy in the high school halls in his ROTC uniform. A boy in a T-shirt and socks in a messy room. A boy.

This is how I want to remember you, Michael comments.

He commented yesterday.

My eyes well up. Michael is also scrolling through these

old photos. But he's scrolling through from the other side of grief. From the inside. From someone who knows Joshua too well, not a stranger who only knew glimpses of him in high school and his last few twisted moments from steps away.

Michael L. I click on him. I'd hardly recognize him as the boy I hardly knew in high school: no glasses anymore, shoulder-length hair, a tight band T-shirt, holding a pair of drumsticks.

HAWT, someone named Piggles Wordsmith comments. That comment has as many likes as the photo.

I study Michael's face. He looks sort of like Joshua, if you really look for it, though his face is longer, a shade darker, and his style is completely different. It says he works at Amoeba. That's a funky record store on Telegraph near UC Berkeley. So I guess everyone under the sun didn't leave the area for fancy schools.

I close my laptop and go out to greet my mom. I just heard her come in the front door. I'm about to offer to make breakfast for dinner when I see her expression. She's not smiling. She throws her purse on the sofa and makeup, keys, her wallet, balled-up tissues, and pepper spray all fall out of it.

"What?" I ask.

"Shandra Pensky died."

Shandra Pensky. It sounds . . . kind of familiar. Or maybe I'm imagining that because it now has the weight of death on it. I flex my brain for an answer, blinking.

"Victim from the shooting. The one in critical condition."

"Oh no, she *died*?"

"Yes. Does Joy know?"

"Who knows what Joy knows?" I shake my head. "How sad for that woman and her family."

"I'm going to send them flowers and donate to MAGS in her name."

"That's nice of you."

Mom gets on her stockinged knees and puts everything back in her purse. As I watch her, guilt spreads hot through me. I spent the last hour poring over Joshua Lee's Facebook page. Meanwhile, a victim died, and I didn't even know her name until I knew she was dead. I get on my knees beside my mom and hand her the pepper spray, the lipstick.

I do make breakfast for dinner. Mom tells Joy about Shandra Pensky and Joy doesn't say a word back about it. She changes the subject and talks about how Lex is coming through California on his tour in a month, how they have a new album—a real album, on a label, not just something on Bandcamp. Joy also tells Mom she went to therapy today. I don't know why she would lie about this, but Joy's keys are in the exact same spot they've been for days, dropped off the nail that holds them up into the potted spider plant in the living room. Her purse is still in the same spot under a coat of mine I haven't worn in a week on the coatrack. So I don't believe her.

After dinner's done, Mom goes to her room and calls some MAGS person about the Shandra Pensky news. I love my mom, but her voice is so loud, I can hear her through the walls. Am I ever glad she's never brought a boyfriend home.

I go to Joy's room and knock. She opens the door. She's burning incense and watching *Star Trek*, some alien frozen with its mouth open on her screen. A long time ago, when Joy was in junior high, she was obsessed with *Star Trek*. I would go so far as to call her a Trekkie. She was also a mathlete, played chess all the time, and had a pet rat. Then she dyed her hair blue over the summer before high school, went to her first punk show, and switched to horror movies. There's something endearing about her watching *Star Trek* now.

"I'm just going to say this," I tell her in a low voice. "Please don't be offended."

"Oh, fantastic. People only ever say 'please don't be offended' when you're going to say something offensive."

"Did you really go to therapy?"

"Yes."

She doesn't blink and neither do I.

"For reals?" I ask again.

"What are you, the shrink police? Yes."

"Why is your purse in the same place, then?"

"You are the nosiest bitch," she says.

Bitch can be fond, it can be mean, it can be neutral with my sister.

"It was a virtual appointment," she says. "Now get out of my room, please."

"How do you feel about the Shandra Pensky news?" I ask.

"Are you auditioning for a role as my new therapist, is that what this is?" She takes me, gently, by the shoulders and guides me out into the hallway. "This," she says, sweeping her hand toward her room, "is a stress-free zone. Understand?"

She shuts the door. I open it again.

"I'm sorry," I tell her. "For not believing you."

She shuts the door again.

"Can I watch *Star Trek* with you?" I ask the shut door.

After a moment, she opens the door. "Stress-free zone," she emphasizes again.

"Yes, I got that."

We sit cross-legged together on her bed in the flickering light and she lets me share her fuzzy blanket. There is something to this "stress-free zone" thing. It's a haven in here, sandalwood smoke thick in the air, red Christmas lights strung along her low record shelf. This feeling of delight to be invited into her space and into her company seems like it will never fade. I'm a kid again, we're safe again, when it's just us sisters.

EIGHTEEN

Shandra Pensky is dead. That's why the I Glam story boomerangs back into the news. The death tally went from one to two. There are tributes to her posted on social media, graphics with her photo, smiling, sparkling brown eyes. She was in nursing school, only twenty-three. I stare at her picture so long, it stings. I don't know her, but I can imagine I do. If I stare long enough at pictures of strangers online, dead or alive, I feel like I know them.

My mom attends a memorial for Shandra, followed by a rally in Sacramento marching for gun safety in her name. I don't attend, but I watch it clipped online. My mother takes the mic again and ends up all over the internet. The videos shared are overlaid with these headlines:

MUST-WATCH: ACTIVIST DESTROYS THE GUN LOBBY IN THREE MINUTES

SHOW THIS VIDEO TO ANYONE STILL ARGUING GUNS ARE SAFE!

"THE NEW NORMAL IS UNACCEPTABLE": SHOOTING SURVIVOR SPEAKS OUT

"Activist." "Shooting survivor." Strange how an incident you had no control over can change your identity forever.

It takes an hour to break ten thousand views this time. Good for her. I shut my computer. I shut my heart, or try to, anyway. I take out my sewing kit and get to work fixing loose buttons.

I hear Joy in her room, singing with a loud song on the stereo. I long for the days when I used to have a moment here alone. When Joy used to go out with her friends and stay late studying near school. I tell myself she'll get there again. She seems so much better. Weirdly, though, that's what worries me. She seems fine. I see more smiles from her than I did before. And yet, she won't leave the house. It makes no sense.

I shouldn't make it sound like she's peachy. Of course she's not peachy. There are still nights I wake up hearing her crying in my mother's room, the two of them holding one another in bed in a fit of panic I can't completely comprehend. There are the mornings I see her put her hand to heart and pop a pill at the breakfast table, closing her eyes and swallowing and waiting for the heavy breathing to pass. There was a day someone lit fireworks in the street and she started screaming. But really, mostly, she's in her room trying on fur coats or playing her bass or talking to Lex in low, sweet tones late at night. She seems more in love with her room and herself than she is with the world anymore.

"We all deal in our own ways," Mom says, touching up

her lipstick before another MAGS meeting. She smiles at me and I hug her. For the first time in my life, I don't inform her she has lipstick on her teeth.

I go to work. A welcome distraction of glossy catalogs and long, impassioned discussions on high-waisted pants and copy that is cheap poetry. *A breezy clover-printed dress with ruffled sleeves would be an exquisite pick for wine tasting on the summer solstice.* I find myself staring out the window at Lake Merritt, splashed in the middle of Oakland like a mirrored puddle, wondering if I should have gone into writing Hallmark cards.

"BB, you're spacing out again," Antonio says to me.

"Mmm?" I ask, turning around.

"You said you were getting up for coffee five minutes ago," he says. "But there's no coffee."

"Sorry."

I look back out at the city that from here looks like it could be a diorama.

"How long have you been interning?" I ask Antonio.

"A year and three months," he says. "But I started getting paid at a year."

Sigh.

"I don't know if I can do this for a year," I say. "For what? To do what you do? To be a paid intern? No offense, but you're a Lyft driver on the weekends to make ends meet. The pay must suck."

We're practically whispering now, even though the

cubicles and open office couches and tables are at least fifteen feet away.

"It does suck," he whispers. "But I like it here. This is what I want to do."

"All my friends went to school," I whisper back. "They're all writing papers and living in dorms and going to art shows."

"Calm down. You're too young for a quarter-life crisis."

Tammy comes out of her office and spots us at the window, looking alarmed.

"Everything okay?" she asks.

"Great!" we both yell.

Tammy hesitates before heading toward the restroom, looking back over her shoulder once as she disappears around the corner.

"Betty," Antonio says decidedly. "We have to work. But I think I'm ready to bring this relationship to a whole new level. I think I'm ready to make you a take-home friend." He leads me to our desks. "Let's hang out this weekend. We can dish. My last date with the guy with the pet monkey, your quarter-life crisis, everything."

"Pet monkey?" I ask.

But he's already put on his headphones and opened his computer. I can hear the classical music from here. Maybe he's right. Maybe that's what my life is missing: friends.

Later, at home, Zoe and I have a long FaceTime call where she introduces me to her new boyfriend, whose name

I immediately forget because, let's not lie to ourselves, she'll likely be over him next week. Zoe is a serial romantic, and she's not picky. I swear she could fall in love with anyone. She says I'm the opposite. She's right. I'm willing to wait for it.

"You haven't had your titty grabbed in like a year, admit," she says.

I'm glad her boyfriend left her dorm room for this part.

"Why a single titty grab is a measurement of anything—"

"You know what I mean," Zoe says.

She's got her hair in a messy topknot and is spitting sunflower seeds into a napkin. She sits in the middle of a rainbow pile of laundry.

"I hope your roomie's not a neat freak," I say.

"Oh, my roomie complained about me and my snoring and now I have a single room."

"I've slept in the same room with you dozens of times; you don't snore."

"Yeah, I was faking it."

This is so Zoe, right here. Zoe, who believes rules are for everyone but her. Queen Zoe, her parents call her. It sounds obnoxious, but somehow she commands it like she deserves such treatment. I remain ever in awe of her.

"You faked snoring," I say.

She picks at a sunflower seed in her teeth. "Mmm-hmmm."

"For how many nights?"

"Three. It was worth it, Betty. She was uber religious, she only eats protein bars, she wears socks with sandals. Oh! And she lifts these tiny weights at night." Zoe pantomimes lifting, struggling, making exasperated noises with little chipmunk squeaks.

I laugh. This is our relationship: I've been her best friend my whole life, but really, I'm her greatest audience.

"She's also totally racist," Zoe goes on. "First thing out of her mouth when we met was 'Where did you come from?'"

"And you said . . ."

"'My mother's vagina.' That shut her up for a bit. But then she asked later if I was from China. I was like, *girl*. Not today."

Zoe was born and raised in Berkeley, like me. Her family emigrated from Japan four generations ago. Even in the progressive Bay Area, people assume she doesn't speak English, or that she's from China, or that she's an exchange student. People can be so stupid. And racist.

"Okay, convinced. I forgive the snore tactics now," I tell her.

Just like when I talked to Adrian, this conversation inevitably veers to Joshua Lee.

Zoe remembers the same red flags I do from our high school years—the trash fire that has become legend—and wonders why no one thought to get him help. What kind of help can you give someone, though, for basically being a giant asshole? I repeat what Adrian told me, about 4 percent of Americans being psychopaths.

"Dang. And I'm pretty sure there's no cure for that," Zoe says sadly.

How terrifying to think there are 4 percent of people out there with no feelings, no remorse, and no hope of ever getting better.

When I remind Zoe I was in a couple of classes with Michael Lee, she suggests I reach out to him and find out why his brother "flipped."

"Um, I can't just reach out to some guy I hardly ever talked to and ask weird questions about his dead murderer brother," I say. "That's . . . so tacky."

It's exactly the kind of thing Zoe would do, though, not going to lie. Nothing is off-limits to her.

"You deserve answers though, don't you?" she asks. "Don't you want to know the motive? Doesn't your family?"

Not sure what the point is in chasing motives when the damage is done. I tell her this. But I'll admit it: deep down, I want to know anyway. As if a reason could protect me. As if a reason could protect any of us.

NINETEEN

My mother is so busy lately I barely see her, and when I do, she's scrambling around the kitchen in the morning, sucking steaming coffee down with desperation before work. Or muttering to herself about Republicans as she does her red lipstick in the bathroom mirror, getting ready for some event. The calendar on the wall is full of commitments: a MAGS lunch, a speaking gig at a local city college, a rally at city hall. She comes home so late, I hear her from my room each night as I'm in bed, a sweet relief flooding me as her stockinged footsteps *pat-pat-pat* to her room. Silly, I know. I'm a grown-up now. But there's something unsettling about my mom being out at meetings and fundraisers deep into the night, in crowded, public places—I'm afraid she's a target. I'm afraid something bad is going to happen to her.

Google verifies what I suspected was true. "To the best of medical and psychiatric knowledge, there is no cure for psychopathy." It also says that it's more like 1 percent of the general population are psychopaths, not 4 percent, but that doesn't make me feel better; one in 100 is still way too many psychopaths.

Then Google also leads me to an article reminding me that not all psychopaths are violent, that some seek treatment, and many live normal lives. I search for information about mass shooters and it turns out not all of them are psychopaths.

Thanks, Google. Now I don't know what the hell to believe.

Not going to lie, it crosses my mind to take Zoe's terrible advice and reach out to Michael Lee. But that would be so wrong.

I want to be smart like my mom. I want to be interested in making the world a better place. But in a world this dangerous, I don't have a clue how to begin.

And yet, when I close my computer, when I instead settle under my covers and open my fashion magazines smelling of fresh ink and perfume samples, I gaze upon bleached smiles and airbrushed legs and advertisements and Splenda-cheerful copy. A wailing sense of emptiness opens up inside of me, of not just unease, but boredom, of this not being enough.

I throw my magazine across the room.

TWENTY

Joy's birthday is this weekend. She's the hardest person to shop for, Queen of England picky, and usually I rely on Mom to give me ideas. Mom's one of those thoughtful people who notices everything. "Oh, didn't she love that black-and-white-striped skirt she saw that girl on that show wearing?" or "Wasn't she just saying she wanted to grow some purple tulips in pots someday?" This year, though, I actually have an idea. Joy's been listening to records and spending so much time in her room, I'm going to get her something on vinyl.

Yes, I realize what I'm doing. As I walk the thirty minutes from our pink South Berkeley triplex, through the ash tree–lined neighborhoods, past other funky restored Victorians in pastel shades, past coffee shops with hand-painted signs and an art warehouse with a drum circle thrumming through the open door and grocery staple Berkeley Bowl, where people look like NYC drivers in rush-hour traffic as they try to park in the overswarmed lot, up to Telegraph Avenue with its long string of shops with vintage clothes and posters and dancing shivas and saris in the windows, I know exactly what I'm doing.

I'm going to Amoeba Records.

It's for my sister, I tell myself. And it's true. I am getting my sister a birthday present. That's also not the whole truth. I'm going because I know Michael Lee works here. And some morbid part of me wants to see him, wants an excuse to run into him. I know this without even really knowing it, knowing it only in a dark corner of myself I won't look fully at for more than one second. I stand outside the door, a Black man with dreadlocks and a lazy eye manning an incense-and-beanie stand giving me a nod and smile. There are robot sculptures in the window playing musical instruments. I stare at them curiously, at their beaded eyes and dull silver limbs, before heading in.

I walk into the postered, flyered, rock-and-roll chaos that is Amoeba Records. A steady plunk of a drumbeat, a dirty guitar, and a snotty but melodic boy voice emanate from hanging speakers. I haven't been in here in years. I have a Spotify account. I'm not even exactly clear on why people still buy records, but Joy loves them, so here I am. The place is enormous, causing immediate consternation. Signs everywhere, signs scrawled with words like *Metal, Jazz, Hip-Hop, Classic, Rare*. Where do I begin?

A white girl with green hair and a tattoo of a mermaid on her arm flips through the section labeled *New Releases* peacefully, one by one, the records making soft slapping noises as she goes through them. She seems to know what she's doing. I mimic her, sauntering to the other side of the display and perusing through the shrink-wrapped albums like I belong here too. I stop to pause and look at album covers, as if they mean something to me, crinkling my brow at one with a cartoon frog smoking a blunt, squinting at one that looks like a band of goth clowns, pondering the band name "The Boo Boo Girls," three pouting girls with Band-Aids on their faces.

The world is so weird.

One album cover features a dude pointing a gun at the camera, spiking my blood pressure. I'm about to move on to another section when on the display up top, in the featured spot facing me, I notice a name on an album I recognize: Electric Wheelchair. A black-and-white, intricately drawn skeleton in a wheelchair with sunglasses on and an electric guitar on his lap. There are five copies and a sign points to them, yelling *STAFF PICK*. I grab one and flip it around.

There he is, long-haired and thrashing in the live pic of them onstage: *Lex Dude, guitar and vox*, the label below him says. "Lex Dude" sounds so much cooler than his given name, "Alexander Doody." So weird to be holding the album of the boy who used to eat our frozen waffles straight out of the freezer, who used to show up half-drunk on our doorstep with crushed flowers he clearly picked from our neighbor's yard as he hiccupped the name "Joy," who broke my sister's heart last year and made her sob in the bathtub every night.

(She never would admit this, but come on, our walls are paper-thin.) Here he is in his major label debut. I've struck gold here; it's the perfect gift for Joy.

I wander around a bit, flip through some posters, contemplate record players that look like suitcases. Out of the corner of my eye, maybe I see Michael, lanky guy with shoulder-length wavy hair. My heart beats wild at the scare of it. Because what would I even say? "Oh, hey, remember me from high school? Also your dead homicidal brother almost shot my sister." The magnet that compelled me here was nothing more than morbid curiosity. But it isn't Michael anyway. I've wandered through the whole store now and not seen him. I approach the register, a guy with a purple-tipped Afro and a single peacock earring and a name tag that says *Max* nods at me.

"How's it kickin'?" he asks.

"It's kickin' great," I say.

Kickin' great? I would like to jump into a hole right now. I swear, my social skills have eroded, first with all my friends shipping off to fancy colleges, and then with the I Glam thing. I put my record on the counter, grab my wallet from my purse. When I look up, someone is whispering in Max's ear. Someone I recognize. Shoulder-length dark hair.

Michael Lee.

He appeared, summoned from nowhere, although now that I look harder, I see a bumper-stickered door that blends into the wall with the words *Employees Only*. There seems to be some dire situation because there's some whispering back and forth right now between Michael and Max and then the Max guy gestures toward me and says, "Ring her up, I'll call the plumber," and Michael is suddenly my cashier. Max disappears. And I feel sick to my stomach. Like I came to flirt with disaster, play some game of chicken with chance, and I lost.

Michael Lee wears a band shirt so faded I can't read the name. He smiles with an eerie semipermanence, a persistent smile like someone stoned, and definitely not like someone whose murderous brother is dead. He has eyelashes so long and eyebrows so perfect, I envy him. We sat next to each other in high school, but he's different than I remember him: taller, more defined, improved skin, better posture. All I can think of are the news photos of his brother and how Michael looks nothing like Joshua. You would never guess they're related. It could be a lie, a story I tell myself.

"Electric Wheelchair," he says as he presses some buttons on the cash register. "You going to the show tomorrow?"

"Tomorrow," I repeat, because apparently I have turned into some kind of a robot.

"At Gilman," he says.

Not sure what he's talking about, exactly. I nod my head and don't make eye contact, hoping the transaction will be over as soon as possible.

"Hey, I know you," he says. "From Berkeley High. Betty, right?"

Welp, there goes my "no eye contact" idea. I look up, perk my lips into a smile. "Oh, hi. Yeah."

"Michael," he says.

"Yeah, I remember you."

"How's it going?" he asks.

Funny you ask, Michael. Have a week to sit down and chat? But I shrug.

"Well," I tell him.

"Right on," he says. "My band is actually opening the Gilman show."

He puts the record in a yellow plastic bag, slides it across the counter. Then reaches in his back pocket and puts a small black-and-white flyer on top. It looks like a ransom note, letters cut from magazines spelling the band names, a picture of that guy riding an atom bomb at the end of that movie.

"We're called Dr. Crusher," he says.

"What kind of music?"

"Heavy, you know, kind of, like . . . Melvinsy. But more upbeat. And eighties."

"Hmmm," I say, in a way that sounds like I might actually understand what he means.

"That guy who was just here, Max, he plays synths."

"Nice."

"Anyway . . . if you like Electric Wheelchair, you should really go. It's the only East Bay show they're playing this year."

"Maybe I will," I say, staring at the flyer.

My throat dries with that lie I told. I know I won't be seeing his band. I glance back up at him—behind the raised counter, and at his height, he's a giant. He beams a smile back down so kind that guilt blooms gross in me for hoping I would run into him earlier. So selfish and morbid, as if seeing him in person would put something in perspective. Instead, it ties knots in my stomach.

"Nice seeing you," I tell him.

I give a dumb little queen wave up at him and back away from the counter.

"Take care," he says, sounding almost surprised.

He smiles—ever-smiling—and I leave the store, the flyer in my shaking hand.

It takes four blocks for my heart to stop racing. Four blocks of bookstores, a sock store, coffee shops, a weed shop, a busker playing a guitar with two strings, a woman in a sweater and no pants asking me for change, and an amateur preacher with a megaphone yelling about Satan. Why is my heart racing? Is it because my mind keeps fluttering in the wrong direction, backward, back to I Glam? Is it Joshua Lee? Is that why I'm clutching my bag close to me and my brow is breaking a sweat? Or is it Michael Lee, who I just objectified somehow—brother of a monster—and turned his tragedy into my own personal exhibition to gape at? Michael Lee is a *person*, I realize as Telegraph's funky shops start quieting into acupuncture clinics and office buildings and quivering maple leaves flamed orange with fall. Michael Lee is a person who lost his brother in a shocking and disgusting way. A person, suffering, but trying to keep going, working a job, finding joy in little moments. Like me.

I should have been kinder, more curious. I should have asked him questions about his band. I should have matched his smile with an equivalent, not a set of pursed lips. I wouldn't have told him Joy was at the shooting—not there, not at Amoeba Records as he rang me up—but perhaps I could have told him I saw the news. Because who hasn't? I could have asked him how he was and told him I have thought of him. Offered sympathy, or empathy, or any kind word with a *path* in it. Not a closed door, an awkward gawking and then going.

I should be better than that.

TWENTY-ONE

Joy officially dropped her classes a couple weeks ago now. Mom supported the decision, which surprised me, because Mom is usually a hard-ass. Then again, tragedies wreak different rules. Joy suffers—officially, diagnosed from her online shrink—from PTSD. So Mom is making concessions.

"As long as you still work" is Mom's condition.

And Joy says she does, Wednesdays and Fridays, ten to two, like she always has. She also waters the indoor plants and does the laundry and cleans the kitchen in the mornings. She does it happily, without complaint. This worries me almost more than Joy not going to school worries me— my sullen, too-cool sister, singing while she does dishes by hand? Seeking out chores like washing windows and scrubbing grout from the bathroom tiles? Who is this person?

At work one silver-skied October morning, I'm about to be pulled into a meeting with Tammy and the marketing team to discuss how we're going to roll out the news that we now carry wallets (which once I would have been excited about, but this revelation rings meaningless today) when the fire alarm goes off and the whole building has to evacuate. And when that alarm starts haranguing its carousel of earsplitting noise, I grab my purse and I fucking *run* for those stair doors.

I am the first one out, without a whiff of interest in what anyone behind me is doing.

I am clattering my oxford pumps down those emergency exit stairs like I am fleeing death itself. Because I am.

All I can think is *There is an active shooting.*

There is a person with a gun in the building and I need to get away, get far, far away.

I hear it in my mind—popcorn, gunshots—and though it's not real, it makes my heart skip and fire the same.

For some reason, as I clutch the railing and descend down the dizzying stairs, my knees noodling, I think of Spain; I think of Namaste House, and my father, like some kind of utopia. If I could only outrun this emergency, then perhaps I would make it there.

Out in the street, it's tranquil, bordering on boring. Parked cars and someone flipping the sign from *Closed* to *Open* at a barbeque restaurant. A woman texting, vaping, walking her Chihuahua in a bonnet. Behind me, I can feel the swell of the crowd of evacuated people, the multitudinous talk that mounts into a hum. I should stay here, wait out the ten minutes I'm sure this will take before the fire department comes and declares there was no emergency, someone burned their lunch again, but instead, I walk fast up the street away toward the free shuttle to get me back to BART and away from here.

What are you doing? a small voice in me asks. *Don't you care about this internship? Don't you care what Tammy will think if you leave and don't weigh in on how to write copy for our wallet selection?*

But I must be a different person, because I keep walking. That little voice piping up, the one I swat away like a gnat next to my ear? She used to be me. That was *my* voice. And now . . . now I'm something big enough to ignore it.

Once I get on BART, my hands are shaking. Antonio texts me.

You fucking *flew* out of there, you ok? he asks.

Honestly, I was triggered, I text back. Can you tell Tammy I had to go home to shake it off?

Of course BB. Anything else I can do?

Can you build a time machine? Can you take me back to a time where we pretend life is safe?

Nothing, I type back. I'll be back tomorrow.

Between the last Oakland station and my BART station, Ashby, I ride the subway from underground to overground. I go from blackness, a tunnel, no idea where I am or what I am blazing through into sudden brightness, a farmers market getting set up to my left, bakeries and homeless encampments and ash trees that seem to speak with their emerald shivering. I go from nowhere into home. The sun is cracking through the sky like an egg yolk, bleeding through the clouds, and I don't know why I feel like crying. There's no reason to cry. I get off the BART train with everyone else, all these strangers, all heading home together, separate.

Maybe this was serendipitous, this fire-alarm hooky I'm playing, because it happens to be Joy's birthday today. She was still sleeping this morning when I woke up. Now I can swing by the vintage store where she works and bring her treats from Sweet Adeline. I pick carrot cake, her favorite, and a black coffee with two raw sugars. I walk the two blocks to Joy's work, swinging open the door that jingles when I open it. The smell—a subtle must of countless closets, stranger-sweat, and time—blends with the burning stick of nag champa. I'm the only customer. The place is so tiny, you could walk five big steps and be up against the wall, and it's absolutely crowded with clothes racks. I've gotten quite a few cute dresses here in the past. Behind the counter a witchy hippie woman sits, shining a pair of cowboy boots over the jewelry case. I know her.

"Hey, Jamaica," I say. "Is Joy here?"

She puts the boot down and takes off her reading glasses.

"What's your name again?" she asks.

She asks me this every time I see her. Joy once described Jamaica as "more ancient than God and higher than him too." Jamaica is older than my grandmother and smokes more weed than a Santa Cruz fraternity.

"Betty," I remind her.

"Joy's sister!" she almost yells, jangling her bracelets in the air with the realization. "Where *is* Joy?"

She puts the boot she was shining onto the floor and steps into it, walking toward me.

"Is she all right?" she asks.

"She's . . . she's fine."

The moment needs to breathe—for me, anyway—because I stand here clutching the coffee and the cake and staring into Jamaica's cataracts and realize that something here is not adding up and I know exactly what it is.

Every once in a while, a moment like this happens, when you realize. And that thing that you realize, you also realize you already knew it deep inside. So really, it's a re-realizing of sorts. Or letting yourself face a realization that had been sitting there with you for a long time. Hi. Hey. I'm the truth, been here awhile. You ready to look at me?

The truth is, my sister hasn't been to work in weeks. In over a month. Since the I Glam shooting. In fact, I would bet Chanel haute couture that my sister has not left the house once since the first time she went to see her therapist. She has not kept her job like she promised she has. She's been lying to my mother, and lying to me.

"What happened?" Jamaica asks, her cold hand on my arm. "Have you *seen* her?"

"Yeah, I see her every day," I say, heart sinking.

"I thought she might be dead, I'm not joking," Jamaica says. "To just not show up like that, not answer her phone, nothing?" She shakes her head. "Are you sure she's all right?"

No, I want to say. *I'm not sure she's all right after all.*

"I'm sorry." I inch toward the door. "I didn't realize any of that. I . . . honestly, I thought she still worked here."

"Can you ask her to call me?" Jamaica says. "She still has a set of keys."

I open the door. "Sure, I'll tell her."

"Two years she worked here and then, *poof*, gone." Jamaica snaps her fingers.

"I don't know what to say."

"She really screwed me, you know that?" Jamaica says, her face visibly melting from disbelief to anger.

"Sorry," I say, and let the door swing shut behind me. I hurry around the corner and away from that incredibly uncomfortable situation.

I stand stunned a moment, in the sunshine, next to a mural of laughing people of all races holding hands. They look so fucking happy. I hurl the container of cake at them in an instant of rage that is so unlike me that by the time the plastic container hits the sidewalk, I have already run to rescue it from the ground like it was an accident.

"I'm sorry," I whisper to the slightly maimed but still intact cake container, picking it up. I look around to see if anyone was watching, but they weren't, unless you count the shirtless guy singing a song about Jesus as he rides up the wrong side of the street on a child's bike, and he seems too day-drunk to care.

I walk home three blocks to our apartment. We live upstairs in the top unit, above our landlord in one unit and his mother in the other. I stand on the porch for a moment and try to figure out what the hell I'm going to say to Joy. The answer is, I don't know, but I have to confront her about this. This has gone too far. She needs help. I go inside and kick off my shoes. I hear laughter, unfamiliar. Or no—déjà vu laughter. Joy's laugher braided with a low male laughter. I edge farther into the living room, and then the hallway. I stand and peer into her open doorway to confirm: it's Lex. Lex is back, and he's with my sister in her room, sitting next to her on her bed. They look like they belong together, both in tight-fitting black clothes and smudged-on-purpose eyeliner. He's showing her something on his phone. They look up at me.

"Hi," I say awkwardly, cutting the laughter into silence immediately with my presence.

"Hey, Crocker," he says.

His old nickname for me. You know, Crocker, Betty. Because I look old-fashioned and like cute sixties dresses or something. Real creative.

"Why are you home?" Joy asks, surprised.

"Fire alarm went off at work," I say. "Why are *you* home?"

"It's my birthday," she says.

She answers so automatically, so unflinchingly, it's really something. Although I guess she didn't lie. It *is* her birthday. But that's not why she's home. She's home because she's always home.

"And what are *you* doing here?" I ask Lex.

"He's visiting, what does it look like?" Joy says. "Jeez. Thanks for wishing me a happy birthday."

Shame flushes my cheeks. I step in and hand her the cake in its plastic container, and the coffee that has gone lukewarm in my hand. "Happy birthday."

"Awww, that's sweet," Joy says, taking them. "But what the fuck happened to this cake?"

"Sorry," I say.

"It's okay, I'll still eat it." She smiles and pulls me into a hug. She smells like perfume and something else—whiskey? I wouldn't put that past Lex. He's always partied hard. We push apart and I see, on her bed behind her, the Electric Wheelchair record I bought her for her birthday. That old stupid feeling swells over me. Joy sits down with the coffee and she and Lex begin devouring the cake with their fingers. I leave them in their disgusting peace, closing her door behind me.

Then I go in my room, take off my glasses, put my hair up in a ponytail, and cry into a pillow for exactly three minutes. I hate crying. I hate letting myself cry. It always feels like weakness, no matter what people tell you. But every once in a while I let myself do it—or more like I allow myself to do it—in order to push out the negative feelings that have built up inside of me. Clear them out. Flush them out, like a clog. Usually it does the trick. Good as new. Ready to face the world again. I go to the bathroom and freshen my face and put my glasses on.

But honestly, this time, I don't feel any better.

TWENTY-TWO

Joy says she wants Homeroom delivered for her birthday dinner. Homeroom is a hipster restaurant in North Oakland that solely serves mac and cheese at absurd prices. As we eat it together at the table, it sinks in that, worse than Joy not leaving the house today or any day anymore—not asking for her usual birthday spa treatments or tickets to stadium heavy metal shows (my sister contains multitudes)—is the fact that my mother is here, devouring the food as we chat about our days, and doesn't even seem to notice her eldest daughter has blossomed into a full-fledged agoraphobe.

I looked up the word earlier: *agoraphobia*. It comes from Greek meaning *fear of the marketplace*, tragically fitting, considering this all started with a deadly shooting in the marketplace. Seeing that etymology stare back at me brightly from dictionary.com made me settle comfortably and then steadfast in my defense of her. So she has a fear of public life. Well, of course she does. Who's the weirder one here sitting at this dinner table teeming with to-go containers of mac and cheese, festively lit with a Jesus candle festooned with a Sharpie top hat—the agoraphobe, or the woman who thinks she's going to save the world?

"I'm honestly thinking we might get to a point where we can repeal the Second Amendment in the next decade," Mom says. "I know it sounds extreme, but I've been discussing it with MAGS, and *this* is my next media-ready talking point. You have terrorists shooting up kindergarten classes, shopping malls, movie theaters, and you have no one willing to pass any meaningful legislation to curtail it—fine, then. You've shown you can't responsibly legislate guns. You've lost your privilege, America."

This, by the way, is Mom's response after I asked her how her day went. I was expecting work news. Instead, immediately, she dove into this sermon. Shows where her mind is. Oh, and happy birthday, Joy. I'm almost hoping my sister is whiskey-buzzed numb from her sit-down with Lex earlier. Her cheeks are flushed, but it could be the buffalo sauce in her mac and cheese, the romantic blitz of his visit, our mother's pontifications. You never know.

"Anyway," I say, steering the conversation away from the diatribe. "Lex was over. How was *that*?"

A smile dances on Joy's lips as she stabs a brussels sprout. "You know when you haven't seen someone in a short forever, and you see them, and so much has happened—and yet—and yet, it's like, with the two of you, nothing did happen? The whole word disappears? Time never passed?"

"I feel that way with your father sometimes," Mom says. "But not in a pleasant way. More like the wound is forever open."

I look up at my mom, surprised by this admission. I mean, I knew it, I detected it, but to hear it said out loud's still a jolt.

Joy chews a brussels sprout dreamily, ignoring what my mom just said. "Well, I feel that way with Lex."

"So Electric Wheelchair's playing Gilman tomorrow," I say.

"I know," she says.

"We should go," I say.

"*We?*" she asks, eyebrows raised.

"Yeah. We should go. I went to high school with a guy who's in the opening band. Dr. Crusher."

I stare at her, without blinking, to see what she'll say.

"Sounds fun," she says flatly.

"How adorable, my girls heading off to a show together," Mom says. "I'm supposed to speak to a group of gun violence survivors tomorrow night."

"Do you ever stop, Mom?" Joy asks. "Sometimes I get exhausted just listening to you; I can't even imagine *being* you."

"We all keep going in our own ways," Mom says, putting the lid back on her leftovers and pinching the tinfoil corners to make it stick.

My mom gives Joy a pair of skull earrings and a journal, which has a cover made of an old record, gifts that make Joy squeal and hug her.

When Joy opens my gift, she laughs.

"I know," I tell her. "I was so proud of myself when I found it. Then I walked in and saw Lex in there today and I realized how stupid it was."

Joy hugs me long and hard, still rocking with laughter. I'm not sure why it's *that* funny. Mom gets teary and tells the story of what it was like on the day Joy was born, how scary it was when she didn't cry at first. Her serious, tiny face with her squinty eyes. She pulls Joy into a long hug and tells her, "I'm so glad you were born, Joy Maple Lavelle."

"Moth-*errr*," Joy says, muffled by our mother's shoulder.

"And I'm so glad you're alive," Mom says.

Her voice catches at the end there. She breaks the hug, gets up, and wipes her eyes with a napkin. She busies herself with the containers of lukewarm, half-eaten food.

After leftovers get put away, Mom gets on a loud speaker-phone call with some MAGS person, and I follow Joy into her room. She lies on her bed, rubbing her stomach, blissful look on her face as she closes her eyes.

"When I was twenty-one, it was a very good year," she sings in her sultry voice.

But was it, Joy? I don't sing back. I kick the door shut behind me and sit next to her on her bed.

"Why are you here and not at a bar tearing up the place?" I ask. "It's your twenty-first."

"You know why," she says, not opening her eyes.

"You haven't left the house since right after the shooting, have you."

There is no question mark. There is no question.

She opens her eyes. She doesn't seem surprised. Her eyes are pink. After a moment, she says, "I like not leaving the house."

"I thought your doctor gave you medication."

"And I take it, religiously," she says, sitting up, the hair trigger of her temper pulled. "And I attend our phone meetings, and I exercise, and I fucking *meditate* now, did you know that, Betty?"

"That's good."

"I am working. I am working my *ass* off, so don't sit there with that look on your face."

"What look?"

"Like you're trying to poop out a feeling."

"I went to High Priestess today."

She falls back on the bed and closes her eyes, instant feigned fainting.

"I can't believe you just ghosted your boss," I go on. "She's been so good to you."

"What am I supposed to say?" she asks, sitting up rigid as an automaton. "I'm a mess because I'm having a very special kind of mental breakdown?"

"Sure, say whatever you want, as long as it's the truth."

"It's my birthday, and you're in here lecturing me."

I open my mouth for a retort, but she's right. I'm in here confronting her and it's her birthday. So I stop.

"I hope you'll consider going to the show with me

tomorrow," I say quietly. "I would love it if we went together."

"I would love to too for a million fucking reasons, including the fact that Lexy is there and I want to see him so bad," she says, her voice breaking a little. "But I . . . I have to be honest that I don't see myself doing that."

"Why?"

"Because if I imagine being there, in that crowded club, in a dark room filled with noise and music, I just, I mean . . . what if someone started shooting in there? I can't enjoy myself knowing that that could happen. I—I can't go places anymore in a world this dangerous."

"Oh, Joy," I say.

The tears start falling down her face. No expression accompanies them. She flicks the tears away like annoyances. It breaks my heart. Three women in this house, none of whom ever allow ourselves the inconvenience of crying. Yet here we are, all three of us breaking down in one way or another in the past few days.

I try to put my arms around her, but she holds an arm up to block me.

"Don't feel sorry for me," she warns. "You'd better not. And please, please don't tell anyone this. I hate this so much, I'm trying to work through it, I swear. Please don't tell Mom."

The begging in her voice is a knife. It hurts to see someone so strong acting this weak.

"You know Mom could help you," I say. "She's been

through it *with* you. She's out there, trying to change the world because of all this."

Joy shakes her head. "She doesn't get it."

"She was there!"

"She doesn't get it, Betty."

"Help us get it, then," I say.

"I don't need a goddamn MAGS meeting. I don't need some political show," Joy says. "I need to understand why this really happened. I need to know how to spot a killer, where to avoid showing up. I need to know how to stop these things from ever happening *to me*."

It seems impossible, what she's asking.

"Can you promise if we go to the show tomorrow night, nothing bad will happen?" she asks, her tears drying, her eyes unblinking.

"No one can promise that."

She sits up. "Well, I can promise if I stay here in my room, nothing bad will happen."

I want to argue with her. Of course, I understand the basis of her fear. But bad things can always happen. House fires, earthquakes, break-ins. I don't tell her this. I don't want to pop this precarious bubble of safety she's constructed, imaginary as it may be. Plus, something in her turned, bad weather blew in. She puts on her leopard-print robe and hugs her arms tight along her chest.

"I told Lexy I'd text him," she says. "He might come over after his show in the city."

"Sounds good," I say.

"This is not how I expected twenty-one," she says. "At home, still living with Mom, a community college dropout with PTSD."

"This isn't how I expected my life to be either," I say.

"Maybe we should stop expecting things, huh?" she muses. "'Cause it doesn't seem to be working out so well."

I leave her to text Lex. I go to my room and brush my hair, heart like a brick. The video player in my brain rewinds, and I go over what she said. I hear it on a loop, repeating.

I need to understand why this really happened.

I need to know how to spot a killer, where to avoid showing up.

I need to know how to stop these things from ever happening to me *again.*

I see footage over the loop—Joshua Lee in the halls, an angry look on his face, his ROTC uniform. The fire alarm going off, smoke snaking upward toward the sun from an ablaze trash can in the quad. Students leaning over and whispering to each other about that rumor that he inappropriately touched a teacher. No one could decide which teacher it was. No one knew if it was true.

There is no cure for psychopathy.

But you know, *I* could have stopped Joshua Lee. *I* could have seen the signals, had I understood they were signals. If my gaze had been more vigilant that day of the shooting, if I had been paying more attention, perhaps I would have spotted him out the window as I ate that cupcake. Perhaps a crazed look on his face, his overstuffed gym bag, something would have tipped my intuition off. I had so many chances to stop this. So many people had so many chances to stop this. But no one did.

We failed.

We failed Joy.

We failed Shandra Pensky.

We should have done more; we need to do better.

The solution must be more than better locks, bulletproof glass. It has to be more than the Second Amendment. All these theories exist about why it happened: guns, mental health issues, misogyny. From my mother, from writers online, and social media soapbox screamers. But they don't know Joshua Lee. None of us did. So what *was* it? What was it that triggered the monster in him? How did he go from being that boy in the Facebook picture, hugging the dog, to an attempted mass murderer? If I can find the answer to this— if I can really find it, the peculiarities of his case, learn about Joshua Lee, reverse-engineer this tragedy—maybe I will discover something close to an answer. And we will know how to prevent this, and Joy will leave the house again.

In a moment so thunderstruck with clarity and self-confidence, it's nearly psychic, I know exactly what is going to happen next.

I am going to go to the show tomorrow.

I am going to become friends with Michael Lee.

PART TWO

TWENTY-THREE

This black shift dress is so shifty, with its batwing-cut cap sleeves; it could marry a beaded cardigan for an ooh-la-la office outfit, or it could rock a concert if perfectly paired with a jean jacket. $220.

Here I am in a designer dress like a living iteration of my stupid ad copy, complete with denim jacket and boots. Lipstick emergency red (borrowed from my mother). Before I left the house, in the dim bedroom light with the mascara and the hairspray, I felt so gorgeous, a girl in the TV of my own mind. Here, I feel like a human lump. Worse, I am overdressed.

I am standing outside a beige sign, cursive lettering reading *The Caning Shop*. This is 924 Gilman, legendary underground punk club. There's a bustle and a crowd. Everyone has rips in their clothing, dye in their hair, or piercings in their epidermis (epidermises? I honestly don't know). There is loudness, boisterousness. A girl with braids

braids another girl's hair against the side of the brick building, some drama about a guy named Scooter is yelled about, a boy with puffy Hawaiian-print pants and a shirt that says *PISS RIGHT OFF* is doing skateboard tricks. There is a lot of black clothing, mostly black clothing, a scene Joy would blend right into. Even though the show hasn't started, the front doors are spitting fluorescent sunshine and blaring stereo music already. Everyone here is young, some younger than me. I keep thinking I recognize faces. And yet, I feel panicked, like I've made a mistake. I should go home. I'm overdressed. I'm here alone. I don't belong, in more than one way. Worse, I can imagine Joy's voice in my head, saying, *What if there was a shooting?* My heart picks up a little, lifted by a fearful inner wind.

I see community now, and I see a target.

I hate it.

"Hey," Antonio says, poking my shoulder.

I am so relieved to be rescued by him, I give him a long hug. He smells good, like something baked and sweet. And I love that he wore a tie tonight, but one with skulls on it; this, I realize, is the first time I've seen him outside of work. And he's exactly the same, but a smidge edgier.

A mirror image, really.

"A nonconsensual hug?" he asks me as we pull away. "That's an HR no-no."

We both laugh because he's referring to a very bad video we were forced to watch at work. Bad actors running through badly scripted scenarios with a voiceover and outdated graphic blaring *That's an HR no-no!* every time something veered inappropriate.

"I'm so glad you're here," I tell him.

"Why?"

"I felt stupid alone."

"Isn't it weird how you're, like, you're alone at home and you're fine, right? And then you go in public and you feel stupid alone," he says.

"Right?"

"I try to fight the stigma," he tells me. "I go to brunch alone, I go to bars alone, I go to movies alone."

"Good for you."

"I guess," he answers. "Is it ever really a choice though?"

I think of my sister, in her room. "It can be."

"True. Look at me, showing up, hi, and then diving ten miles deep." He gives me a squeeze, his arm around my back. I still feel so stupid, so stuck-out and too-fancy here, but he doesn't seem to notice. "What kind of music is this band we're here to see?"

"Like, heavy. You know, Melvinsy, with synths."

"I have no idea what you're saying right now."

"I don't either, honestly." I talk lowly into Antonio's ear. "The guy in the opening band . . . I went to high school with him."

"Oh, it's like that," he says, raising his eyebrows. "You went to *high school* together."

As if "high school" is a euphemism for something.

"I don't know you well enough to read you right now, but if you're inferring something nefarious—" I say.

"I'm always inferring something nefarious."

"—then no. Truth? His brother"—and now I am full-fledged whispering in his ear, because I'm not trying to be rude—"he was the I Glam shooter."

GASP.

"And," I whisper on. "My sister's ex is in the headlining band."

GASP. He resumes a normal tone now, hand to heart. "You did not tell me this show was so laced with history. This is some drama right here. So why did you come, exactly?"

I open my mouth to respond. Somewhere in me, I have an answer. But no words form. On the surface, I don't know what I want or why I came, but somewhere, deep, deep, I know— I came here to make friends with Michael Lee, because he might have something near an answer for my sister's despair. Some key that will unlock her self-made cage and allow her to feel safe.

I'm about to admit this when the band begins to play. Antonio and I move to the door and wait in the line that's formed, take out our wallets to pay.

"When we get back out, remind me to tell you about the guy I went on a date with who was actually a Scientologist trying to convert me," he says.

I raise my brows now.

"Mmm-hmm," he says. "I think I'm going to write a chapbook called *Tinder Hearted* about all these horrible dates I've been on."

"I love that idea! I didn't know you wrote poetry."

"I do," he says kind of shyly.

I tell him about how Zoe used to do slam poetry Wednesday nights at the Starry Plough, an Irish pub on the other side of the Ashby subway station. I have many fond memories of drinking Arnold Palmers and cheering her on from a wobbly table in the front. Then I mention that I once won a districtwide poetry contest sophomore year.

"What?" Antonio asks. "I want to read it!"

I would never let him read it. It mortifies me, that poem. It's an emo sonnet about how much I missed knowing my father and how we were divided by a titular Uneasy Sea. It was drowning in water metaphors. I can't even believe I won a hundred-dollar Amazon gift card for it.

"It's nothing," I say. "I'm not really a poet. I was just trying it out."

"You're a good writer, though. I mean, at work. You're good."

"Yeah, takes such *talent*, that catalog copy."

"Seriously. It does."

I can't tell if his sarcasm is so dry it's undetectable, or if he's serious right now.

Our conversation is cut off as we get in the door, pay for and buy membership cards—apparently we need them here, we're now part of the club—and then go inside into the dark room. The walls are painted black. There's a stage at the end of the room, lit with red lights, graffitied backdrop, where the band is playing. The crowd seethes with excitement. Even though it's warm in here from so many bodies, I get a shiver as a smoke machine spills clouds onto the floor of the stage. I note the exits, the bathroom. I edge close to the exit doors near the left of the stage, thinking, if a shooting happened right now, I could hide under the merch tables. So that's where I stand to watch the show. It sucks that these are the things I think about. I never used to scan every public place for the neon exit signs. I never even noticed they were there, honestly.

At least Antonio's here. I'm glad I'm not alone in this crowd. We slip earplugs in our ears that we bought on our way in and exchange a smile. The band is so loud I feel it through my boots. Their amps are probably taller than I am. There's the guy Max from Amoeba on synths, a girl whose face is hidden by a curtain of red hair on the guitar, and Michael beating the drums, headbanging along with it. I'm not a musical person, and this isn't my genre—whatever it is—but I know enough to tell right away that this band is pretty damn good. It's heavy, but it's hooky, and the synths make it danceable. Their singer, a girl in sunglasses with some Red Bull energy, commands the stage. People in the front are rocking along with every note of it, some are dancing, and when the song is done, a swell of appreciative screams fills the air.

"They're really good," Antonio says in my ear. "Which is the guy you went to school with?"

"Drummer."

"I *like* them," he says, sounding surprised.

"Me too," I agree.

Michael clicks off his drumsticks and another song begins. I've never been to a show like this before. I've been to the Greek at Cal's campus to see a couple concerts, but those had seating. Adrian and I went to the symphony once, and I went to a reggae show with Zoe. This, here, is entirely different. Everyone is *electrified*. It's like the music is moving through us, sparking something within each of us. I can't help but bob my head and find the beat with my heels. I forget about the exit signs. I forget about danger. I wish Joy were here to forget about it with me.

Joy has been to so many shows at this venue. She even volunteered at Gilman early on in high school. By junior year, she had graduated from punk to metal, grew her green Mohawk out and dyed her locks black, and started going to stadium shows with Lex. If anyone would understand this electricity I'm experiencing, it would be Joy.

When Dr. Crusher's set is done, the overhead lights come on and the exit doors blow open. We ride the people river out to the side of the building facing a quiet industrial street. The blue night air hits me, cool and relieving on my sweaty face. Antonio and I stand against the brick building and take a selfie together. Screw humility, we look cute as hell. Cliques, couples, skaters, smokers mingle around us, the buzz of their collective conversation tingling along with the ringing aftermath of Dr. Crusher in my ears.

"How well do you know the drummer?" he asks.

"Not well. We sat next to each other in school, but he was super shy."

"So . . . why'd you come?"

"I ran into him at Amoeba. He works there. He gave me a flyer. I don't know, it sounded fun."

"Do you think he's cute?"

"I haven't really thought about it."

"I'd cuddle him."

"You'd cuddle anyone."

He sucks in a feigned *I'm offended* breath.

It's true. I don't know Antonio that well, but I do know his bar is much lower than mine.

"Oh, and you're so high and mighty," he says. "Who would you cuddle, then?"

"The barista."

There's a barista at a coffee shop across the street from Retrofit who I have a well-known (to Antonio, anyway) crush on. She's got these big almost-black eyes she draws on with perfect cat-eye liner, light brown skin, and lips she glosses up pink as a Popsicle. She bleaches her short hair platinum and has an incredible sense of style.

"Okay, who else?"

I think. "I don't know, that guy who used to work in sales,

the one with the really blue eyes."

"*Nick?* He was so preppy. He liked *baseball*."

I shrug.

"Your taste is utterly unpredictable," Antonio says.

"You should see my exes." I give him a rundown of Hassan, Molly, and Adrian, the three of whom are so different they could star in a remake of *The Breakfast Club*. The one thing they had in common was they were all really smart.

It's hard for me to crush on people for looks alone. I mostly crush on people's brains. Half the reason I like the barista so much is because she labors over a sketchbook in her downtime, and her drawings—I've peeked—are gorgeous. And Nicolas, well, he had one of the most amazing vocabularies I've ever encountered. I downloaded the Merriam-Webster app to my phone after talking to him in the break room one day.

Antonio starts to tell me about the Scientologist as the band comes out, one by one, carrying equipment to the van parked about fifteen feet away in a parking spot against the building. They wheel their enormous amps, hurry past with instruments in cases. Michael catches my eye and gives me a nod as he carries a stack of drums. This friendly exchange equals progress in my mission. Box checked. I wave and smile, thinking, *I can't believe your brother killed a total stranger. And tried to kill a whole lot more. You, Michael, are the key to me understanding why.*

Then I feel guilty for the thought, because Michael just

thinks I'm some nice girl from high school who came to see a show. He doesn't know that my sister and mom were almost shot that day, that we have this sordid connection, that that sordid connection is what compelled me here in the first place.

How could two people share DNA, be closer blood-relations-wise than mother and daughter or father and son, be the closest you could be to a twin, really, without being a twin, and end up so different?

"You weren't listening to anything I said, were you?" Antonio asks.

"I'm sorry," I say, turning back to him. "I'm ... distracted."

"It's fine. Short version is, I thought he was taking me home to make out, but instead he tried to get me to do an E-meter reading and watch a propaganda film."

"Oh dear."

"I pretended to have a family emergency and got the hell out of there."

"Good move."

I scan the crowd to see if Michael's anywhere. I can't just let him slip away and have this whole night be for nothing. The van they loaded into is closed. Something else, though, has caught my eye. Another van parked next to Dr. Crusher's van, with smoke billowing out the windows and a familiar hacking sound. I would know Lex's 420 cough anywhere. Plus, the Electric Wheelchair skeleton logo is spray-painted on the van. I can't see Lex, but I know he's got to be in there.

"You get nervous at all?" Antonio asks. "Being out in public after . . . everything?"

This, by the way, is a weird thing that happened after the shooting. Most people don't want to name it, don't want to call it a "shooting." They say "after what happened" or "after the incident" or even "after, you know." Little do they understand that naming it couldn't possibly make it scarier than what it already was.

"I do," I say. "I mean, you saw how that fire alarm triggered me."

"Which is why I asked." He speaks gently, like I'm breakable. "So . . . is there anything that *does* make you feel safer?"

I watch a girl doing skateboard tricks off a curb while someone films her with their phone yelling, "Sick! So sick!" Inside, someone tunes their guitar onstage.

"Like if they had metal detectors here?" he asks.

I shake my head.

How to tell him nothing would make me feel safe, except to know how to spot a monster? That that is precisely what compelled me here tonight?

I'm rescued by the band beginning. Antonio turns and follows the crowd around the corner to the entrance. I'm right behind him. But then I hit a snag. My sleeve is pulled from behind. I turn around and it's Michael. Gold struck. I step aside and let everyone flood forward toward the music, including Antonio, who doesn't look behind him to notice. All I can think as Michael smiles at me is *I hope he didn't hear*

Antonio and me talking. But of course he didn't. We were murmuring to each other in a spot against the wall away from anyone else. Michael looks invigorated, his hair wild from sweat, his eyes dancing.

"You came!" he says.

"You were great," I say.

Great. Of all the adjectives in all the thesauruses in the world, I had to go with *great*.

But he doesn't seem picky about his compliments. He grins. "Thanks."

In a moment or two, the last of the people have trickled in to see the next band and the bustle has evaporated. It's just Michael and me here, under a floodlight, my heart pounding louder than the drummer inside. This is it, my chance. I feel a little sick from how excitedly he looks at me, like I'm a genuinely kind person interested in his music and personhood and not a lost soul exploiting him for answers about his dead murderous brother.

"I've never been to a show here," I say to silence the silence. "My sister used to come here all the time."

"How do you like it?"

"It feels . . . I don't know. Spirited."

He grins. I shouldn't even note it, because Michael never seems to stop grinning. Even when he was drumming, his smile was a permanent fixture. "I've spent way too much of my wasted youth here."

"Doesn't seem wasted to me. Hey, at least you're part of a community. I spent my wasted youth in fashion club meetings and befriending people who all moved away to fancy schools."

"It's weird how many people leave the area, huh?"

"Privilege provides some distance."

"Amen. My family's only managed to stay here because of EBT cards and rent control. College wasn't an option. Funny how being poor means I'm stuck here in the most expensive city in the country."

"The irony," I agree. "My family's *exactly* the same."

A moment stretches. My mind fills it with the realization that his mother, living off EBT cards and skating by on rent control, already living a not-easy existence, recently lost a son. When life deals you hard hands, it seems it just keeps dealing you more of the same. But then I shake my pity, reminding myself to stop feeling sorry for a murderer. That's not why I'm here.

It's not Joshua I feel for, though. It's who he left behind. No one wants their son or brother to become what he did.

"You play music?" Michael asks me.

"I wish. I'm not creative like that. I'm an intern at Retrofit."

He blinks with a blankness that clearly says he has no idea what Retrofit is.

"It's a fashion company. I write ad copy. For free!" I give him some jazz hands.

"Oh, one of those coveted unpaid internships," he says.

"Exactly. A great 'opportunity.' A stepping-stone to an underpaid internship."

"Between my friends who flew off to out-of-state schools and are digging themselves into crisis-level student debt, and you and your unpaid internship, I'm not feeling so bad about my dead-end record-store job."

"Hey, you get a paycheck. More than I can say."

Michael is so immediately easy to talk to. He's eager and interested, he's sharp-witted and self-deprecating, he's humble and a little goofy, too. We stand against the brick wall and talk about our parents, oddly similar—both single moms with chickenshit dads who live far away. He laughs when I tell him about Namaste House.

"My dad ran off to live in a commune in Oregon," he says. "They make hammocks and wind chimes."

"You're joking."

"If I was, believe me, I'd come up with something more original than that. Seriously. It's a vegan gluten-free utopia that has their own monetary system based on acorns."

"Sounds like your dad has my dad beat."

The conversation skirts dangerously close to siblings. For a moment, his grin falters and he kicks his Vans on the gravel. "I guess we should go inside," he says.

"Yeah, my friend's probably wondering where we are."

But we both shuffle slow and get caught in conversation again. We talk about high school and what a dimwit our

English teacher was, always wheeling those old-school TVs in the room and showing us movies of Shakespeare adaptations instead of reading Shakespeare. And how he read excerpts of *Catcher in the Rye* in some indistinguishable accent.

"What *was* that?" Michael asks.

I'm laughing so hard remembering, there are tears in the corners of my eyes. "I don't know."

"Brooklyn? Boston? He was trying way too hard to embody Holden Caulfield. Remember how he even wore a hunting cap? That guy was like if Michael Scott taught English. He was either skating by with movie versions of classics or he went all in to a mortifying degree. . . . There was no in between."

Everything he's saying is so true. I had no friends in that class and honestly never sat down and thought about it since. I simply endured it, like most of high school. In retrospect, though, it seems hilarious.

"How far away all that seems now," I say.

"I tested out of senior year, so it feels even farther away from me," he says.

"Oh yeah? Why'd you do that?"

"Trying to be the knight in shining armor, making money for my mom, working to save my brother."

My smile falters at the mention of the word *brother*. I remember my mission here, why I sought him out. For a while there it was like we were two normal people. Inside, the music blares. Out here, it's just noise. "Oh," I say.

"My mom got to keep the apartment, but we lost my brother," he says. "So ultimately it was a failure. But it got me out of high school."

We lost my brother. So different than the story I've been telling myself, the story I've seen printed everywhere, that his brother was an aggressor, a perpetrator. He was not lost. He sought hatred and violence. He found it and ended there.

I guess all of these things are true.

I am thinking that I should write these things down at some point before I forget them. My tongue is trying to locate a response when a burst of laughter and car door slamming interrupts our conversation. I look up and see a girl in a long black gown arm in arm with Lex aka Alexander Doody. They have cigarettes dangling from their mouths and eyes redder than Mars. Lex stops in front of me and points a finger in my face.

"You," he says.

"Always so eloquent," I say. "Hi, Lex."

I'm trying to keep my eyes on him, but I can't help the urge to give his goth floozy the stink eye. She's such a cheap replica of Joy, only probably younger, and I'm sure nowhere as near a catch as my sister. I wonder if Lex has mentioned this girl in texts or late-night visits to my smitten sister. My heart hurts for Joy, because I know if she were here, she'd be on his arm. And if not, she'd probably be starting a fist-fight with this bitch (she would call her a bitch). Instead, she's probably popping a benzo and watching *TNG* reruns by herself in her room, Christmas lights atwinkle around her.

My poor sister.

"You know him?" Michael asks as Lex passes.

"My sister's ex," I say.

"He's in Electric Wheelchair."

"Right."

"He's . . . well, sounds like you already know him. He's got no shortage in the self-esteem department."

"What my sister sees in him is truly a mystery."

"I mean, he's sexy," says Michael. "I get it. He's charismatic. I'd make out with him. Would I trust him within a millimeter of my life? Hells nos."

"Plural hells, plural nos."

"That's what I'm saying."

Michael and I keep inching toward the front, then staggering to a standstill as we keep talking. By the time we make it to the front door (since the side is closed while bands play), the band is done and people come out again. I can't believe how hungry we were to talk. And yet I still didn't even get a minute of what I came here for: some insight into his brother, some perspective there. It's like I've been chatting with an old friend, like when Zoe and I get on the phone so starved for each other there's so much said, it seems to breed more of the unsaid.

Antonio comes out and shoots me this look, a capital-*L*

Look with eyebrows like carets. Michael's bandmates and their crew join up with us, and all at once, here we are, a hodgepodge group.

"This is Max," Michael says.

I reach my hand out for a handshake, but Max gives me a weird fist bump and I say, "Oh." It's so awkward we both laugh.

"And his girlfriend, Vera," Michael finishes, pointing to a girl with a vamp haircut and baby-doll dress, arm in arm with a wavy-haired blonde in a fur coat and ballet slippers.

"*Partner*," Max corrects him.

"Hi," Vera says, waving. "I'm . . . whatever. Max's human. This is my friend Anna."

The girl in the fur coat waves and answers in a raspy voice, "Hi! Hey! What's your name?"

"Betty." Everyone watches me like I require further explanation. "I knew Michael back in the day."

"Back in the day of high school," Michael explains.

I smile at Max. "You were really good."

These people all seem a few years older and much more at ease with themselves than I am. For the millionth time tonight, I wish Joy were here. She'd impress everyone just being herself. Here I am barking "good!" and "great!" like a puppy.

"Danke," Max says, and moonwalks backward for no reason.

Everyone laughs. Antonio joins him and asks if he's doing

it right, and they do it together. For a minute, a sweet burst erupts in me. Here I am, unexpectedly, sharing laughter with people I have never met until tonight. This scene is so foreign and yet familiar, conjuring something buried backward in time, and then it dawns with a pop what it is: for the first time since those gunshots, since life became mere survival, I can catch a glimpse of something more in the barely discernable road ahead—something unpredictable and full of life and melody and the ever-nearness of strangers who could be friends. For the first time since the shooting, I can fathom a future for Betty Birch Lavelle. And it strikes me like a blow to the gut to realize this, because to do so is to realize I have been missing myself all this time.

TWENTY-FOUR

Fall has always been my favorite time of year. Though we are in seasonless California, Berkeley is well populated with trees that yellow, orange, redden, brown, then bald. The air shifts, a gentle chill bittering evenings and early mornings. The clock turns backward and darkens our dinner hours. Pumpkin mountains jut up at grocery store entrances, Halloween shops explode on street corners grinning with skeletons and faux spiderwebs. And, most importantly, the fashion adds so many layers of possibilities—scarves and fingerless gloves, knee-high leather boots, stockings and peacoats. *This cashmere sweaterdress is your coziest electric blanket dream, alive and walking the working world. $299.* At night I fall asleep to the hum of the space heater, or better yet, the tiptoeing of gentle rain.

There's no way to really trace when and how a friendship is born. Is it in high school classes, when I sat next to Michael and shared the same space without interacting? Was it in Amoeba, when I took that flyer for his show and dared to make eye contact, or was it the night he played and we had our first burst of easy conversation? I don't know when a friend officially becomes a friend, but as the weeks pass and fall deepens, we text back and forth enough that if I don't hear from him in a few days, I begin to worry. I haven't learned anything that clues me into his brother yet (not exactly something to broach over text), but I have kind of accidentally become his friend. We haven't actually met up since the show. Mostly our conversations consist of him recommending music to me, or me complaining about my internship, or us making fun of the absurd Bay Area. He sends me a picture of a person dressed as a pig on a Lime scooter, I send him a picture of a church sign that spells *JESUS HAD TWO DADS AND TURNED OUT JUST FINE*.

On Halloween, he invites me to a house show Dr. Crusher is playing, but I decline, because Joy is at home in a witch costume handing out candy. Joy, who used to celebrate Halloween with the fervor of a five-year-old at Christmas during her teenage years, who used to go out all night long party-hopping. Who, a year or two ago, would have been the one at a show. Now she's handing out peanut butter cups to kids and pretending it's fun. Between doorbell rings, we half watch a bad, outdated Halloween movie with teenagers getting knifed by some dude in a mask. She clutches my arm and screams at the scary parts. I sit, laughing, glad for her nearness, sad for her nearness. She checks her phone more than once—momentarily, glancing at it with instantaneous disappointment, then pressing a button to darken it.

Lex is on the road again. Europe. He hasn't reached out much.

"Time differences," Joy says.

Right. That must be it.

It's weird to have to be the one fake-yawning and making excuses for bed, my wide-eyed sister ready to watch the slasher sequel with her finger poised over the *rent now* button onscreen.

"In this one it's his son who returns!" she says. "Shit gets next-generational. We could order pupusas."

"Joy, I have to work in the morning," I say, standing up and stretching. "We have a meeting on the spring line."

"Oh, the spring line, cool, what's that?" she asks.

She says it so genuinely that I assume it's sarcasm, till I see her dewy, moisturized face and big eyes. She smiles wide, red-lipsticked for no one but me. My heart breaks a little at her happiness. I miss her meanness. I miss her absence. They seem such odd things to miss. But they were hers. This person, willing to get excited about hearing about such mundane things, she's not the person I used to know.

"It's just a stupid rundown of what's next," I say. "Sitting around trying to get people to get excited about spending their money with us."

As I say this, it lands with a heaviness, almost a thud; apparently I am not who I used to be either.

The biggest red flag, though, is when Dad's care package

for Joy's birthday arrives, almost a month late, of course. It's a running joke at this point; every year, he sends some random box of stuff we have no use for that shows how completely out of touch he is with us. It arrives so late, we've forgotten the birthday ever happened. One year he sent me a pair of used clogs not in my size along with a hand-carved wooden doll missing an arm. Another, I got some expired Swedish candies and a plastic package with soap, an eye mask, and a washcloth that was clearly from a hotel room. We've learned to laugh about it over the years, because if we're not laughing about it, the fact our dad barely knows us or remembers our birthdays would probably make us weep.

This year, Dad sends Joy a dusty candle with the word *Relax* printed on it in gold, a self-help book called *(L)Affirmations: Jokes for the Woke*, and a macramé kit. I expect some sarcastic comment, but Joy says, "How sweet of him!" By the end of the day, her candle is half-burned, she has completed a knotted doily with the kit, and she recites a joke to me from her book about what Buddha said to the hot dog vendor.

"What did he say?" I ask.

"I'll have one with everything," she says, chuckling.

I nod and smile, thinking, *This is it. I can't pretend Joy is okay any longer.* Rock bottoms look different on everyone, I guess, and this here—laughing at such a stupid joke, making *doilies*—is hers.

I'm worried about Joy and I can't talk to my mother about

it at home. Our walls are too thin and Joy is ever-present. Besides, Mom's been so distracted with some boycott MAGS is working on, I've hardly seen her. I still haven't told a soul my sister stopped going to her job, and Mom hasn't asked. Everything lately has been "next semester," this vague someday of a phrase Joy and my mom exchange that holds infinite possibilities. Next semester she'll retake her classes she dropped, or next semester maybe she'll start research-ing universities, or next semester she could take off and work full-time. I hear these conversations from my room, sound-ing so obnoxiously normal, and close the door.

After the Doily Incident, Mom and I meet up in down-town Oakland one night for pizza slices after work. She's still in her suit, and as she talks about the dangers of silencers, I focus on the fact she's wearing what I would consider to be an excess of blush, and that I think she rocks shoulder pads surprisingly well in that thrift-store blazer. I wonder if shoulder pads will come back. She talks about how many decibels silencers shave off gunshots, and lists off assassinations they've been used in, and the states where silencers are banned, and I nod and will myself not to panic and think of guns as real things right now. I am in a pizza restaurant, sitting over a steaming, lovely, gooey-cheesy triangle of dreams. I burn my mouth on the pizza. It's weird to be thankful for pain, because it's a relief from the anxiety.

"You're awfully quiet," she says.

"I was just listening to your talk of silencers," I say. "In silence."

"Ha," she says, with no smile.

"It's truly amazing to me you have the stamina for this. I mean, you work all day, and then every night it's MAGS."

The word *MAGS* drips with something embarrassingly close to jealousy. Why? Is it because I want her attention, or because I want her passion for something bigger than myself?

She takes a moment to swallow her pizza, and then replies, "I do this for *you*."

"Really."

"For my girls. Because you deserve this," she says, pointing out the window, where people walk and laugh and ride scooters and pigeons strut merrily on sidewalks and cars laze to a stop at a yellow-then-red light. "You deserve to feel safe here. I'm going to make sure you feel safe."

She's genuine, and yet I'm reminded of her on a tiny screen, preaching.

This, right here, is a perfect segue.

"I don't think it's me you have to worry about," I tell her.

She gives me her crust, our unspoken agreement since age five. I chew it with a crunch.

"You mean Joy," she says.

"Mom, she made a *doily*," I say. "With a *macramé kit* Dad

sent in his birthday package."

"Yes, I saw," she says with concern. "It was a nice doily, though, you must admit."

"Dad sent her a self-help book of jokes, and . . . Mom," I say. "Mom."

"What?" she asks, leaning in.

"She laughs at them."

Mom puts her hand over her eyes in what looks like pain.

"She's not herself," I say.

"She's not," Mom agrees, taking her hand away and offering not quite a smile, but a little wistful lip swish. "None of us are. Have you considered, Bets, that maybe we never will be?"

I press my tongue to where the pizza burned the roof of my mouth raw, a secret meaty pain.

"So what, you're okay with her being like this forever?" I ask.

Mom shakes her head, checks her phone. I'm about to tell her Joy no longer has a job—the information sits ready in my throat, despite the fact I swore I wouldn't tell. But then Mom shows me the screen. Her hand just barely shakes, and even the slightest whiff of her weakness kills me. I remember, in that moment, what it was like to realize, as a child, she was human and capable of error. It turned my whole world inside out.

"This is what I'm dealing with right now," Mom says.

I'm not even understanding what she's showing me—an

article? Is this some goddamn MAGS thing? I take the phone and adjust my glasses, squint at the screen. It's an email from diebeverlylavelle@gmail.com, dated today.

ALL YOU LIBS TALK ABOUT IS GUNS! COUNRY IN THE CRAPPER! CANT WAIT TO EXERCISE MY 2ND AMEND-MENT RIGHTS AGAINST YOU CNT! GOT MY AK OK AND IT WONT BE LONG TIK YOU MEET ME
ALBERT SMITH

"What is this?" I ask.

She shows me another email, dated a couple days ago, same sender. It says:

SAW IN GTERVIEW TODAY AND WALTNED TO PUKE! FOUNDING FTAHERS ROLLUNG OVER IN THEIR GRAVES! I SHOOT TARGETS GOING TO PRINT ONE WITH OUR FACE ON IT! PRACTIVE
ALBERT SMITH

"'Practive,'" I repeat, trying to quell my overeager heart, which is thudding blood in my eardrums.

"I think he means 'practice,'" Mom says.

"Or 'proactive'?"

"Either way."

"How disturbing. Also, Albert Smith? Who signs hate mail?"

"Who knows if it's a real name? This guy has been emailing me this bullshit all week," she says. "I've had seven emails so far."

"So now you're getting hate mail," I say. "With threats. Badly spelled in all caps. Great."

"This goes with the territory," Mom says, returning her phone to her purse. "You've read story comments."

"I've tried to avoid the stories."

"Well, trolls are everywhere."

My heart is still thudding and I hate it. I wish I could teleport home in a blink. If trolls are everywhere, they might be here. They might be those guys with baseball caps watching a video together on their phone. They might be the man with the comb-over and slippers staring into space as he chews his pepperoni. The trolls, the psychopaths, the murderers. They slip by us and don't give us the right clues at the right time. The world is never safe.

The pizza remembers itself in my belly with a nauseating turn.

Mom stacks our plates. Fluffs her hair. Reaches for her scarf, ties a double knot. "You try to avoid the stories," she says as we get up.

"I do," I say as we exit the restaurant, the chill of November welcoming us on the twilit street.

"Even the ones I share? Even the ones about MAGS and the work we're doing?"

"Mom," I say. "To you, it feels productive, all this. That's great. But to me, I just open those articles and think about all this stuff and feel like I'm drowning."

"So how do you pay attention? What do you do to make the world a better place, then?" She's not asking in a challenging way. She sounds curious. But her question rings like a challenge to me, one I am in no way fit to meet. "And what makes you so different than Joy and her doilies?"

Joy and her doilies. Joy and her woke jokes. Me and my magazines. Me and my catalog copy. I ride home in the car in silence, soaking in my mother's righteousness, stinging with my meaninglessness, trying to ignore my dumb reflection in the window and to see the world instead. But I am so distracting.

TWENTY-FIVE

Turns out, Michael and I live pretty close. In a normal world, I would invite him over to my house at some point, but the *normal world* ceased to exist a few months ago. Now inviting him would be unthinkable. First, my sister would be there, because my sister is always there, and what if she recognized him and connected the dots and realized I was hanging out with the terrorist's brother? (My mother said MAGS wants to "shift the narrative" and call mass shooters "terrorists.") And imagine if Michael came over and connected the dots and realized that my sister and mother were in the shooting—how stunned and weirded out would he be if he knew that twisted connection was what compelled me to find him in the first place?

So when we meet up for the first time after a month of texting, we get tacos at a place right near the BART station. It's a tiny building with colorful flags decorating the outside. It smells pretty good, but I notice the words *textured soy protein* appearing with alarming frequency on the menu and no mention of cheese. I turn the menu over a few times before it truly sinks in.

"Michael," I say. "I believe this place is vegan."

"Yeah, it's great. I'm vegan—is that okay?"

"Sure."

Vegan Mexican food is never okay, but I'm not about to be disagreeable. I order a couple taquitos and then he tells the cashier "we're together" and orders tamales and pays for our meal.

We're together? I think, biting my lip. *Oh no.*

We sit down at a table.

"I figure if I'm going to disappoint you with vegan Mexican food, I might as well pay for it," he says.

"Do I look that disappointed?"

"An expression on Betty's face is worth a thousand words."

I grimace and smile. "Sorry."

"Don't be."

I'm at least relieved he didn't pay for this because it's a date. Because it's definitely *not* a date.

"So . . . why vegan?" I ask.

"The inevitable question," he says, putting his wallet on the table, which is duct-taped together so much, I can't even tell what the fabric is underneath. "Well . . . first, there's the whole 'it's disgusting and cruel to eat factory-farmed animals' thing."

"Yes," I agree, because, well, he does have a point.

"But then my mom has had some health scares, and I do most of the cooking and I kind of forced us all to adopt a vegan diet because I don't want her to die. I kind of like having her around, you know?"

"What were the health scares?"

"Too many to name."

The silence stretches, and I can tell he doesn't want to answer, and maybe I shouldn't have asked.

"It's not as hard as you'd think, going vegan," he says. "And it's good for the world. Climate change and all that."

"Right."

I can't help but think how weird it is that Michael is preoccupied with his carbon footprint and never hurting a feather on a chicken's head, and yet his brother was a mass shooter. Terrorist, I mean. I smile at him to show him that everything is fine and I'm not thinking about guns and dead brothers and traumatized sisters. He smiles back, and I wonder what his smile is hiding.

The taquitos are greasy and crunchy. They don't taste like meat, nor do they taste healthy, but they are okay. We eat silently and a mood seems to settle in over our table, an invisible cloud that blows in with the lunch crowd, sucking the joy out of whatever this is between us, making me wonder if this is awkward, if this is like a bad platonic date. What is in his head, what is in his heart? We've texted and joked, but I am aware in this moment that I know very little about him.

When I get home, I decide I am a yucky, fake person for going out on that friend date with Michael. But then I hear Joy in the next room, watching a horror movie we've seen so many times, I know it from the *ree-ree-ree* soundtrack through the wall. All alone with *Psycho* in the middle of a Saturday. And I think, it's okay, because what I did today was detective work. It was collecting information, like an investigative reporter. The more I learn about Michael, the more I gain his trust, the more I will maybe learn about Joshua, and eventually, I will come up with a list of requisites for a killer—a list of reasons this happened, a list of features and attributes and circumstances to avoid in a human being. And I will be able to tell Joy exactly why this happened, and then we can stop it from ever happening to us again.

After I graduated in June, after I started my internship and what I thought would be my new shiny life, I bought myself a journal. I hoped to start writing something other than copy about flowery sundresses and gingham rompers. I hoped to write a life into being. I thought I was beginning at that time, a grown-up, an internship, not quite a story, but the promise of one. Instead, I have one entry, written in my embarrassingly forward-slanty, bubbly handwriting.

July 1. Today is my first day at Retrofit, riding the subway like some kind of grown-up, clad in a pencil skirt. I got a blowout and a manicure yesterday. I want this to be perfect!

And then a bunch of smears of ink as my pen leaked all over the page. That is the only entry. I feel that says just about everything that needs saying.

Today I open this journal back up and reread this entry—this hopeful, ink-stained entry. I think of everything that has happened in these short four months. I tear the page out and ball it up. I throw it in my tiny trash. Then I get up, remove the ball, and walk it to the recycling bin in the kitchen. I pause at Joy's door, hearing the low hum of movie dialogue, before returning to my room.

My journal is now fresh and clean, full of bright white nothing. Fresh slate. Clean start. I write a short list of things I know about Michael:

He plays drums and is teaching himself guitar.

He hates school and has trouble concentrating, but he occasionally busts out a good vocabulary word like "boondoggle" or "flabbergasted" or a random historical fact that impresses me.

He is a collector of records and set lists.

He takes pictures of ridiculous graffiti, like the word "quinoa" spray-painted on the shuttered Pizza Hut, or the word "hoghag" painted in pretty cursive on the side of a corner market in our neighborhood.

He has a very small gap between his front teeth that would probably go unnoticed with most people, but because he smiles so constantly, it's hard to ignore.

He rarely checks his social media.

His dad really does live in Oregon on a commune, and he sends him postcards occasionally made out of some sprouted paper that you can plant in the ground and grow wildflowers from.

He has a small balcony at the apartment he shares with his mom filled with container plants of these half-dead wildflowers.

He took out a small loan last year to pay for his dog to get chemotherapy. His dog's name is Maverick.

He is vegan, apparently.

His mom is sick.

His brother is a dead monster.

I look at the list. My belly feels gross and I kind of hate myself. Why? Because I like Michael. When I see all these random snippets of his personhood arranged this way, it only affirms that I do actually *like* him. I like what he adds up to. I don't like the fact that I feel compelled to add him up this way, that essentially all he is is a means to a monster. A monster, by the way, he hasn't even mentioned yet.

When I go in to say hi to Joy, she seems drunk or something. I'm sure she's not drunk. I eye the pills on her windowsill, orange, proud, prescribed. *I'm allowed to be here*, they seem to say. *A doctor invited me.*

"Never trust a man who loves his mother too much," she says, pointing to her computer screen, where Norman Bates in a wig rocks on a rocking chair.

"Is it really his mother's fault?" I ask.

"Everything's a mother's fault."

"Mmm."

"Like, would we have gone to I Glam that day if it hadn't been for Mom?" Joy asks, sitting up and pushing the bangs from her eyes to really look at me. "You ever think of that? Moms, they're supposed to *protect* you. But what if they do the opposite?"

Mom, right now, is at a weekend-long conference about banning assault weapons. I remind Joy of this fact. She basically works a second job to protect us.

I do remember, after I say this, after the silence swells, that my mother had those threats she showed me on her phone. What if by trying to protect us, she invites danger? But I dismiss it. Because to live in fear of tiny people in your phone is like living in fear of germs. Sure, they're real, but *how* real? If you can't see them, can't feel them, can't smell them?

Michael texts me, Was super fun! Let's do it again soon!

Is lax with exclamation points, I add to my new-old journal.

Definitely! I respond, not without a sprinkle of self-hatred.

TWENTY-SIX

Every year, about two hours after the store-bought Thanksgiving pumpkin pie is devoured, we bust out the three-foot-tall atrociously pink Christmas tree and plug in its permanent lights, and bam, it's Christmas season. Growing up, my mom, Joy, and I, we loved Christmas. Mom has all these old Elvis Christmas records she put on, and we made janky gingerbread houses, and wore terrible Christmas sweaters. It was a joke we'd lived out so long, it became dead serious. Even Joy participated, though she passed on the sweater. She owns a Judas Priest Christmas album.

We have certain traditions. We visit the Tilden carousel every year, for example, an old historic merry-go-round nestled in the redwoods on the hill, decorated with elaborate inflatable Santas and dozens of decorated Christmas trees. This year, though, Mom's busy in the evenings, and Joy is housebound. Mom is so oblivious, she still doesn't know Joy hasn't left the house, and Joy lies to her constantly in my presence, almost like a dare to me.

"How was work today?" Mom asks.

"Oh, so boring," Joy says. "No one bought anything."

She watches me and I chew my food.

I don't say anything. But I burn with resentment.

Joy is testing me. I know she is. She's testing my loyalty, and I always pass that test.

"Joy, you want to go to the carousel with me tonight?" I ask.

She chews her food now, extra slow.

Mom is scrolling on her phone, whispering "you assholes" to invisible, faraway people, her potpie untouched.

"No thanks," Joy says. "I'm too old for that nonsense."

I chew my chicken for so long, it loses all its flavor. I do it to keep my mouth occupied, because I want to say something cutting back to her, like, *But you're not too old to live at home forever, unemployed, a city college dropout too scared to leave?* The disgust I hold for her in that moment is a shock, a cold wind blowing into my soul I am not accustomed to, and I do not like myself for it. It blows out again, and I'm left ashamed.

Michael and I text nightly, though I haven't seen him since last month when we went out for vegan Mexican food. That outing was unspectacular, but our text messaging makes us something like close friends. It's hard to explain. I think I'm a better person when I'm reduced to words only.

I have added pages to my journal, more facts under Michael, but also some facts now under Joshua. Michael never discusses what happened to Joshua directly. He never says, "My brother went on a shooting rampage and then killed himself" or anything. Instead, he talks around him. He mentions him in passing. So I have some random entries like:

> *Joshua had a different father. He mentioned this in a text conversation on November 13. Michael's dad was a folk singer who was married to his mom for only three years before leaving his family for the commune. Joshua's dad has only been described as a deadbeat.*

> *Joshua was kind of a bully. From our conversation on November 19, Michael just mentioned his older brother once shaved Michael's hair and eyebrows while he slept. Joshua also said "racist, homophobic shit" to Michael. (Joshua's dad was white, Michael's dad was Indian American.)*

> *Joshua spent a lot of time alone in his room on the computer. From our conversation November 21, I told him my sister hardly leaves the house either.*

> *"Oh my God, I'm so sorry!" he responded. "Is she in therapy? I hope she's in good therapy." I told him she is. "Did your brother have agoraphobia too?" I texted him, pivoting back. It's only after I sent it that I realized I used past tense, revealing, possibly, that I already know his brother is dead. My cheeks flushed like I exposed myself as a double agent. But Michael just texted back, "No. He had a lot of other problems, though." My heart raced—I'd*

struck emotional gold. I was about to text back and ask,
"What kind of problems?" When Michael texted, "Good
night, Elizabeth!" (He gave me a nickname: my full name.)

I have taken to hiding my composition book under my
bed, because honestly, I know how weird this looks, and I'm
preemptively ashamed. There are things I don't put into the
book too, like the fact Michael is pansexual, like me, and that
there are times I've wondered if our joking edges on more.
Where does friendliness end and flirtation begin? I've never
been good at telling. I've had intentions misinterpreted in the
past. So there's one more thing I also didn't add into my book:
the fact that I lied to Michael and told him that I was still with
Adrian, long-distance, to make things simpler. To make sure
Michael knows nothing is going to happen between us.

Yeah, same, he responded.

It seemed such a bizarre response, I stared at the glow of
my phone for a moment before typing my response.

. . . same how?

I'm with someone long-distance too.

Oh!

Yeah, I met her online.

cool cool. Same boat then

I was so bothered by this conversation, and I didn't know
why, and that bothered me most of all. Who knows, maybe he

was lying, saving face by making up a pretend long-distance girlfriend so I didn't think he liked me. (But would that be any worse than me making up a long-distance lover as a buffer between us? Maybe I was projecting.) And then part of me was suspicious he'd never brought this person up until now. (Again, guilty as charged.) And then lastly—and this part was more felt than realized—I was a bit jealous of this long-distance person and the connection they had with Michael. Because to me, as much as we might text, Michael was clearly still a mystery, one I was semi-obsessed with, judging from my composition book's entries. I mean, it was Joshua I was supposed to be obsessed with, but somehow, it was mostly Michael's name that spent my ink.

Does it ever get lonely for you? he asked.

Eh, I've been lonelier in other
IRL relationships.

I hear you. Or . . . I read you. 😎

What I did not respond with is this: I am lonely. I'm lonely all the time. But honestly, the more I think about it, the more it seems I'd be better suited for a long-distance relationship anyway. Maybe I should try one. Because with Hassan, Molly, and Adrian, something was always in the way—not miles, but me. A distance I carry.

Speaking of which, my father is calling.

TWENTY-SEVEN

I shut the door to my room, heart aflutter as I answer. It's been weeks—months, even?—since he's called. There he is, the word **UNKNOWN** captioning his face as I open the video call. I fix my hair, adjust my glasses to minimize reflection. He's sitting at a table outdoors, a backdrop of green, a fountain flowing behind him. He's wearing what looks like a workout shirt. You can see the faded peace-sign tattoo on his shoulder. There's always such a contrast between us: him in some lush paradise, me against the white walls of our apartment.

"Lizzy!" Dad says.

"Dad!" I reply, mirroring his tone.

"Did you get my messages?"

"No . . . you texted?"

Dad never texts. He's never even owned his own cell phone—too many radio waves. Letters aren't his thing either, just the occasional (late) birthday card. His spelling, his handwriting, are shockingly crude, considering how articulate he is.

"No—no texting," he says. "But did you have the dream? The one on the beach?"

"The . . ." I'm not sure how to keep going with verbalizing my thought here. "What?"

"I went to this workshop centering on astral projection," Dad says. "Are you familiar with the concept?"

Oh, Dad, I groan on the inside. *Please don't be serious.* I keep a smile plastered on my face and beg my eyes not to roll.

"I've heard of it," I say. "An intentional out-of-body experience."

"Well, according to this workshop, a lot of people who live far distances use it to communicate, even people who are distanced by being 'existentially challenged.'"

"Existentially challenged?" It takes a moment for this to sink in. "You mean dead?"

"That's what they called it at this workshop—an interesting concept, right?"

"I love you, Dad, but this sounds ridiculous."

"My little skeptics," he laughs. "All three of you."

At some point, when everyone around you is a skeptic, you should probably wonder if you are the anomaly, I don't say.

Instead, I laugh too. "So are you joining an astral-projection cult now?"

"Listen, a wise man entertains all ideas without necessarily believing them."

"Buddha?"

"Aristotle, paraphrased. Listen, the astral-projection

workshop was a bit over the top, but the dreams did lead to something. Every night, I found you and Joy," Dad says. "I had this same dream every night of the workshop—seven nights in a row."

"And what happened?"

"We sat together on this gorgeous beach—a topaz sea, sand that sparkled for miles, palms so tall, their fronds touched the clouds—and you kept telling me there was something you needed from me. You kept telling me, with urgency, there was something you needed. You kept pulling my shirtsleeve like you did when you were little."

Strange to think of a time when he would be physically close enough for me to tug a shirtsleeve. The strangeness pangs.

"And then you turned into a little blue crab and you darted into the ocean waves."

"This is sounding pretty silly."

"And then *Joy* turned into a crab and ran after *you*."

I continue smiling, even though this dream is much less exciting to me than it seems to be to him. "Let me guess: then you turned into a crab and ran after both of us."

"No! Then I started shouting to the ocean, 'Lizzy, I'm here! Lizzy, I'm right here if you need me!' And then the dream ended."

"Intense."

"Same dream, every night. You didn't have the same dream?"

"No."

"I'll ask Joy—maybe she did."

"Maybe it's less about us and more about you."

"How so?" he asks, leaning into the screen.

"Like, maybe it's not about us saying something to you in those dreams—astral projection or whatever—and more about you and your feelings."

"Ah," he says. "My own helplessness. I hear you. Yes, that does make sense."

I mean, I'm no psychologist, but the symbolism there is embarrassingly obvious.

"I was thinking there was something you needed from me," he says.

"I'm good. It's after midnight now, so what I probably really need is to go to bed."

"Right. You have school in the morning—I forgot."

"An internship, but yes, I do have to go there in the morning."

"You're so wise," he says. "So grounded. An old soul. I hope you know how proud I am of you."

"I love you," I say, and then we exchange goodbyes.

I turn off my light and get into bed. I can hear Joy through the wall—Joy stays up all hours of the night now. Her music blares. Then I hear her say, "Dad!" And I know he called her next.

I lie here in bed, unable to sleep for a few minutes. I turn white noise on my phone to drown everything out. The sound reminds me of the ocean, and I imagine myself on my Dad's astral plane beach, and I suddenly feel so angry at him for calling me at midnight about a stupid dream where he thought I was sending him telepathic messages about needing something from him. What on earth would I need from him? Everything I've ever needed from him, he couldn't give me. Needing him was a bad habit I long ago gave up.

Can you cross an ocean to be here for us, Dad?

Can you help me make sense of a senseless world?

Can you do even the bare minimum—be reachable? Remember how old I am? Calculate the time zones correctly?

No, I didn't think so.

TWENTY-EIGHT

My dad left us a decade ago, which means I've been without him longer than I've been with him now. When he left, mostly what I remember is how crushed my mother was, how she lost so much weight, I could see her collarbones, her eyes permanently red from crying. She broke out in unexplained rashes. And yet she insisted she was fine. It was better this way. We would move to a cheaper place, she would up her hours at work, everything was fine, fine, fine.

The more she said the word *fine*, the more she smiled and told us not to worry, the more I worried. I watched her fill cardboard boxes with his art books, dreamcatchers, and the clothes he left behind—suit jackets and button-up shirts, the ghost of the person he used to be before he decided to dive fully into the new age and abandon all semblance of the man who once worked at a tech company. You can see his transition in the few pictures Mom saved on a drive for us to revisit: him clean-cut and baby-faced in his wedding picture, handsome in a gray suit, my mother pregnant with Joy and aglow in her flowing white dress beside him; Dad with toddler Joy at his side, me a baby wrapped like a burrito on his lap, his eyes tired, his beard starting to grow; Dad smiling on a beach, the peace tattoo new and fresh on his arm, a self-help book on how to be happy splayed beside him on the sand; Dad doing a yoga pose with me standing on his back; Dad standing at the top of Half Dome in Yosemite, grinning, alone. I remember we went to Yosemite as a family that day, and when we couldn't keep up with him, he hiked to the top of Half Dome alone and a stranger took his picture there. We waited for him at the bottom, my mom silent with rage. When he saw us, he told us he had a spiritual awakening, but it seems to me when I look back, the "awakening" had taken years. He quit his job and left us the very next day.

I don't know if it takes guts to leave your family and everything you know in pursuit of some bigger spiritual truth, or if it makes you a selfish asshole, or if both can maybe be true. I do know it takes guts to pick up the pieces of a family and keep going when you've been left behind. My mother bought thrift-store blazers and went to job interviews, found us an affordable place to live a block from our school, and built new traditions. We celebrated Christmas that first year with a fervor I'd never known—we went caroling. We went ice-skating at Union Square. We drove to Christmas Tree Lane, we strolled through Zoo Lights, we walked around Mountain View Cemetery with its cherry trees strung with golden lights and sipped apple ciders. These were things we never would have done with Dad, who called Christmas "consumermas" and treated the entire holiday season like a giant trick being played on us by capitalist pigs. Mom made it fun again. We had new traditions now, ones Dad had no role in. Through the years, many of those traditions faded, but one that stuck, at least until last year, was the Tilden carousel.

Tilden Park is an evergreen jewel in Berkeley, one you can see from a distance topping the hills. It's a sprawling universe of redwood trees, creeks, hiking trails, picnic spots, a lake to swim in, a train to ride, a farm to feed animals, and a historic carousel. The carousel is magical during the holiday season, lights strung everywhere, holiday music piping through the stereo, the lawns adorned with various festive inflatables. Inside, dozens of decorated Christmas trees circle the carousel, kids in puffy coats line up to meet Santa, people sip hot cocoas in line. Last year, I was here with Joy and my mother. We sat on a bench watching the painted ponies circling around and talked about what awaited us in the coming new year—how Joy was going to take full loads of classes so she could transfer soon, and I was going to graduate and get an internship, and Mom was going to get a new job. Now, of course, even though some of those things happened, life's not at all how I imagined it would be. It seems if there's one thing that stays the same in life, it's this: nothing stays the same.

Here I am now, on that same bench, only I'm sitting next to Michael. On a whim, I asked him if he wanted to go to the carousel tonight. He said yes. He picked me up in his mom's minivan, with leopard-print seat covers that smelled like dog. It was my first time in this car, driving with him, and another glimpse into his life. I scoured the inside of his car for clues, for something Joshua might have left behind, but judging from the glittery *Brandi* ornament hanging from the rearview, and the many empty sparkling pink lemonade cans on the floor, there's no trace of him here.

His mom's name is Brandi, I imagine writing in my composition book later. *She likes leopard print and sparkling lemonade.*

I hate that I think these things. I tell myself to focus, to *be here now.* We sit side by side on a bench in the chilly air next to the glowing, singing Christmas display. Here Michael is, eating a soft pretzel and humming along to "You're a Mean One, Mr. Grinch," and he has no idea about my disgusting curiosity.

"I can't believe you've never been here," I say to him.

"Yeah? I strike you as the carousel type?"

"I mean, obviously."

He frames his head with his hands. "Is it my horselike face?"

I laugh. "Haven't you lived here all your life? Didn't your mom ever take you up here?"

"My mom didn't do a lot of typical mom things," he says. "Bringing us to carousels is only one item on a very long, depressing list."

"I'm sorry."

"Please never say that to me." When Michael stops smiling, you really notice two things about him: the still blue at the centers of his otherwise hazel eyes, and the laugh lines already formed around his mouth.

"Okay. I didn't mean to offend you."

"I'm not *offended*, it's just—I couldn't stand the thought of you ever being sorry for me."

Before I can respond, he gets up and throws his pretzel wrapper in the trash.

"Shall we?" he asks, gesturing toward the carousel, smile reappearing.

"We shall," I say.

Michael picks a rooster with an engineer hat on and I pick a cat with a ribbon on its neck. We ride side by side. The carousel begins its rotation and the room blurs in a splendor of twinkling lights, a rhythm of trees and reindeer and happy people. I remember what it was like to be a child in a world that was both safe and thrilling at once. For a moment, the memory occupies more than my mind—it's humming through my body, in tune with the Christmas music. It's holidays and the coconut smell of my mother's embrace and the simple beauty of a decorated tree. The hum blooms up my limbs, up my throat, fills my cheeks with warmth. I imagine my mother waving from the crowd, and Joy by my side, but when I turn to see my sister, it's Michael there, quiet and smiling in awe at the spinning scene in which we're smack-dab in the center.

As the ride slows again, the hum cools on my face. It sharpens, behind my eyes, and I draw in a breath and hold it tight in my lungs. The bell rings for us to get off the ride, and at that moment, I recognize someone in line: Is it really? Yes, it is, I'd know that hair anywhere. Adrian, in a long velvet skirt, with fingerless gloves. They're with their dad. They look beautiful and grown up. Have they spotted me? I'm going to be sick. Imagine if I run into them with Michael— what a mess. Michael would quickly figure out that I lied about being in relationship with Adrian, and Adrian would see me hanging out with Michael, who they know is Joshua Lee's brother. . . .

As Michael and I step off the ride, he asks if I want to go again.

"No!" I almost yell. "We should take off."

"Are you sure?" he asks, showing me a booklet. "We bought all these tickets."

"It kind of upset me—upset my stomach," I say, pulling his arm to go toward the parking lot.

Michael looks down at me pulling his arm, surprised; he hooks his arm deeper into mine as we go farther into the parking lot. It's weird how natural it feels, arm in arm. He unlocks the minivan with a *beep beep* and I get in. My heart is beating wildly. I wasn't lying to Michael about the feeling-sick part. I do feel sick. I feel guilty. I feel like I'm a bad person for so many reasons, and I don't deserve his kindness, and that the more I try to make sense of the messy world, the bigger messes I end up making. I wish I'd never gone to the carousel, never left the house tonight. I should have stayed in like Joy. It makes sense to me right now why she never leaves the safety of her room.

"I'm sorry," I tell him as we drive away from the laughter, music, and lights and into the night, black with trees.

"What did we talk about earlier?"

"Sorry I say sorry so much."

"I'm going to kill you," he says cheerfully.

He's joking, of course, but the joke falls flat in the air and I wonder if he's thinking of Joshua Lee and what he did too. I reach out and touch the *Brandi* pendant hanging from the rearview.

"My mom has impeccable taste, doesn't she?" he asks.

"I mean, I too am a fan of leopard print."

"Leopard print isn't a pattern for my mom, it's an identity."

"As someone who works in fashion, I can tell you it never goes out of style."

"She'll be happy to know that."

I've always thought you could learn a lot from how someone drives. The way my sister revs the engine and comes to abrupt squealing stops, the way my mother follows every rule and never exceeds the speed limit but swears at everyone, and me, of course—the fact I never drive because I never got my license, which falls in line with the fact I still live at home and don't know where I'm going with my life. Michael, on the other hand, drives with his seat leaning far back, one hand on the wheel, the other drumming along to Metallica. He drives easy. He drives slow. He comes to a complete and full stop at every sign.

"You should come over and meet my mom sometime," he says as he pulls up in front of my house. "She'd like you. And she'd want to talk leopard print and hear about Retrofit. I think you'd get along."

"Sure," I say, surprised. "I'd love to meet her."

"Not in some weird 'hey, come meet my mom' way," he says, putting on his hazards as the car sits parked in the middle of the street. "I know you're seeing someone." He looks at me and raises his eyebrows.

For a split second, I wonder if he saw Adrian too—if he recognized them. If he's calling me out on my lie.

"Right, and so are you," I say.

"Exactly."

That feeling I had before—the guilt—it has disappeared, and something else has occupied its space. Something warm and okay, something captured in an exchange of smiles I share with Michael. It's almost like he knows I haven't been honest with him, and he doesn't mind. Like we share something so deep and effortless, even lies are permitted. I've never had a friend like him before.

"See you in text messages," he says. "It was nice to hang out with you IRL."

"IRL always sounds so weird when you say it IRL."

"Thumbs-up emoji."

"Thanks for the ride."

"Anytime."

He waits until I get all the way up the stairs and into the house before he drives away. My mom once told me that's the mark of a decent friend—one who never leaves before they know you're safe.

TWENTY-NINE

The weather outside is frightful, but this snowflake-patterned A-line dress is SO delightful. Holiday print in an icy-blue color that does you all the favors? Check. Dainty, detailed lace collar and sleeves? Check. Cotton sateen that warms like a dream? This dress checks all December's boxes and then some. Boasting a full petticoat, you will feel like the Snow Queen of the Nutcracker Ball! $399.

I wake up, pull on my festive dress, pen my lips with red lipstick. It's Christmas morning and the world is supposed to sparkle. All the elements are there—Elvis croons on the stereo, Mom cranked the living room's space heater, and the smell of pancakes fills the air. (Mom cooks once a year: this is it.) But when I pull back my paisley curtain and look outside, the world looks the same: rained on, sleepy, a woman on a phone walking her dog, another woman in a duct-taped poncho with a shopping cart filled with cans digging through a recycling bin at the curb. Where's she going, what does she celebrate? Why am I here and she's there? Shandra Pensky's picture comes to my mind, with a startled pang—her mourning family. Michael Lee's mother, Brandi, without a son this year. It seems sometimes a charade that we continue celebrating in the face of relentless tragedy. How dare we? But then . . . what else is there to do?

I snap a selfie and hit send.

Merry Christmas, if you're celebrating, I text Michael. Otherwise . . . merry normal day!

You're adorable, he texts back. Thank you! I needed that!

He returns the favor with a selfie of him and his dog. Jackpot. I zoom in on the background, hoping to study the books on the bookshelf for . . . I guess, clues? But I can't read their spines. I see a photograph of what looks like Michael and Joshua as children.

I FaceTime with Zoe, who's in Hawaii on her annual family Christmas vacation. They've all been drinking mimosas and are raucously playing Monopoly. Zoe and her brothers don matching Christmas onesies, which is both cute and kind of disturbing. She passes me around to her family and I say hi, and then Zoe shuts herself into her room. She has been there three days, and there are piles of clothes, overflowing shopping bags, and an inexplicable giant stuffed kangaroo wearing several leis on the floor. As she talks to me, she gesticulates so wildly her mimosa keeps spilling. She doesn't seem to notice.

"Also, he smelled weird," she continues, telling me why she broke up with the guy after the guy she introduced on that call. "Like bananas when they get spotty. And he never seemed like he was listening, even when he was. It's hard to explain."

While Zoe's less picky in terms of finding a mate, she quickly finds about ten thousand reasons why they aren't right for her long-term, and moves on. So I guess she *is* picky in the end. I'm relieved to see that, even though she's living thousands of miles away and getting educated, she's exactly the same.

"What about you, you little gorgeous minx?" she says. "Look at you! All sexy and Christmassy!"

"Um, thank you?"

"How's your fam?"

"Oh, they're fine. Joy's—"

"I have a confession. I am totally fangirling over your mom. Did she tell you about our interview?"

"No," I say, so slowly the word *no* comes out like a polysyllabic word.

"I'm going to profile her for a journalism class! I want to talk about the intersection of feminism and anti-gun culture. I want to sell it to *Bitch*."

"*Bitch*," I repeat.

"Magazine."

"Oh."

"Isn't that awesome?"

"Totally," I say, internally yelling to myself to keep smiling.

"Have you talked to Adrian, by the way?"

"No," I say, relieved for the change in subject. "We've texted, but . . . I haven't seen them yet." *Unless you count me running away from them at the carousel*, I don't say.

"Well, they had some New Year's party they wanted to invite us to. Apparently they're house-sitting? I don't know. Could be fun. A little high school reunion."

"That does sound fun," I say.

One of Zoe's brothers comes in and yells at her. "Everyone's waiting!"

"Ew, did you just fart in my room?"

He laughs.

"Olfactory harassment!" she says, and then turns back to me. "You should be so glad you have one sister and not two stinky disgusting brothers. I'M COMING, GOD!" she shouts offscreen. "Anyway, tell your mom I say hi and I'm her biggest fan! Merry Christmas!"

"Merry Christmas," I tell her, but she already hung up.

We eat pancakes, we exchange small gifts, we watch a Christmas movie. But I am distracted. I'm thinking that Joy hasn't left this house in months now, and my mom still doesn't seem aware or think it's a problem. I'm thinking that my mom is now more than my mom: she's this figure who people, even childhood friends, want to profile and interview, a person who receives death threats from strangers in her email account. I'm thinking of the big, wide world, of the families missing loved ones. When Lex comes to visit with Joy and they giggle and kiss in her bedroom, when Mom opens her laptop and closes her door, I sit overdressed and stare at the little pink Christmas tree. All these years living in this house, all these Christmases for the three of us. This could be our last. The darkest, brightest thought rings loud as a bell: *I hope, I hope it is.*

THIRTY

On December 26, our family car dies in a parking garage in downtown Oakland. Mom and I have just met up after work to drive home together. I'm sitting shotgun as Mom turns the engine over and over again with her key. After about five minutes of excruciating grinding noises and my mother intermittently coaxing the car with an odd sprinkling of obscenities—"Come on, you little piece of shit, you know you can do it"—I pat her hand and ask her if she has considered the fact that this car has surpassed 200,000 miles and might be past its expiration date.

"Stop it, Betty, I'm so sick of your incessant negativity!" she yells.

In this enclosed space, this small cube of silence that is the car's interior, her yell rings in my ears. My fingertips tingle.

"Jeez, why are you snapping at me? And what do you mean 'incessant negativity'?"

"You're *constantly* pouting and morose. Even yesterday,

we're supposed to be celebrating the holiday, and you spent half the day quarantined in your room."

"What are you even talking about?" I ask, heat flushing my cheeks. "I was looking through the vintage *Vogue* covers book you gave me. I was *enjoying* your *gift*. And you were working in your room at the time, and Joy was in her room making out with Lex."

"Your attitude is constant darkness and despair. You exude it. The car is *not* past its expiration date."

"Fine," I say, holding my hands up in mock surrender. "The car's fine."

"It's just slow to start." She puts the key in and tries to turn it again, but this time it makes a sad little clicking noise. Mom closes her eyes and sits back, a mannequin mother. She looks peaceful, but when my mom does this—gets quiet and inward-facing, Zen-looking—it means she is so enraged she is trying to control herself from exploding.

"Mom," I say. "We can take BART home. It's not a big deal."

"I cannot afford this," she murmurs. "I cannot afford one more thing." She shakes her head. Her cat-eye eyeliner is smudged on one side, but now is not the time to tell her. "I'm about to lose my mind. Please give me a minute."

We sit in the loud silence, my mother with her eyes closed and hands on the useless wheel, as people in fancy suits with well-kept hair beep open their cars around us and exit the parking lot. I open my phone. There's a news alert of another school shooting. Sometimes I want to throw my phone out the window, as if that's where all the world's danger and discontent lives.

How's your day? Michael texts.

> Sitting in a parking garage with
> my mom, who is losing her mind because
> her car is broken. Fun times!

Shit. Where?

> Garage at Franklin
> and 14th.

I'll come get you both and
take you home. I just got off work.
I'm super close.

> No!!!

Too late, I'm already on my way.

> Michael, seriously. Stop.

No response.

> MICHAEL!!

Nothing.

I groan. Mom opens her eyes and looks at me. "What?"

"A friend of mine is coming to take us home," I say.

"What friend?"

"His name is Michael."

"I didn't even know you had a friend named Michael. How nice of him."

I feel sick. I don't want my mother to meet him—in fact, this is a goddamn nightmare. She can't shut up about the I Glam shooting and guns. They're bound to figure out the sick connection.

Michael, really, we can take BART. I don't want you coming all the way out here.

No response.

"I got reprimanded at my work today," Mom says.

I put my phone down.

"It's a second warning," she goes on. "Third warning and I'm going to be let go."

"For what?"

"Taking too much time off. I took time off last week for that interview, a week before for the San Francisco rally, and then did a MAGS event the week before. This morning I had to go talk to Berkeley PD, and I guess that was the final straw."

"What were you talking to Berkeley PD about?"

"I got a disturbing voicemail message this morning from a guy who said he knew where I lived and can't wait to see me. He said he wants to—and I quote—'show me his gun collection.'"

"What the hell, Mom?" I ask, my stomach turning. "Is it the same guy?"

"Yes. He said his name was Albert Smith."

"That is so scary."

"Apparently it doesn't count as a threat, though, so Berkeley PD couldn't do much about it. So I'm in trouble with my work for nothing."

"How is that not a threat? And how can police not do anything about it?"

"The message was long and bizarre and from a blocked number. He said he lives outside of Vegas, and if that's true, he's not even in their jurisdiction, and he didn't technically threaten me. They said if he left any more specific threats or shows up at our house, I could issue a restraining order."

"Shows up at our house?!"

"He's not going to show up at our house."

"Then why did you call the police?"

"I don't know, Bets, I'm trying my hardest, okay? My car's shot to shit, I'm on thin ice at my job, Joy's dropped out of school and isn't pulling her weight, my liquor is mysteriously missing. . . . Did you drink my liquor?"

"Did I— No."

"Yeah, well, I went to make myself a drink last night and it's all gone."

"Lex was there. I wouldn't put it past him. Or maybe Joy drank it."

"I don't know why I'm worrying about my whiskey, it's the least of my problems. If I lose my job, I don't know what to do," Mom says. "I don't even think Joy makes enough at her job to buy us groceries, and you've got an unpaid internship. We're screwed."

Now is *not* the time to correct my mother with the information that Joy is, in fact, unemployed and hasn't left the house in months. I still cannot believe my mother hasn't figured this out, but then again, look at all the crap she's dealing with.

"I'm sure if you told your job that you were getting death threats, they'd cut you some slack," I tell her.

"Oh, I'm sure they'd love that. Knowing I'm a target—what a great addition to the office."

"Mom, I'm really worried about these threats now. This is too much."

"It is too much. It's all too much."

"Have you considered . . . stopping the MAGS work? Just lying low for a while?"

"Bets," my mother says. She thinks for a moment, collecting her words, before proceeding. "The work I'm doing with MAGS is the most worthwhile thing I've ever done with my life. It's like—I know this is going to sound strange—but that shooting, and my role in it, it woke me up. It made me feel real, and urgent, and like I have *purpose*. And it wasn't until I woke up that I realized that purpose—that urgency—it's been missing my whole life."

"Wow. Thanks a lot," I say.

"Of *course* you give me purpose," she says. "But a bigger purpose, one directly connected with the world in a different way." She holds my hand, squeezes. "You know how much I love you. The vastness of my love for you, it's the engine driving my want to make the world a better place. Do you understand?"

I nod, though I don't fully.

"I don't want to go back to the way things were before," she goes on, taking her hand back. "That fucked-up incident made me realize how delicate, how precious, my life is. How little time I could have. I don't want to be quiet anymore and just go to work and . . . punch my time card, click another mile on the odometer, another *X* on the calendar. . . . I want to be a part of something outstanding. And I finally feel like I am, completely by accident, but what a gift, you know?"

I don't know, I don't say.

"I know," I say.

I'm alarmed at her ability to stand still in the face of threats of violence. But more so, I'm jealous of her conviction. Sometimes I can't believe I'm her daughter. It's like a shark gave birth to a jellyfish.

"I understand if you want some distance from my work," she says. "That's okay. And you and Joy are adults now—soon you'll go your own ways, and I'll go mine. I would never do anything if I really thought I was endangering my girls. But I also have to be able to do the things I know are important."

I sting at the thought of her going her own way, even though it's the inevitable conclusion of, well, everything.

My phone lights up. What floor are you on?

I hold my breath for a moment before replying, Second floor, near the elevators. It's a little old gold car with a bunch of bumper stickers on it.

"My friend's here," I tell Mom. "Let's wait outside."

A minute later, Michael pulls up in the minivan and waves, permanent grin illuminating his face.

"Handsome friend," Mom says to me.

"Please don't."

"Just saying."

"Well, don't say."

"Hi, Michael," Mom says, opening his door and climbing into the front seat. "I'm Beverly, Betty's mom."

"So good to meet you," he says, turning down the heavy metal music and shaking her hand.

I get in the back, praying to a god, any god that might be listening, to not let Michael recognize my mother from any of her interviews—to not let my mother talk about guns even for a second—to not let them figure out the connection.

"What a pleasure to meet you too, Michael. You're so generous to come pick us up."

"It's really no big deal," he says as he drives. "I'm happy to help!"

"And at rush hour—you're an angel. Truly."

"Anytime! I mean it."

"Where'd you find this guy?" Mom asks me in the rearview.

"We went to high school together," I say.

"Really?" she says.

"We were in a couple classes together," he says.

"Did you see that news about the shooting in Texas that happened this morning?" says Mom, right on cue. "Horrible."

I cringe. Oh, how I cringe.

"Oh, wow," Michael says.

I search his eyes in the rearview for some flicker of pain, but his eyes are on the road. "Mom," I ask, "can we talk about something less depressing?"

"I'm sorry. What do you want to talk about, Betty?"

"Well, at my work, we're about to unveil the spring line," I say. "And apparently empire waists and pastels are back in." Anything, anything to fill the air and steer away from the news. "And we're releasing clutch purses and wallets for the first time, so that's exciting."

The silence in the car tells me this is far from riveting for them.

"We're doing a whole collection of capri pants with floral prints," I go on anyway. "I'm writing the copy for it."

"That's great, Betty," Michael says. "I didn't know you write."

"Yeah, ad copy."

"She's a spectacular writer. She wrote poetry in high school," Mom gushes. "She could be a writer if she wanted."

"I am a writer," I remind her.

"I mean a writer who writes more than ad copy," she says, turning around.

"Thanks."

She turns ahead again. "Don't give me that look. You know what I mean."

"Ad copy's important," Michael says. "I work at a record store, and ad copy in distro catalogs is what makes our managers decide what to buy."

"Words are the most powerful weapons," Mom agrees. "This is our house, the pink one with the lights on."

Michael stops the minivan in the middle of the street. "I remember."

"Oh, do you?" she says, and I can hear her eyebrows raising in the tone of her voice. "Thanks again."

"Yeah, thanks," I agree.

"It was great meeting you, Beverly," he says. "Have a good night."

"You too, Michael," she says.

We go upstairs and he waits until we get inside before pulling away. "He's a keeper," Mom tells me, peeking through the blinds.

"He's a *friend*."

She puts her purse down, her coat away. "You said the same thing about Adrian."

"Seriously, stop. No, really. Stop walking." I pull Mom's sleeve and whisper. "Don't tell Joy about the threats."

"Why not?"

"She's really scared still. Haven't you noticed?"

A ripple of two different tones of laughter fills the air. It's Lex and Joy. We can hear them through the wall. Apparently they never left her room since yesterday, or he's back again.

"She sounds terrified," Mom says with a wry smile.

"Well, not right now."

"I won't tell her," Mom says. She reaches out and smooths my bangs, just the way she did when I was tiny, except she has to reach up now instead of down. Because I'm not tiny. She is. "You stop worrying, okay? If I get another threat, I promise I'll tell you *and* the police. Just keep the doors locked. We're on the second floor. We're very secure."

"That does *not* make me feel better."

"Go take a bubble bath," she says. "Stop worrying."

I do take a bubble bath, and it does help, except I can hear Lex and Joy through the wall playing a song together. It's not a very good song, and they play it over and over again. My mother told me I was negative. Maybe she's right. I begin to hate the song that Joy and Lex are playing, the generic riff with no drumbeat. Maybe something is broken inside me.

I should be happy for Joy, because I know she loves Lex more than anything on earth except maybe the color black, but I don't trust him. Lex comes, Lex goes, Lex is always buzzed on something. Lex is forever promising her things—they're going to be in a band together, or she's going to follow him on tour. He drifts in like a season, he blows away again. And he doesn't even know her. All they do is laugh and play in there. He doesn't check on her when she cries in the middle of the night. He doesn't keep her secrets.

THIRTY-ONE

Adrian invites me to the New Year's party Zoe told me about, and I decide to go. Honestly, I would rather not. I'm going to see people from high school I haven't seen since high school, and besides Adrian and Zoe, I haven't kept up with anyone. They all have been away at their fancy out-of-state schools. Many of them know my sister and mom were involved in the I Glam shooting, so that's inevitably going to come up. In the olden days, as in last year, I would have gone without even thinking about it. But in these not-at-all-olden days, I think. Too much. I would go so far as to say I have a thinking problem.

Thankfully, Antonio is going with me. Last month he started dating someone, so we haven't hung out much, but his banker boyfriend is on some business trip in New York City, and my friend is back again. Ever since he lost his single status, Antonio won't stop gushing about Banker Boyfriend. I had been enjoying my noise-canceling headphones at work with increasing frequency; then a couple weeks back, Tammy moved me to another part of the office, closer to the marketing team. The plus side? My work has improved. Tammy told me I seem more focused. There's a noon on the opposite side of every midnight.

"Why didn't you bring your drummer boy?" Antonio asks. We're in the back seat of a Lyft, on our way up the hills. The buildings go from apartments to condos to bungalows to mansions. They still have their Christmas lights up, and we pass them in glitzy flashes.

"Stop calling him that."

"Ba-rum ba-bum-bum," he sings.

"I didn't bring him because Adrian and Zoe know him and know his brother was the shooter and it would just be weird."

"Didn't you all go to high school together?"

"Yeah, but Michael wasn't part of my world there."

"So? High school was months ago. You make new friends. Like, hi."

"Yeah, I didn't mention him to Adrian and Zoe yet. It's hard to explain."

"Why are you keeping him such a secret? You must like him."

"I don't like him."

"You *must* like him."

"Look, just because you're all in a tree with your banker guy doesn't mean I am with Michael."

The silence tells me he's willing to drop it, though the one raised eyebrow tells me he has not dropped it for good.

"You look snazzy tonight," he says. "That tie and blouse? So andro."

"Thanks," I say, grinning. "It's good to see your face. I feel like we've been ships in the night, even though we're in the same office."

"It's lonely since you moved nearer to marketing. Plus, that whole team is made up of such bros."

"They're not that bad."

The Lyft driver stops in front of an enormous colonial, with pillars and a lawn sparkling with sprinkler dew and a long driveway that has about a half dozen cars.

"Holy shit, you've got some fancy-ass friends," Antonio says.

"They're house-sitting," I remind him. "This is not normal."

"No, no it is not."

When we ring the doorbell, it sings a whole song, and when Adrian answers the door, they're holding an open bottle of champagne with one hand and restraining a Great Dane with another. They look amazing: bell-bottoms, a half-buttoned polyester shirt, their hair is pure seventies, only their perm is au naturel. Their eyes sparkle as they hold back the dog, a wry little half smile on their face.

"Well," they say. "Not late, exactly on time, but oh-so-fashionable."

"Adrian," I say. "This is my friend Antonio."

"Nice to meet you. Now get inside before this beast drags me out with it," they say.

We step in and the dog barks at us. Antonio gets on one knee and starts petting it. "Look at this sweet little baby," he says.

"Whoa, Napoleon loves you!" Adrian says. "This is a horrible, unintelligent, slobbering monster who barks at everyone. So feel special, 'cause you are." Adrian's voice turns to a baby voice as they lean down to talk to the dog. "And your breath smells like feces, doesn't it? Doesn't it?"

"He's perfect," Antonio says.

"I was just about to put him downstairs because he won't stop barking." Adrian gestures to the open doorway from the foyer to the living room, a sea of cream-colored carpet and leather furniture. "The kitchen's past there. Go grab a glass of whatever. I'll be up in a second."

We go into the kitchen. There are six people in there, three of them people I know from high school and honestly haven't thought about since we sauntered out of there in our graduation gowns. I greet them with hugs anyway and introduce them to Antonio, and they pour us glasses of champagne in regular wineglasses. This kitchen has multiple espresso machines, marble countertops, and a chandelier. Adrian's family rolls with an untouchable crowd.

"You. Gorgeous. Wench," someone yells from across the room.

I look up, midsentence, and see Zoe barreling toward me. In a moment, I'm almost knocked to the floor in an embrace of fake fur and vanilla perfume.

"Look at you! God, she is so sexy. Please tell me you're dating this sexy woman," Zoe says to Antonio as she pulls back and looks at me.

"I would if I had even one ounce of attraction toward her gender," Antonio says. "Alas."

"This is my buddy Antonio," I tell her. "Antonio, this is my friend Zoe."

"Friend? You mean *best* friend. We go back to fifth fucking grade. We pricked our fingers and were blood sisters."

"True story," I tell him.

"Intense," he says.

I'm not sure if he means the "blood sisters" comment or Zoe's general energy. Works either way.

Adrian comes upstairs without a dog and with a poker set and a few inflatable pool animals. More people come in, and we shout hellos and introductions at each other over the music. Glasses are refilled, beers are opened, pizza is ordered, and the pizza guy joins the party. At some point, everyone moves outside and someone busts out a keyboard and a guitar and everyone is singing half-drunkenly to Disney songs. Someone takes the pool cover off, Zoe jumps in with her clothes on and begins making out with the pizza guy. I am not drunk enough to swim, but I do take my shoes off and sit with my feet in the pool.

Adrian sits next to me and puts their feet in the pool and we start talking, sharing a bottle of white wine at this point because I don't know where I left my glass. We talk about my sister. I tell them she's fine in one way, and in another, she's not fine at all. I tell them she takes a lot of antianxiety medication and doesn't leave the house, but other than not being functional in the way she used to be, she's pretty content. Then this guy we went to high school with, big-shouldered dude who looks like he could have played football but instead was the best tap dancer in our theater program who everyone called Spaz, joins the conversation, swimming up to us. Spaz is wearing some glittery sunglasses that Zoe had on her head an hour ago.

"I hear you were in the shooting!" Spaz shouts.

"No, not me, my sister and my mom were," I say.

"That guy Joshua Lee was a total freak," he says.

"Hey, as a proud freak, I'm offended that you're calling him that," Adrian says.

Spaz splashes Adrian. Zoe comes swimming up to us now, in her bra and underwear, her red lipstick all over her face and also all over the pizza guy's face, who is now floating on an inflatable flamingo a few feet away.

"Are you talking about me?" Zoe asks us.

"Yeah, of course. Because that's the only thing there is to talk about," Adrian says, rolling their eyes.

"I'm getting déjà vu right now," Zoe says, treading water and smiling up at us. "Give me a drink."

Adrian hands over the bottle and Zoe glugs. I decide I should stop now. I so rarely drink, I'm not very good at it; I usually either drink too little or too much. Right now I feel just right. The new year rings in with a few small fireworks, kisses, and screams. And in a second, the year is supposedly over, and yet everything feels the same as it was before.

We reminisce about high school, about who is doing what, and soon the conversation circles back to Joshua Lee. I take the bottle of wine back from Zoe and drink more, quickly, looking around for Antonio, who is still playing poker across the yard under the veranda with a pink-haired girl who laughs, shrilly, at everything. I can hear her from here, but I can't catch Antonio's gaze to save me as the conversation turns. First Zoe starts talking about how my mom is so badass and how she's going to interview her, and the pizza guy floats over to us, and Zoe backs up and tells him the whole story about the shooting, in detail, and how my mom is semi-famous now. I sit here the whole time with a slight smile plastered on my face, watching the pale blue pool water dance like glass under the strung-up lights and the stars that ache like cheaper imitations. I nod and drink more as Adrian interjects, wondering aloud if these shootings are a media distraction to the advantage of the powers that be, and Zoe begins arguing that that's conspiracy theory bullshit, and Adrian says the media coverage of them and activists' hyperfocus on these incidents is actually even potentially harmful—*sorry*, they say, to me, hand on my arm, and I realize they're implying my mother is part of the problem—and that they perpetuate copycat killings and it's a cycle that keeps spinning. Zoe yells back something about patriarchy needing to be reminded of its casualties by heroes like my mother, and Adrian says something about false flags—not that they believe it, but *what if* we do realize that while the recent school shooting happened, a scandal related to the president broke out and universal health care was dealt an enormous blow in the courts and it's better for those in charge that we're shooting each other and mad about it than it is that we're paying attention to the people who make the rules. I drink the last sip of the wine and look around and realize I have probably drunk too much. And I open my mouth, and finally I speak.

"You both talk so confidently, so *prolifically*, and yet you say nothing," I tell them.

Everything gets quiet. It seems Spaz and pizza guy long ago left the pool. I look up for Antonio, but the glass table on the veranda is empty. I can hear everyone laughing, watching a movie inside. I'm sitting between Zoe, shivering in her fur coat and dripping, and Adrian, our legs in the water.

"You're the one saying nothing," Zoe says. "I thought you had drunk yourself deaf."

"Tried to," I say.

The trees aren't in focus. The words feel thick in my mouth.

"I hate this conversation," I go on. "You're both wrong, you're both right. Zoe, my mom's not a hero, that's the whole point of her parade—I mean crusade." I burp. I should say *excuse me*, but don't. "Adrian, what the hell is wrong with you? False flags? I was at the fucking store and my mom and sister were there!"

"I didn't mean *that* was a false flag!"

"The fact that you're saying anything like that is—it's shocking. It's stupid, Adrian. It makes you sound stupid. And it precipitates—*perpetuates*—people not believing in reality. And if we can't agree on what reality is, civilization's going to implode."

"God, Betty, you're drunk, aren't you?" Zoe asks.

"She is drunk," Adrian agrees. "I've seen her drunk once and she gets like this."

"Right?" Zoe agrees. "All logical and opinionated."

They're talking about me like I'm not here. I get up, under the strung lights and the oak hissing with wind, and walk in the straightest line I can muster; I walk through the open sliding glass door and pass people watching cartoons and eating cookie dough. I am drunk and my body is leading my mind. I go down a set of stairs into a warm basement filled with boxes of stuff and comfortable mismatched furniture. Antonio is here, on a couch, asleep with the giant dog under an afghan. I take off Antonio's glasses and put them on the table. I climb onto the other side of the couch and curl up next to him and the dog and try not to throw up as the world spins.

THIRTY-TWO

When I was a kid, I cried every New Year's Day. Celebrations croaked to a silence, the sky silvered, my mother stuffed the little pink tree and stockings back into her closet again. There was a mournful air about the first week of January—brown, thirsty, naked Christmas trees, still as corpses, appearing on curbs, trash cans overflowing with ribbons and crumpled wrappings. The air tickled me cold when I walked to school in the mornings, the sun sly in the clouds.

Our elementary school was a two-story building adorned with colorful murals and surrounded by edible gardens. Joy and I walked together in the mornings. One particular year, I remember Joy and I shuffling along the chain-link fence together on the outside. There on the inside, our schoolmates played on the blacktop; there was the sound of bouncing basketballs and jump rope chants, a distant whistle, shouts and laughter. We stopped and looked at it from the sidewalk. Back then, she was already inches taller than me, with hair in two neat braids. Rather than wear all black, she was obsessed with rainbows. She carried a yo-yo around and did tricks with it.

"I wish school weren't starting again," I said.

"What would you rather be doing?"

"Staying at home all day. Sewing." I'd recently gotten my first sewing kit and had learned to sew by hand. I sewed skirts at first, ugly skirts I wore to school anyway.

"Home would get pretty boring if you never left it," she said.

"No it wouldn't."

"You'd never see your friends anymore."

"But I'd see you and Mom. I wouldn't be alone."

"You get like this every year. I think you have a complex." She smiled at me and straightened my glasses on my face. "Here, in January, it's the coldest time of the year. But did you know in the southern hemisphere, it's the hottest time of the year? Somewhere, people are sweating and so hot, they can hardly think. I'd rather be cold than hot, wouldn't you?"

"Is that where Daddy is?" I asked.

The year or so after Dad left, he sent only a few postcards from random locations. He headed to South America first, meandered north again, then at some point took that transatlantic flight that was his last. The strangest thing about when my dad left was how little we missed him. I worried more about my mother's mental health than I did about not seeing him again. He had worked a lot and been snippy with us, had spent his spare time chasing yoga, meditation, chakra cleansing on the weekends. His mind left us years before his body did.

"Who knows?" Joy answered.

I liked imagining my dad was somewhere hot, too hot, sweating and moaning under the sun, thirsty for water. And here we were, Joy and I, together—in our cozy matching jean jackets with the fur lining.

She linked arms with me and led me to the school entrance.

"Someday, when we're older, we'll go to the southern hemisphere in January, and you'll be happier then," she said.

"We'll swim at the beach."

"Picnic under a coconut tree."

"Scuba dive."

"I'll drink one of those fancy drinks with the tiny umbrella in it," she said. "When I'm twenty-one."

The school bell rang, and I was smiling now, because Joy had cheered me up. We parted ways and I held on to that picture—that beachy postcard in my head, those promises we made—and I was warmed.

Now it's January again, and Joy is twenty-one, but we're not in the southern hemisphere. In fact, being an agoraphobic in the northern hemisphere is about as far as one could get from the southern hemisphere. Those promises were non-sense, empty as New Year's resolutions.

"My resolution this year," Joy tells me, "is to start a band."

I'm in her doorway. Joy is standing, her bass strapped to

her and plugged into her amp. It's buzzing so loudly. She has a microphone on a stand and another small amp set up for her vocals.

"I came in to ask you to please turn that down."

"You hag," she says, not meanly at all. Then she turns it down. "Are you hungover?"

"I went to a party last night, and I drank too much. My head hurts. So . . . probably."

"How adorable!" she says ecstatically. She puts her bass on the bed with a *plunk* and runs over to hug me. "The little Girl Scout lived on the edge! What was the party like? Did the cops show up? Did you make out with anyone?" Her eyes are bright and curious.

"Joy . . . I want to lie down, and I don't want to hear that song anymore."

"It's my opus. I'm writing it so Lexy can hear it later."

"Was Lex here last night?"

"No, he's been busy. He was out at a show last night. He'll be over later."

"You should have gone with him."

"You know why I didn't," she says, a cloud passing over her expression. "Stop pressuring me. You really want me to have a panic attack?"

"How do you expect to start a band if you can't even leave the house for a show?"

Her face goes completely expressionless. I went too far.

"Get out of my fucking room," she says.

"I'm sorry. I'm trying to help."

"Well, you suck at it."

"What if you and I, we just went for a walk? Just a walk, to our old school around the block? What if we did that and started there?"

"You know there was a mugging right on that corner two weeks ago. And closer to the BART station, there were a dozen incidents last month, two assaults with deadly weapons."

"How . . . do you know that?"

"There are crime maps online. I'll show you."

"I don't want to see them. This is why I don't read the news, Joy; if you look at all the bad stuff happening in the world, you'll never be able to leave the house again."

"Or you'll know how to avoid it," she says. "I know which streets are most dangerous from looking at those maps—I know the safest routes to walk."

"But do you walk them?"

Her eyes turn to slits, thick with black eyeliner.

"Remember when we said we would go to the southern hemisphere in January?" I ask.

"I didn't say that. I hate the heat. Why would I say that?"

"To make me feel better. When we were kids, you said, when you were twenty-one, we'd go to the southern hemisphere. We'd sit on the beach and you'd drink a fancy drink with an umbrella in it."

"You're making shit up."

"Joy," I say. "Just a walk around the block. I'll be there

with you. We'll take your pills, and I'll have my phone—broad daylight."

"You are the most irritating person alive. Get out of my room."

I leave her room. I pushed her too far. The thing with Joy is, you can't push her into doing anything. In fact, the more you push, the more she goes the other way. I've never learned the art of getting her to do what I please. Eighteen years on this planet, she's still a mystery.

I go back to my room, and she goes right back to her song, screamed operatically into her mic, her distorted bass grinding over it.

"An army of witches on broomsticks from HELL
Are coming to seek their revenge!"

My sister is recording her metal opus this morning, I text Michael. Loudly. About an army of witches on broomsticks from hell. I am hungover and looking forward to death.

Immediately after sending it, I wish I could take back the last part. I was joking, of course, but death seems like a thing we can't joke or even talk about. It's the unsaid thing between us—the invisible ocean we ignore.

Hahaha! Your sister sounds badass! Can I bring you some Gatorade? Soup? Also tell your sister I have an old-school 8 track for demo recordings if she wants to borrow!

Sweet of you, but we're good.

His infinite kindness makes me hate myself. I get back in bed, not responding, and flip through the composition book. My sister looks at crime maps to try to make sense of the bad things that happen in our neighborhood. I write things down about Michael to try to figure out what was wrong with Joshua. I've filled pages and pages with information, but I haven't even gotten close to an answer.

Yet.

You want to come over Friday night for dinner? Michael asks. My mom is excited to meet you.

My sister bleats another lyric of her not-song for her not-band that will certainly play a ton of not-gigs.

Yes, I text back. Sounds fun.

THIRTY-THREE

Day after day, I go to work and try my damnedest. I zero in on my screen and lose myself in the minutia of catalog copy. I get enthralled by patterns and prints and previews. My heart beats faster when a blank page opens and my fingers linger, ready, over the keyboard, and I know I get to take the picture of a chevron-striped jumpsuit I would never wear but deeply aesthetically appreciate and put its striking singularity into words. And then a relief blooms, something like endorphins, as the words take playful shape in my head—somewhere in my brain, yes, but dancing in a smile behind my lips—and out my limbs, into my fingers, onto the computer keys and onto the page in front of me. I know I'm only writing about clothing, but clothing is important; it's how we choose to show up in the world. The rest of ourselves, we're born with. My useless dusty-blue eyes; my wild, wavy hair; my poor posture; my small boobs; these things I was born with. These fabulous outfits? This

Mondrian dress with go-go boots? These winking rhinestones in my glasses' corners? Choices.

I do have to admit, since I was moved across the office from Antonio, productivity skyrocketed. Tammy's funneled more and more copy my way. I started as a proofreader, then she had me sitting in on meetings taking minutes, and the final jewel: writing catalog copy. I submit my pitches (suggested copy for each item in the upcoming catalog) alongside the other writers with full-time jobs. We're in the marketing department, technically, and Antonio is in the customer service department. Antonio wants to write too, but hasn't been given a shot at ad copy yet. Instead he writes soothing emails to prima donnas unhappy with our product.

"You're getting groomed for a copywriter position, I can feel it," Antonio says over lunch. We sit at Jack London Square, shrouded by plotted palms, watching the shiny blue water from a bench. We share a turkey sandwich wrapped in paper. It's so cold, we haven't taken off our scarves, but the sailboats, the sun bleeding through the clouds, it's worth the air's chilly bite.

"Are you bitter?" I ask.

"Yeah, honestly. I've been there longer. Kissed all the asses. Why does no one groom me?"

"Grooming is such a creepy concept."

"It so is. Listen, I'm happy for your success, BB. And you're good at what you do. I just—I know they're going to offer you some silver-platter shit, and do you even want it?"

"Of course I do. And they're not offering it to me—there isn't even a job open for a copywriter right now."

"You are such a mystery to me," he says. "Like the other night, you bring me to that party, you flirt with your ex the whole time—"

"Antonio," I say, hands up, as if I'm under imaginary arrest. "I was *not* flirting with Adrian."

His mouth is full of sandwich. *"Wha* ah you—"

"Antonio, my love, I'm feeling like we are misunderstanding each other."

He swallows his sandwich, hand out asking for time, and downs half a bottle of water. Out there on the water, so many sailboats. I watch his gaze linger. I know his banker boyfriend is dodging him suddenly and painfully after weeks of sleepovers and gushes of forever talk; I know Banker Boyfriend sails as a hobby. I imagine Antonio imagining these things.

"You're with that guy, Michael, but you're not; you flirt with Adrian, but you don't; you don't want to live here, but here you are; you don't even care about that copyediting job, but you do. You fascinate me. Who are you, Betty? Do you even know?"

I shake my head. "Absolutely not."

Antonio puts his arm around me and we sit there a moment, throwing crumbs at seagulls. Then we both scroll on our phones in mutual comfortable silence.

Back in the office, Tammy drops by my cubicle. It's less a cubicle and more a table with a mesh wall, but it's mine, my workspace, and I have a cactus there and a vintage *Vogue* cover with Wilhelmina Cooper in a red patent-leather turban pinned to the mesh wall to mark my territory. Anyway, Tammy drops by.

"How are you?" she asks.

"Doing well," I say, opening my computer. "How about you?"

"Living the dream!" she says.

She's drinking out of a coffee cup that says *Living the dream*. So I guess she really is.

"Swung by to say fab job with the copy for the granny-pack line," she tells me.

Granny packs are a line of fanny packs with patterns I would describe generously as grandma wallpaper; it was truly a challenge to come up with compelling copy for those. I'm surprised to hear this.

"We ended up using most of what you submitted on the website," she continues. "I can't *wait* to show it to you. I'm literally dying."

You are figuratively dying, not literally dying, I don't say.

"Really?" I ask.

"Abso-fruitly!"

"Wow, thanks."

"There may or may not be another copyediting job opening up this year—no promises, of course—but if it does open up, I sure hope to see you submit an app for it."

"Yeah, sure, I'd love to submit an app." Sounds so weird, abbreviating it like that. "Lication," I finish. "Application."

"Wunderbar!" she says, and leaves my desk.

Across the room, I see Antonio's bespectacled gaze peeking over his mesh cubicle wall. He shakes his head at me.

"What?" I mouth.

My phone lights up. Wunderbar. I've never been called wunderbar!

Stop eavesdropping.

There's no such thing as
eavesdropping in an open office.
Anyway, I told you so, BB.

I should be happy. I know I should. Tammy just came up to me and encouraged me to apply for a real job. Sure, it's a ghost job, one that doesn't exist yet, but she doesn't tell all the interns to apply for full-time jobs. But instead, I feel undeserving. Antonio has been here longer. He wants it more. He's earnest and a better person than me, more talented, more qualified. Why do I get all the luck, when I didn't even ask for it? Why did I barely miss the I Glam shooting? Why do I get offered the job? I should be so happy.

"Nothing good ever came of a *should*," my dad once told me.

Oh, shut up. I push him from my mind. I open my computer—glancing at my social media feed, seeing I've been invited by my mother for a march for gun safety in Washington, DC—and push that from my mind too. I get to work studying a line of bell-bottom pants, thesaurus open, looking at synonyms for a bell shape. Sometimes there are no synonyms.

THIRTY-FOUR

The Bay Area is so crowded, so void of space, squeezed between the water and its bridges and the hills and its forests and mansions, that traffic is a steady disease. Michael lives in Crockett, another town on the northeast edge of the peninsula. My phone tells me it's nineteen miles away, and yet it takes us over an hour to get to his house. He came all the way out to Berkeley to pick me up. He made a playlist of local bands for the occasion. He is too damn nice. As we crawl along the freeway, I am rotted with guilt. I watch the sun sink behind the San Francisco silhouette. I have earned Michael's trust. I don't deserve it.

"Beautiful, isn't it?" he asks, watching me watching the sunset as we sit in a moment of gridlock.

"It is," I say, adjusting my focus and watching him watching me in the window. Through the window, the sky goes from pink to a cool blue. I think I know how a sunset feels.

Perhaps I have made a mistake, but I can't turn back now.

"Have you always lived out here?" I ask him.

"We moved a few months ago," he says. "Downsized. Needed a change after . . . after."

He doesn't finish his sentence. *After* becomes its own continent.

"We needed a change," he says again.

Usually this would be the place where I ask for more, where I pry for detail, but my mouth is dry. I can sense him, thinking, heavy with it. He turns up the music.

Crockett, though only a handful of miles from the nearest subway station, seems like a town that belongs in another state or time. The downtown area is quaint and unoccupied. The bridge, so close, looms like a steel colossus in the background, and a sugar factory puffs smoke beside it. There is a park we pass, long and grassy, with no one in it. Michael's apartment is above a corner saloon with red-painted doors and a neon sign that says *Toot's*. We go through a door, up some stairs with faded floral carpet, and then another door, the inside hallway stinking like decades of cigarette smoke. As Michael fusses with his keys, I hear a television behind a wall. Their wall? What would she be watching? I'm collecting this information. Later, I will jot down notes. One day I will make sense of all the factors that added up to Joshua Lee attempting to murder my mother and sister.

Michael hesitates. "My mom is . . . I don't know how to put it. She's a lot."

"So's mine," I say. "I've had tons of training in moms with big personalities."

"No, but . . . um. Betty." He puts his keys back in his pocket. "Betty, walk with me."

I follow him down a set of stairs toward the back of the building. We open the door and go outside, to a cement porch with two milk crates. We sit on the milk crates. Tangles of vines, morning glories, climb up the porch barrier and spill all over the ground. There's a can with cigarette butts at my feet. My heart is pounding. Michael is sweating, not smiling, not making eye contact.

In the silence that follows, it hits me—this is it. This is the moment when he's going to say the thing neither one of us has said yet. My stomach tightens as I wait for it, like I'm at the top of a roller coaster and there's nowhere to go now but straight down.

"The I Glam shooting—that was my brother," he says. "He was the shooter."

I'm not sure how to react. Relief begins to bloom in the silence that follows, to hear the truth laid bare.

"Joshua Lee was my brother," he says.

Those five little words have the potential to shift everything.

"Okay. Wow." After I say it, I realize what a lie my tone implies, like I'm finding this out for the first time.

"I'm sorry, this was not the right way to explain this. I've been meaning to say something. I just—I don't know how to talk about it. I thought you wouldn't want to be my friend if you knew."

I swallow. I search for his eyes, but he still won't meet mine.

"I still want to be your friend," I tell him.

He looks up at me and I didn't realize how thirsty I was for our gazes to meet again until I get a drink of him. I'm suddenly weirdly attracted to him, witnessing him in this different emotional state. He's different to me, in his shame, in his fear I might go away. Also, I know this is where I'm supposed to tell him my sister was *in* the shooting. That I already knew Joshua Lee was his brother, that I sought him out exactly because of that, but I cannot say these things to him—especially when he grabs my hand and intertwines our fingers and squeezes. He lets go and smiles a tired smile.

"I'm so glad you still want to be my friend," he says.

"And I still want to meet your mom," I say.

"Good. She really wants to meet you, too. But—I had to tell you. Because probably my mom will mention it. It comes up."

"I understand."

We exchange a long look. I do understand, and he thinks he understands, but really, I understand far more than he does. And I still don't understand enough.

We stand up and the secrets I'm keeping weigh more than they did before we sat down. Of course he has no idea about my sister being in the shooting—how would he? Joy's name wasn't printed anywhere. My mom went viral, but I doubt he's seeking out clips about gun control, and most people wouldn't even make the connection anyway. He bared his soul for me, and what did I do? I kept pretending.

I am invited into his house, and instead of being honest, I stalk.

His house smells like fake mangoes, I imagine jotting down the second he opens the door. It does. It smells like manufactured fruit, and there are vape clouds swirling in the lamplit air. His mother sits on a purple velvet couch with fake-fur cushions. She's bony, with gelled, spiky hair and bright eyeshadow, like some rocker from another age who never changed up her style. She sucks on a vaporizer, blowing out another candy cloud, and puts it down. She stands up, saying, "I'm Brandi. Nice to meet you, so nice to meet you!" and clasps my hand. As promised, she is wearing leopard print— a pink leopard-print top.

"Hi, I'm Betty," I say.

"I've heard *all* about you, Betty," she says, giving Michael a wink. Brandi has bloodshot eyes the same color as Michael's. She smiles, revealing a silver tooth. She smells strongly of mangoes and something else—something almost antiseptic. I don't like the fact she winked at Michael, like they share some secret about me. Immediately, I notice the pictures on the bookshelf, Joshua's senior portrait. I try not to stare at the portrait, but it's there, screaming in my line of vision. I feel his presence, the presence of evil. I cannot believe I came to this house today.

I've got a nauseated soul.

Brandi wants to know all about Retrofit as Michael fixes dinner in the kitchen (chana masala, smells incredible). I sit at the Formica table in the dining room with his mother, my hands folded in front of me, explaining how I came to write catalog copy, and Brandi is leaning so far into the table, I'm afraid she might break it. She is making me feel very fascinating, certainly more fascinating than I deserve.

"You know, I worked in fashion," she says. "Did Michael tell you?"

I shake my head. She has a careless tone, an irreverence that shaves years off her age. *The things she and Michael share: the shapes of their noses, the cheekbones. The things that differ—how much more olive-toned Michael is than she is, how much plumper his lips.*

"I worked in New York City in the midnineties," she says. "Moved out there from Kentucky." She gets up and cracks a window, flashes her vaporizer at me. "Mind if I puff?"

"Go ahead," I say.

She blows a plume out the window. Fake mangoes, everywhere.

"Yeah, I worked as an intern at *Sassy*," she continues. "You're a baby. You've probably never even heard of *Sassy*."

"No."

"A teen magazine way before your time. I got hired just months before it folded. I wanted to write about fashion."

"Where'd you work after that?"

"After that, I met a cabbie, fell in love, got knocked up, had Joshie, and got a job doing medical transcription. Then I left that husband—he was an abusive prick, excuse my language—and moved to California. That's where I met Amir and had Mikey."

My head is swimming. Joshie. Mikey. Brandi is a bit of a gusher. She gushes information, important information, too openly and quickly for my brain to catch up. All of this must be written down later.

"I had dreams of going back to New York City and going to fashion school for years," she says. "But my first husband, he was such a *stain*, you know. Such a shit. I still can't look at a yellow cab without flinching."

I nearly flinch at that remark. "Gosh, I'm sorry," I say.

"But, oh, I love New York," she says, like a walking, vaping T-shirt. She shuts the window and sits back down at the table with me again. "So you went to high school with Mikey, right?"

"Yeah," I say.

"You two . . . friends then?"

"No, we weren't."

"You know Joshie?" she asks, clear-eyed, but I sense a sudden quiver of ready tears.

"I didn't."

"Ah." She nods, as if this makes her sad.

"I wish I had."

I'm not lying, but I am shocked at the boldness of saying this thought aloud. The moment hangs in the air. In the next room, Michael is listening to Slayer, screeching double guitars, and I can hear the clatter of plates and silverware.

Brandi wipes under her eyes, even though nothing is there. "I wish the whole world would have known him—known the best parts of him, anyway."

She gets up and goes into the kitchen and returns with a beer. Michael follows her with a stack of plates, napkins, and forks and starts setting the table. He leaves for the food. Brandi drinks her beer.

"I wish there wasn't such focus on him—on Joshie," she says in a tight tone, like she is barely containing her rage. I get the sense, watching sip after sip, her drink is slowly extinguishing a fire.

"Right," I say.

I don't know what is right, what I am saying, how we got to this place in the conversation.

"What happened to him was an epidemic," she insists. "Yes, he committed a crime. He was also the victim of an epidemic."

"Epidemic of . . . ?"

"Social media," she says. "I've been trying to talk to lawyers about pressing charges against these hate groups online. Boys don't radicalize themselves, you know."

"Oh, not this," Michael says, coming in with two bowls. He puts them on the table. "Anything but this."

"Why shouldn't they be held accountable?" she asks him as he spoons us our food.

"Because people are responsible for their actions," he mutters. "Okay, we're done talking about this. I wanted to hear you geek out about fashion, Ma. You said you were going to tell her your idea for a purse, remember?"

"I don't care about purses anymore," she says quietly, staring at her food.

"She has this idea for a purse that doubles as a defense weapon," Michael tells me. "To help women feel safe."

Brandi gets up and her chair makes an excruciating scraping sound. She goes to the kitchen, gets another beer—she drank the other one in practically an instant—and she grabs her vaporizer.

"Very nice to meet you, Betty." She makes a namaste gesture with her full hands and leaves the room.

It's very awkward, and I am positive I made a mistake in coming, and that Michael silently agrees with me. But then I look up and Michael is enjoying his meal, grinning at me like his mom didn't just have some weird mood crash after talking to me about her dead son and leave the room. Like it's only ever been us in this room.

"I told you my mom was a lot," he says.

"She's been *through* a lot."

"She's always been a lot, even before all that." He blows on a steaming bite of tomatoes and chickpeas on his fork. "I really want her to be okay."

"So she doesn't work?"

"She's on disability. Depression, fibromyalgia. She barely leaves the house."

"We've got some things in common, you and I," I tell him.

"That's why I like you so much." He takes a bite. "As a friend," he adds with his mouth full.

"Of course." I wait a beat. I cannot tell if he is being facetious or not. I don't know about me, either. "I can't believe you're so . . . joyful, after everything."

"I can't believe you're not eating my food."

I stir my food around in the bowl, then get a bite and blow on it just like he did.

"There's no other way to be, honestly," he tells me. "Smiling is the glue that keeps me together."

"Have you always been like this?"

He thinks. "Yeah, I guess I have."

"I don't remember you smiling a lot in classes we had together."

"It was zero period. Too early for smiles. And don't pretend you even noticed I existed."

"You didn't notice me either."

"You don't know what I notice."

His food is quite impressive, and this odd conversation seems to border on flirtation, or maybe it's just in my head. Maybe I'm so love-starved, I see it in places it's not. Either way, I am impressed by how at ease I feel here, even after the interaction with Brandi, even with framed pictures of the dead terrorist—boy, I should say, Brandi called him her boy—in the living room. Joshua probably sat at this table, and then he tried to shoot my sister. And here I am, enjoying a meal, and only half-sick about it.

After dinner, I help load the dishwasher and Michael shows me his room. At first I get nervous, like he's going to try to make out with me, but instead he puts noise-canceling earmuffs on me and plays drums. This enormous drum set is squeezed next to a mattress in the world's tiniest bedroom. There are posters from the floorboards to the ceiling, and even *on* the ceiling—the whole place shines with patchwork gloss. I watch him, how hard he hits the skins, how he spins the sticks on his fingertips like a magician. I clap when he's done.

"Amazing," I say.

"Thank you, thank you," he says.

"Do the neighbors ever complain?"

"The neighbors are a bar downstairs, and the landlord next door is literally deaf. So no, they don't. Although when Joshua lived with me, he hated it. I could never play with him around at our old place."

"What would he do?" I ask, unable to contain my curiosity.

"Oh, come in and punch me. I had a dead bolt on my door." He puts his drumsticks back over the snare, signaling he's done playing. "He was always coming in and starting shit. Hey, did you know about my first band? Let me show you our seven-inch . . ."

He shows me his record collection and plays a few records for me. Behind the music, my mind is whispering, *Punch me*. I imagine Joshua bursting through the door in a fit of violence. I wish Joy were here; she'd have so many more interesting things to say to Michael about his records than I do. Instead

I ask questions about why that band name, how funny is that cover, is this heavy metal? And Michael answers them with the patience of a kindergarten teacher.

"Ready for me to take you home?" he asks after a while.

As he drives me home, I wonder two things. First off, is he *not* attracted to me? Because it's not like I want to be with him, but the prospect of him really being this close to me, this edging on flirtatious, and yet not attracted to me . . . makes me wonder if I have no sparkle or allure for other human beings. And that terrifies me.

The second thing, the important thing that I wonder, I ask. I have to ask it. Or what has any of this been for?

"Why do you think your brother did what he did?"

He doesn't answer for a long time, so long I become quite sure it was not at all an appropriate thing to ask him.

"He did it because he was fucked up and needed help. And nobody stopped him," he says.

"What kind of help?"

"He had problems. He was on and off medications for ADHD, anger issues, a bunch of crap. He was always unstable, even as a kid. Threw fits, tantrums. Was violent. His dad was abusive, I don't know, maybe he picked it up when he was a child. Honestly, I don't know what would have helped him, I'm just sure it didn't happen."

"Sounds like you feel a lot of regret."

"I'm learning to live with it," he says, and then adopts a much chipper tone. "Hey, have you ever noticed that sign?"

He points to a large sign we pass on the freeway. It says *Acapulco Rock and Soil.*

"For years, I passed that and thought it was some amazing club," he says. "Acapulco Rock and Soul. I only recently found out it's a place that sells dirt, and it's rock and *soil.* I misread it."

"That's funny," I say. "I guess we see what we want to see."

He grins and drives, drums his hands on the steering wheel. There are moments in life where you wonder what incalculable math got you exactly where you are, and this is one of them. I'm glad I know Michael, even though I don't quite know what is inside him. I wish that Joshua had never existed. That his criminal act and his death weren't always there eating the space between me and Michael. Of course, without Joshua, Michael and I would have never even known each other. I look out the window at the bridge, where the traffic glitters like a strand of Christmas lights. Look at it out there, sparkling with lives I'll never even know, faraway headlights on roads to strangers' homes. It's so big, and I'm so small.

"You know you chew your cheek when you think hard, Betty," Michael says softly. "Don't eat yourself alive."

"Do I?" I ask, touching my cheek.

"You do," he says.

I rub my cheek. He's right.

"I didn't realize," I say.

I keep my eyes steady out the window. The night is the color of all I do not know.

THIRTY-FIVE

Since the New Year's party, I haven't had any in-depth conversations with Adrian or Zoe, only meaningless group texts gossiping about how our high school theater teacher apparently eloped with the swim coach, and some trashy reality show they are into about people who marry each other after speed dating for one minute. Adrian and Zoe were my closest friends mere months ago. A year ago I thought I was in love with Adrian, and Zoe was my platonic soul mate, but now I don't know where I fit in the equation anymore. Every time our conversation from New Year's Eve replays in my head, my stomach dips thinking of Zoe gushing about my mother, and Adrian's bizarre remark about false flags, and then . . . me. I'm sure I sounded so drunk and stupid. I blush alone in my room just recounting it. And yet, why? It was the truth.

"Guess who I just did an interview with?" Mom asks me, coming inside the door with a plastic bag of Chinese food and a pile of mail in one hand. She kicks off her shoes, hangs up her purse, and puts the mail and the food on the kitchen table.

"Um . . . CNN?" I ask.

"Guess again."

"Fox News?"

"I'm about to disown you."

"Who, then?"

"Zoe Hayashi."

"Oh, great." I didn't mean for it to come out so flat, it bordered on sarcasm, but . . .

"What?" my mother asks. "You not getting along with Zoe?"

"No, we're fine. She's, like, all feminist warrior now and obsessed with you. It's fine."

Mom stands frozen, hand hovering over the Chinese food. "Zoe's getting into a cause, and I think it's wonderful. You don't believe in dismantling the patriarchal system? You don't believe in challenging a culture that perpetuates violence against women?"

"Of course I do, but do we have to talk about it all the time?"

"Are you kidding me? How often do you engage in political discussions?"

"I don't, because honestly, I get so tired of hearing them constantly around me," I tell her. "No offense."

"Okay, Bets, keep plugging your ears and singing *I love fashion, lalalala*. I'm sure that will change the world."

It's as if I've been smacked in the face. I'm so hurt by her remark, I turn around and get plates, pretend to be busy.

"Zoe should be incredibly proud of herself," she goes on, unpacking the food. "She moved across the country, she's going to an amazing school, she organized a protest at her dorm—did you hear about that?"

I put the plates on the table. "Maybe if I came from a family that could afford to send me to school, I could dismantle the patriarchy too."

"Don't give me that—don't push your apathy on me. *Nuh-uh*. That shit might work on someone else, but not me. Did *I* go to a fancy school? Was *I* raised rich? My father was a goddamn *telemarketer*. My mother cleaned *houses*."

"This speech again?" Joy asks, entering the room. She's got her hair piled high on her head, in her robe, and smiles blissfully to herself. "The *grandma was a maid* speech again?"

"It's not a speech," Mom says, sitting down. "And hi, Joy."

"Everything's a speech," I mutter.

"What?" Mom asks, genuinely unable to hear me.

"Nothing."

We spoon our food onto our plates.

"Betty's been a little *sassy* lately, have you noticed?" Joy asks Mom.

"More like moody."

Joy smiles slyly. "I like sassy, moody Betty."

"And you, why are you *smiling* so much?" Mom asks. "You look like you just got back from the spa."

"I had a four-hour nap," Joy says.

"Mmm. You register for classes yet?" Mom asks.

There's a crack in Joy's blissful smile. "Not yet. I will."

Bullshit, I think.

And maybe they're right. Maybe I am moody and/or sassy. I've always been the agreeable one, the nice one. Never pushing back. Never saying what I think. Never wanting to poke or provoke. Not even in my own mind—I would push those thoughts away. I would try to see the good. Now I'm not sure what kind of person I am.

After dinner, to make up for the almost fight earlier, I do dishes and clean up the food. I wipe the counters, trying to leave the place better than I found it. I stack the mail in the middle of the table. As I line up the corners of the envelopes, I notice the return address on the one behind an ad postcard. I pull the envelope out and look closer. In shaky, Sharpied all caps, it says *AL SMITH*. His city? *LAS VEGAS, NEVADA*.

I experience a moment of rigor mortis. I make sure Joy is in her room—she is, I hear her playing her bass and singing *"Let me be your spider woman"* behind her door, her latest hit—and go knock on Mom's door.

"Yes?" she asks.

I push open the door. Mom's on the bed, with reading glasses on, peering into her laptop. "I'm reading this story about a dog that killed his owner with a gun. Can you *believe* this is the reality we live in these days? That this is a news story?"

"How did . . . ? Never mind. Mom, this is really scary."

"I know it's scary. We have dogs killing people on

accident now, *babies* involved in firearm accidents. What kind of sick world—"

"Not that. That is messed up, but I'm talking about this."

I hand her the envelope. She squints at it and then her eyes go wide. "Oh, this flaming sack of human garbage again."

"He knows where you live? Has he been sending threats here?"

"This is the first."

"Open it. What does it say?"

She tears it open and reads it. From here, I can't tell what it says, I can only see that most of the page is blank and I can tell it's more all-caps Sharpie. She crumples it up and closes her eyes. She appears so peaceful, but of course, she is an impending volcanic eruption. I back up a step, in case.

"Mom," I say.

"It's okay," she says, opening her eyes. "We're going to be okay. I am going to contact the police again tomorrow, and I'm going to find a security firm, and we're going to get an alarm. I'm going to look up places on Yelp right now."

"Why? What did it say?"

"Nothing that concerns you. Nothing you need to worry about."

"Let me see it," I say.

But she shakes her head, keeps the ball in her hand.

"Was it a threat?" I ask.

"It wasn't anything."

I go back to my room, fuming. I lie on my bed and stare at

my window. Not out—not at the black night—but at the reflection of my yellow room with its paper models on the walls. For the first time in a long time, I wish I could escape it all. Not just this apartment, where apparently Insane Al Smith knows where my mother lives, but this city, this state, this nation. Buy a plane ticket and hide in Namaste House, chanting with my father. Or farther—to an island away from all other people. Hell, it's my fantasy. I could go to the moon. Although, of course, once you're finally safe, you have another problem; you get lonely.

Want to go to the moon? I text Michael.

Sure! I'll pack right now.

This is why I love him. I didn't text him for two days, and then I text him this, and he responds positively and immediately. Wait . . . did I just say I love him?

I sit with this in my mind for a long time. I take my glasses off and lie on my bed, the cracks on the ceilings now gone, the world my blind, familiar blur. It's really weird the words *this is why I love him* crossed my mind. I don't love him. At least, I don't love him in the way I've ever loved anyone before. I don't want him direly, the way I did with Adrian, at first, desperate when they were away, or the way Molly was about me. I've never even thought about having sex with him until right now—and it's weird. I've never had sex with a boy; I have no idea if I'd even like it or not. And it's Michael!

"It's Michael," I actually say out loud, to nobody.

And then I say, "I love Michael," as if to try it out.

And then I sit up and ask the air, "*Do* I love Michael?"

Movies, shows, they seem to perpetuate this idea that love is one thing. It's mostly hetero, it's passionate and sexy, you pine for it, it's diamonds, white dresses, honeymoons, babies, growing old; it's the ultimate everything, the end goal. I've watched Antonio chase it for months, only to get paired with disasters like baby-doll man and now strung along by the banker. I watched my mother get crushed by love, and my sister get stupid for it again and again. Not love itself, but the idea of it, the promise of it—which always breaks.

What if love is different than that? What if real love doesn't have to include all those things? What if it can be meeting a person who fits with you, someone you can be quiet with and awkward with and it doesn't matter, a friend plus something else entirely special—a connection that can't be replicated anywhere else in your life? Something that even contains secrets and horrible coincidence and tragedy?

What if?

All right, all packed and ready, Michael texts. Meet you at NASA HQ in a half hour.

I don't answer him, but I spend a long time with the light on in my room, eyes closed, imagining that fantasy were true. The moon would be so cold, so blue. And I'm sure, from there, from that distance, with earth nothing but a sapphire earring, nothing would matter, all our rules and histories would no longer exist, and how beautiful that would be.

THIRTY-SIX

Mom went to a march in Washington, DC, the one she invited me to online, the one that I declined. The whirlwind of a human being she is, my mother flew out across the country tonight (Friday), attends the march where she's giving some speech tomorrow (Saturday), and flies back the next morning (Sunday). Before she left, she got some security measures installed. We now have a bunch of H2 locks on our windows. We have a camera outside the door that's hooked up to an app on her phone. She left us a note with her schedule printed out in an actual calendar, and a gold gift bag on the kitchen table. Joy clearly thinks it's going to be something exciting, and when she pulls out the plastic packages, her face falls.

"What the fuck is this?" she asks.

It's pepper spray. It says it in big capital red letters on the front of it.

"Pepper spray," I show her, moving my finger across the lettering.

"Okay," Joy says, putting it back in the gold bag, confusion scrunching her forehead. "I thought it was going to be chocolate."

"That would be way better."

"You know what? I'm gonna order some *chocolate* right now." Joy grins and grabs her phone. "And should we order some pizza rolls for dinner? And, like . . . chips? Let's have a pizza roll party! We can watch *TNG*!"

"Sure," I say.

"What, you're too cool for pizza rolls and *TNG* now that you have a boyfriend?"

"I'm not sure where you got your information, but it's wrong."

"Mom told me about him."

"He's a friend."

"Michael, and you went to high school with him. What's his last name?"

My cheeks flush. "Pizza roll party sounds fun. Order me some sparkling water."

"You're so *fancy*," she sings, pressing buttons on her phone. "Oooh, wanna do facials, too?"

"Sounds good."

I go into my room and get into my pajamas. As I button up, I become aware my hands are shaking. It's a lot to hold on to something people do not know. It feels like a disease, if I bother to stop and notice it. I pull my hair back in a ponytail and hear Joy singing on the other side of the wall. She's singing a song from *Mary Poppins*. How can she be so fucking happy? How can she not ask questions about the H2 locks and the pepper spray? How dare she feel so *safe* in this bubble we call home?

Joy must love me a lot, though, because she shares one of her expensive facial masks that she got last year for her birthday. Strangely, as into fashion as I am, I'm not an aficionado of facials and manicures and other girly things. The wet paper mask is chilly and slimy on my face. I hear these are supposed to make my face baby-skin smooth, but I look like a masked murderer from a horror movie. We both do, in fact, as we set them on our faces side by side in front of the mirror.

"Oh my God," Joy says, degenerating into a giggle fit. "Can we take a picture for Lex? I want to scare the shit out of him."

"How is Lex? He hasn't been by in a while."

"He's in Texas, recording. 'Lex is in Texas'—poetic."

"Are you two officially a thing?"

"We are not a thing; we are two people in love."

"Committed?"

"Betty, you are the most annoying person sometimes. You should be a reporter. Can we take the picture so I can scare Lexy now? Thank you."

I oblige, opening my eyes extra wide for the photo.

"Look at us!" she laughs, showing me.

"Please delete that picture."

"It's *funny*."

"No, it's terrible."

"Excuse me," she says with a sigh. She turns off the light and heads to her room. "But when did you become the joyless one?"

"When you became the one full of joy," I mutter to the darkness.

I follow her into her room and we start an episode. I watch, but don't comprehend. My mind is so much louder than the screen. A year ago, I would have peed my pettipants if Joy asked me to order pizza rolls, do facials, and watch TV with her on a Friday night. But now it's an obligation. And especially annoying because she keeps getting distracted and missing the episode I don't even really care about watching in the first place to text Lexy and snicker to herself at his probably dumb responses, or get up and look out the window for the Instacart person.

"Kiki was on her way fifteen minutes ago. I could have walked to the store in fifteen minutes," she says.

"Then why don't you?"

"You have become such a little smart-ass," she says, but proudly, ruffling my hair.

I push her hand away.

A minute later, Kiki calls Joy's phone and says she's there but we're not answering the door. Joy and I get up and go to the door and open it; no one is there. As I stare out at the empty, well-lit stoop, I get a shiver, thinking of Al Smith. Beyond our front porch, the world is dark, shadowy, swishing trees, dim-lit sidewalks, and parked cars. What if he's lurking out there?

"But you're *not* here, Kiki," Joy says into her phone. "I'm right here staring at the porch and you're not here." She pauses and rolls her eyes for my sake. "Okay, if you see rose-bushes, you're at the wrong house, you're clearly at the corner house." Joy mutes it for a second. "This twat is absolutely use-less. I'm about to explode if I can't get my pizza rolls."

"Put your shoes on and go out to the sidewalk. It sounds like she's two houses away."

"You do it."

"I don't want to."

"Betty, please," she says.

And she says it in this pitiful way, *pleading*, her eyes big, no jokes left, that it flutters through me and lands with a gen-tle pain.

"Joy, come on. It's two doors away. You're too scared to walk two doors away?"

"Just do it for me, one favor. Please?"

Our eyes are locked. She still has her phone in her hand, muted. The woman is saying "Hello?" over and over. The TV is still rolling on, some life-and-death battle scene that hardly matters to me.

"No," I tell Joy. "You do it."

"Why are you such a bitch from hell?" she explodes. "Seriously—I order us food, and you can't walk outside to pick it up?"

"I want to see you do it."

"Fuck you, Betty. Seriously. Fuck you." She looks terrifying with her mask on as her eyes go wide with anger. "Get out of my room, and guess what. No pizza rolls for you. Our party is over."

"Okay," I say.

I go back to my room and close the door. I sit on my bed doing nothing, waiting. Finally, I hear the door open, and shut. What a sweet sound, the silence that fills the air. For a moment, I think I could float. My sister just left the house for the first time in months. Joy! But then, after a minute, I hear sobbing. I hear it out my window. I try to open my window, but these goddamn H2 locks are still confounding me and instead I yell a string of expletives that would make my mother proud and then get up and go to the front door. I open it. My sister is sitting halfway down the stairs, sobbing into her hair. She did that as a little girl whenever she got particularly sad—she bundled her hair up in her hands and cried in it like a handkerchief. It's disgusting and endearing and it's a version of her I haven't even considered in at least a decade.

"Hey," I say, sitting next to her.

"It's not like I don't want to," she says into her hair. "It's that I *can't*. I can't even move right now. I can't even look up. I just want to disappear."

"I'm here, okay?"

"You know how you are with heights, how you get so

scared, you get dizzy and want to ball up and close your eyes?"

"Yeah," I say, even though I got desensitized to heights after I got an internship in a tall, tall building.

"That's how the whole world is for me now. Imagine if your whole world were twenty stories high." She sobs. "I hate this so much."

"I didn't realize it was so bad," I say. "Or . . . I mean, I did, but Joy, you seem so content, you make it easy to forget."

"I *am* content, if I never have to leave." She sniffs, but doesn't lift her head. "Honestly, I'm afraid I'm about to have a panic attack."

"Want me to get your pills?"

"Yes, but I also don't want you to leave." She starts sobbing again.

"How about you stand up and keep your eyes closed, take my arm, and we'll go inside and get your pills. I'm so sorry I made you come out here."

"I'm a fucked-up imitation of a person," she says into her hair.

"Let's go back inside."

I help her stand and she keeps her eyes closed. Down on the sidewalk, a man in a trench coat stands at the bottom of the stairs, looking up at us with wide, horrifying eyes. My body rewards me with a shot of adrenaline as my mind whispers the name *Albert Smith*.

"Get inside, Joy," I say as calmly as I can, stumbling a

bit as I hurry her back up the stairs and toward the door. I notice, in a glimpse as I shut the door, the man is walking away with a dog on a leash. After I lock the door, I see myself in the foyer mirror and realize I'm the one who looks like a murderer, with my facial mask still on. No wonder that man was staring.

"Where are the pizza rolls?" I ask Joy in the warm, womb-like light of our lamplit living room.

"Kiki left them on the doorstep of the house with the rosebushes." Joy pulls her mask off, squinting with blood-shot eyes. "My eyes are burning, I have to wash this shit off."

"I'll go get them, okay?"

"Okay. Thank you, Betty."

I run back outside and scare another random dog walker as I retrieve the groceries from someone else's doorstep and come back inside. I open the bag. There are pizza rolls, chocolate, sparkling water, and a bottle of whiskey.

"Joy?" I ask, standing in the bathroom doorway and showing her the whiskey.

"Oh yeah," she says, taking it. "Want some?"

Her pills are on the counter, next to an empty water glass.

"You're not mixing this with your pills, are you?" I ask.

"Oh, shut up," she says.

She goes back to her room. She opens the whiskey, takes a sip, and flops onto her bed. "Excuse me if I want to relax on a Friday night after having an embarrassing panic attack. Did you put the pizza rolls in?"

I put the pizza rolls in. I look in the cabinet at my mom's whiskey, which is almost empty, and everything suddenly makes sense: where the whiskey went; why my sister is so happy, despite her circumstances; her moods, her raucous laughter, everything.

I know better now, though. I know the more I push her to be better, the more I push her away. So I say nothing. I watch a few more minutes of the show I never cared about with Joy. She doesn't drink much more, maybe a few sips, and puts the bottle under the bed. I pretend I'm not watching her. I wash my face and go to my mom's room for a new towel. I step into her bathroom and wipe my face off, and for some reason it makes me sad being in here with my mother's creams and her dried rose in an empty blue bottle and her perfume spray bottle on the countertop. It makes me sad because I feel like my mother is gone for longer than a weekend, and we are all not the people we were, and I can't imagine staying here and I can't imagine leaving.

My lower back hurts from sitting on Joy's bed all night, so I take a pillow from my mom's bed before I return to Joy's room. First, though, I notice a balled-up piece of paper in the tiny space on the floor between my mom's nightstand and her bed. I pick it up, heart on sudden overdrive. I know exactly what this is. Do I really want to read it? I don't. But I have to. Once upon a time, maybe I could have left it there. But I'm different now.

I flatten out the white piece of paper in my hands,

crinkled, crumpled, cracked with shadows.

WHAT LOVLEY DAGHTERS YOU HAVE, it says.

That's it.

A compliment with the sting of a threat. I consider vomiting.

The oven timer dings. I ball the paper back up, press it to my heart, close my eyes. For a moment, I am so afraid, I might implode. Which is good for me, maybe. Now, for the first time in a long while, I might know how my sister feels.

PART THREE

THIRTY-SEVEN

IN BOLD PUSH, GUN GROUP AIMS TO REPEAL AND REPLACE SECOND AMENDMENT

GUN SAFETY GROUP SPOKESWOMAN: "OUR FOUNDING FATHERS DESIGNED THE CONSTITUTION TO CHANGE"

MOTHERS ALIGNED FOR GUN SAFETY BREAKS FUNDRAISING RECORDS AFTER DC MARCH, NEW STRATEGY UNVEILED

My mother returns from Washington, DC, with a blaze in her tired eyes, her voice a laryngitic croak.

"Oh my God, poor Mom," I say to her, giving her a hug.

"I was shouting and talking so much," she says in a rasp. "Where's Joy?"

"Still sleeping," I say.

"At one p.m.?"

"You're surprised?"

She kicks off her ankle booties and collapses on the sofa

next to her rollaway suitcase. "I've been up since three thirty East Coast time, so pardon me if my mind is blown."

"Your voice sounds so sad," I tell her. "Let me make you some tea."

"Thanks, Bets," she says, closing her eyes.

I fill the turquoise teakettle, flicker on the gas flame. Out the window above our sink, next to our neighbor's house, there's a small, bare plum tree. Every year, I watch its gradual bloom, burst of fruit, paling leaves, and wintery skeleton. Here we are again. There's so much I need to tell my mom. Where to start? The note from psycho Al Smith I found in her room, how betrayed I feel that she neglected to warn me or Joy, the fact Joy is a mess who can no longer be ignored? I want to tell my mother that seeing her headline and picture and "brave speech" and "bold pushes" all over the news this morning enraged me, because it now feels selfish, her campaign a personal affront to my and my sister's safety. Who knows how many more death threats we are going to get now that she's battling the Second Amendment of the US Constitution?

However, my mom is much like Joy: a gentle, thoughtful approach, easing into a difficult discussion is the only way to go. If I come at my mother with criticism or anger, it will only make her more stubborn.

So I make sure my sister is still asleep in her room with a peek down the hall, then bring Mom a steaming cup of chamomile tea.

"Here you go," I tell her.

She opens her eyes and takes the tea. "Thank you," she says in her hoarse voice.

I sit down next to her. I'm going to start with Joy's porch breakdown. That's how I'll open the conversation, then mention I saw the threat Al Smith sent via US mail, as a kind of summary of why my mother needs to do something, change something, make things right for us. Because, after all, she's doing this MAGS work because she loves us and wants a better world for us. If I appeal to us needing her, she has to listen. She's our mother. Protecting us is her job.

"Mom," I begin.

"I have some news," she begins instead, and takes a sip of tea. "This is really hard for me to tell you, but I'm just going to rip off the Band-Aid: MAGS offered me a full-time job on this new campaign in DC, and I'm thinking of taking it."

This news paralyzes my ready words. My tongue goes numb and I have a hard time locating a response. The logical part of myself says, *Betty, control yourself. Don't tell her how you feel.* But it seems like the logical part of myself is on a losing streak lately.

"I can't believe what you're saying," I tell her, in a tone so controlled it sounds unusually low.

"Did you even follow the news of the march and our announcement?" she asks, and then mutters, "Of course not, why am I even asking."

"Yes, *Mother*, I did." Strange how like Joy I sound right

247

now. "You're going to push to repeal and replace the Second Amendment. The Founding Fathers designed the Constitution to be interpreted and adapted over time, and you want to put the 'well-regulated' back into the 'well-regulated militia' the Second Amendment proposes to protect."

I have to say, I'm not sure who's more surprised by my articulate snapback—me or my mother. But I didn't realize I had such a well-informed answer inside of me. I guess browsing articles on my phone doesn't count for nothing.

My mom raises an eyebrow. "Well said."

"That's all great, but what about *us*?" Tears form behind my glasses and I close my eyes, begging them to stop. But soon they're spilling down, hot on my cheeks. I will myself to vanish. With my eyes closed, I can pretend my mother can no longer see me. But these tears keep coming. I bite my lip to not sob, to keep myself quiet. My mom sees everything anyway.

"My baby girl," she whispers, and puts an arm around my shoulder. "Is it that bad?"

"An unhinged man who hints he wants you dead sent us a letter that said 'what lovely daughters you have.' Joy has lost it, Mom, *lost it*, and do you even see it? She hasn't left the house since the shooting. She stopped going to school, her job, everything. She drinks whiskey secretly in her room. How do you keep pretending we're fine?"

"You think I think we're fine? No offense, my love, but you don't know *what* I think." Her voice sounds so strange to me, some blown-out, sick version of herself, all from yelling at the top of her lungs about gun safety.

"Did you hear me say she hasn't left the house in months?"

"Do you think I'm blind?" Mom drops her arm from me to look at me. More like to show me she sees me.

"Then why don't you *do* anything?" I ask.

"I do everything I can every fucking day," she says. "All this MAGS stuff, every moment of my work—you girls are the flame I hold ahead of me to light the way, to help me remember *why* I'm in this fight."

This is the moment I realize my mom's eyes are also full of tears.

"How can you talk about leaving us, then?" I ask.

"Because I have to ask myself, where can I do the most good?"

"Here, with *your lovely daughters*!" I almost yell.

"Bets," she says in a sigh. She puts her hand on my braid and pulls it once, playfully, and lets go. "You are eighteen years old. Joy is twenty-one. I can't take care of you forever."

"It's your fault this psychopath is after us, though," I say, my voice climbing. "You have to protect us."

"As much as it kills me to say this, honey," she says (and when my mother drops a generic term of endearment like *honey*, you know the worst is coming), "the best way I can probably protect you is by moving across the country. Away from you. This shit's only going to get worse."

"You're going to leave us," I say flatly, feeling the tears begin to cool tight on my cheeks.

"So dramatic," she says, pulling my braid again.

"Stop," I tell her.

"You're an adult now," she reminds me. "It's time to think about your next steps."

"I work an unpaid internship and Joy is unemployed. You're going to make us homeless if you move to DC."

"Don't catastrophize. I wouldn't move to DC for at least a month. And I could, of course, leave you the apartment for several months after that, long enough to give you time to figure something out."

"Mom, please don't." I look at her pleadingly. I use the tone Joy used yesterday that saddened me so much; it seems love is just another kind of desperation, another opportunity to degrade us into beggars.

"Elizabeth," she says my full name and puts her hand on my hands, and that's when I know she's not going to listen to me, no matter what I say. "This job is more than a job to me. My time here is so brief, *so* brief—all of our time is; the idea that we have all the time in the world is a luxurious illusion. I feel lucky that I almost got shot, because it made me realize that the only thing I ever truly did, that I ever loved, that I ever would die for is you and Joy. My girls—my entire life—you are everything to me." Her eyes are dripping, charcoal rivulets compelled by gravity. She wipes them with her shaking fingertips. "Please give me permission to do what is best for all of us. To fight this fight. To make this world better than what it is. Give me a chance to do something I finally realized I'm good at, and that matters, so someday, when you have babies—if you choose to have babies—those babies will grow up in a world where they don't face danger in shopping malls, where they aren't getting shooter drills in elementary school, where they aren't debilitated by PTSD to the point where they can't leave the house. I am doing this not just for you, but for your children. Can you see that?"

I nod, although it's hard to imagine a world where I have children, when I can't even grasp my own sexual and romantic feelings for other people, when I mistake closeness with Joshua Lee's brother for love. But I nod. Because deep down, I know what she's saying, in a place without words. This is a long game she's playing. I respect that.

"But what about Albert Smith?" I ask.

"I already contacted a private detective to figure out who he is and keep tabs on him, since the police have been useless. I'll hire private security if I have to. But I'm sure once I live on the East Coast and you and Joy have your own places, you won't even be on his radar. You can always use your dad's surname, too, if you want."

"You know I'm not going to do that," I say. "Dad doesn't deserve us having his surname."

She laughs, her hoarse voice rocketing through her and making me laugh too. She pats my knee with her hand, manicured, with a chip on her index finger.

"You are certainly my daughter," she says.

I put my hand on hers there, and then reach out and hug her, hard. I bury my face in her shoulder. "I'm going to miss you."

She squeezes me, inhales me. "I haven't taken the job yet; I'm thinking it through."

"Seems like you thought it through already."

We pull back and look at each other. For the first time, to this degree, anyway, I see myself in her. I see my almond eyes in hers, and the round shape of our cheeks, and the coarseness, the undecided half-curly, half-straight nature of our hair. Does she see the same as she stares back—a younger, wilder-eyed, less assured version of herself? Perhaps I am of her, and she is of me, and thousands of miles can't do anything. This is not like my father and his unsurpassable sea; my mother would never leave us, not that way.

"I'm leaning toward yes," she says. "But I need to figure a few things out."

"I'm leaning toward yes too," I tell her, rubbing her arm.

She nods, opens her mouth to say something, and then, as if emotion ate the word up, clamps her mouth closed again. "Thank you," she says, finally, in a rasp. "That means a lot."

"I'm so proud of you," I tell her. "I hope I can be like you someday."

"You already are. You're more than me. You're *better*. Don't you know that? At your age, the only dream I had was to fall in love and have babies, maybe get an associate's degree. Look at you—ready to take over Retrofit, vying for a staff position at a successful fashion company less than a year out of high school, all from grit and determination. Nobody handed you anything."

"Thanks," I say, smiling.

The truth is, though, I know what it feels like when she says that life is not enough, that we need more purpose, and when it comes down to it, perhaps I'm more envious of her sense of purpose than I am resentful she is leaving us for said purpose. Retrofit is fine. Retrofit has been a good opportunity. Maybe, like Tammy hinted, a job will open up and I'll soon get a legitimate full-time position. But still, a small voice asks in me, *Is that enough? Is that what I even want?*

What I'm left with, after this conversation with my mother where my world was shattered, is the sense that it's quite possible I don't know who I am, or what I want, or if I even want the things I am working so hard for. I don't know what I believe; or maybe I do, but I don't know how to articulate it. Deep as a heartbeat, though, a purpose thrums—a purpose with rhythm and place, a purpose mine, a purpose humming low beneath the doldrums of everyday. It's there, somewhere. And now that I know my mother might be leaving us to follow the beat of her heart's drum, maybe it's time to start actually listening to my own.

THIRTY-EIGHT

It rains for a week straight. On the plus side, I get to bust out my rainbow raincoat and red rain boots, my headscarves; on the negative side, our apartment has sprung multiple leaks and our kitchen is filled with pots and pans.

Joy took my mother's news of her cross-country move in stride—too much stride, in fact. She listened to my mother's heartfelt explanation and just said, "Cool! You should do it." And went back into her room to play her bass guitar for her "new album." She probably drank a bunch and maybe took a pill. I reached out to Lex on social media, wanting to know if he thought my sister was okay. He sent back a nonsensical message at three a.m. in what seemed like a free-verse poem form.

hey crock, your sis is an uncontainable spirit, even if
she's not leavin the house or what
is worry for? we still talk, shell always be my queen
anyway on the road tryin to drive the van right now
your profile pic looks hot

tell Joy i'll listen to those tunes soon

I don't tell Joy about this disappointing exchange, which taught me nothing except Lex is exactly as much a loser as I thought he was. I don't know what I was hoping for—someone to intervene? Someone to help pick up the pieces? To be her new roommate? I browse job listings while biting my nails late at night because I don't know how I'm going to afford life here with my mother gone, and I know that I'm going to have to figure out something for not just me, but for my sister. I don't understand how Joy can keep watching TV and singing songs and taking pills and pretending the world beyond her four walls doesn't exist. Doesn't Joy know? Even the safe planet of her room is doomed. I look out my curtain often, expecting Albert Smith; I imagine him with a duffel bag and an unhinged look on his face.

One night I have a nightmare there is a man with a gun in my room and I wake up gasping for air. The H2 locks and security cameras can't protect me from Albert Smith following me into my dreams. I flip through my book of what I've learned from my months with Michael—pages and pages of notes in different-colored pens—and try to discern some lesson I can carry to this situation. But it seems I've made no real progress. I open my computer, conduct a search, scroll through a sea of Albert Smiths; all of them could be harmless, or dangerous. It's just like staring at Joshua Lee's picture. Context is what makes a monster look monstrous. Another search tells me there are signs for how to spot a psychopath.

I jot down some notes, but sigh when I read them back to myself. *Lying, using charm as a tool for manipulation, lack of empathy*—yes, there is a checklist. But it's all abstract patterns of behavior. None of these are things I could spot easily or quickly in a stranger. This checklist wouldn't have helped me to prevent Joshua Lee from shooting people in I Glam that day, or to assess the level of danger in profiles of Albert Smiths. Frustrated, I throw my book across the room.

My mother leaves for another weekend in Washington, DC, the day the rain finally lets up. The sunny skies do not match my insides. Michael asks if I want to go on a hike. He's got a New Year's resolution to go into nature more, and the resolution stuck: he's been sending me selfies from forests and shorelines and creek beds regularly. He picks me up Sunday morning in his mom's minivan. He has brought us homemade sandwiches and thermoses of herbal tea, because he is too good to be true. Also, he got a haircut, and I can see the shape of his neck now and his jawline better. He is handsome, and he is too nice, and I hate him for it. Or maybe I don't hate him. Maybe it's exactly the opposite.

"Hi," I say, clipping my seat belt. As he drives, I touch the hanging *Brandi* pendant on the rearview. "How's your mom, anyway?"

"In a deep depression," he says cheerfully. "How's your mom?"

"She's planning on abandoning us for a job in DC, and my sister is a basket case pretending everything is fine."

"Fun times."

"Also, Joy's secretly drinking."

"It just keeps getting better, doesn't it?"

"It really does. I am living the dream," I tell him, thinking of Tammy's mug.

We both laugh. I realize that this way Michael is—ever-joyful in the face of the seemingly insurmountable—is not just a survival mechanism. It actually brings relief. Especially when you're not alone.

Michael drives to Redwood Regional Park, up in the Oakland Hills. It's a hidden forest, one that makes me forget the mad tangle of freeways, the screaming BART trains, the violet metropolis and its cancer of skyscrapers. As we get out of the car and start walking into the thick of it, the smell of trees and fresh earth fills my lungs. A calmness spreads throughout my body as I follow Michael down an unpeopled path, into the green shade, my hands in my pockets, his in his, our steps in sync. We walk for some time without a word between us, just exchanging a look now and then, a smile; he points to a hawk above us. I stop, look up at the grace of its wingspan. When I look back at Michael, he's not looking at the hawk anymore. He's looking at me.

Something about him right now—the shadows cast from the redwood trees, maybe, or this sweatshirt I've never seen him wear, or his haircut—something seems different. I imagine pulling the buttons of his coat with my fingers, or running my hands through the side of his hair. I imagine my arms around his neck. As if we are of one mind, he reaches out and puts his arms around me. I can smell him—lemon soap—as he looks deeply into my eyes. The desire is a rush from my toes to my cheeks. I have never wanted my lips on another pair of lips so badly in my life, and the anticipation is singing through my nerves. Very softly, he leans in. I close my eyes, feeling the pinch of the moment. But then panic jolts me and I open my eyes and break free from him before it happens.

I can't ever have this with Michael; I shouldn't even be here with him.

I have been dishonest with him, this whole time I've come to know him, befriended him, and whatever else this is I feel for him. I can't keep going.

"Oh man," he says. "I think I misread the moment."

I shake my head. "You didn't."

"Betty," he says, and tries to hug me, but I push him away.

"No," I say.

I take my glasses off so I can wipe my eyes with my scarf, return my glasses to my face.

"I'm sorry," he says again. "I was just—"

"This is all wrong," I tell him.

"What's wrong?"

"I am not a good person," I finally say. "I haven't been good to you."

"Betty," he says. "You've been not just good to me, you've been the best part of what has been a very shitty time for me."

I open my mouth to speak, and I know I'm about to say everything I have been holding in for months. This must be what it feels like to pull a pin from a grenade.

"The only reason I became your friend in the first place is because I have this . . . sick fascination with your brother," I say, unable to meet his eyes, instead focusing on a branch above his head. "Because of the I Glam shooting. My mom and sister were in the shooting—not shot, but they were there. And when I found out it was Josh who did it, I remembered you were his brother. And I became . . . obsessed, I guess. Looking him up online, trying to figure out why he did what he did, so, I don't know, I could get some answer that might help my sister feel safe in the world again. I found you online. I found out you worked at Amoeba, and I came there, and you gave me that flyer for your show and you were so nice to me. You were so *nice* to me." I squeeze my eyes shut. "And I didn't come to that show because I wanted to see you—I mean, I did want to see you—but mostly I came because you're Joshua Lee's brother."

I look at him, finally, expecting him to be angry. But he's nodding at me like this is perfectly okay. How can he look at me that way? His kindness is maddening. This is *not* okay.

"I understand," he says. "Thank you for feeling open enough to share with me."

What is he, a robot?

"You don't get it," I say. "I have been using you to collect evidence, Michael. I have a composition book where I take

259

notes on things I learn about Joshua, to try to make sense of this—to give my sister some explanation for why he did it."

"Has it helped?" he asks.

I'm flabbergasted at how calm he is right now. In fact, I think I'm growing angry. "No! It hasn't."

"I'm sorry."

"Why the fuck are you apologizing?" I ask, stamping my boot on the ground. "Seriously? Aren't you mad at me? Don't you think there's something wrong with the fact I became friends with you because your brother was a murderer?"

"Betty, sit," he says, pointing to an enormous, moss-covered fallen tree. "Please."

I'm shaking. I want to scream. But I do as he says and sit next to him.

"I knew your family was in the shooting," he says. "And to be honest, when I saw you in Amoeba, I wanted to be your friend for weirdly similar reasons."

I'm not even sure how to respond, so I don't.

"After the shooting, I saw a clip of your mom talking about the shooting online," he goes on. "I saw the last name Lavelle, I remembered that name, I looked her up online. I made the connection that she was your mom, and Joy's mom. I read Joy's social media update about being in the shooting. I realized you were her sister, and obviously I remembered you from high school. When you came into Amoeba, it was like . . . the universe gave me a chance to make something right that was so horribly wrong. I thought, 'Hey, maybe I can be her friend. Maybe I can make her life better, after what my brother did.'"

I haven't had a feeling like this, like the air has left my body, since Joy sucker punched me in third grade. It takes a moment to recover my breath. "*That's* why you wanted to be my friend?"

"Mostly," he says. "At first."

A couple passes us by, hand in mittened hand, murmuring hellos. Michael and I straighten up and smile and say hello until they pass, and then both of us drop the smiles. I look up at him, not sure what to say. Not sure if I'm mad at him, or hurt, or vindicated.

"See," he goes on, and I detect a bit of shakiness in his voice, even though he still sounds like his usual cheerful self. "Um. How do I say this? Um." He smiles, looking ahead, but then I realize he's holding back tears. "You want to know why my brother did what he did?"

"Michael," I say.

"No, I mean, you went to all this trouble, right? Looking for an answer. Here's your answer, okay? *I* am why my brother shot all those people. It was me. Yeah, you know, it was social media and guns and his shitty medications no one regulated very well and everything else. But guess who was with him the afternoon before it happened. *Me.*"

"That doesn't make it your fault."

"Betty, Betty, Betty," he says, wiping his eyes. "You don't understand. My brother warned me, and I ignored it."

"How?"

"You really want to know this? You're going to hate me."

"What did he say?"

Michael turns to me, transformed by his new serious-ness. His face isn't his. "He said, 'I am going to kill myself today, and I'm going to take some bitches down with me.'" The words land heavy, sink fast. "I was sitting on the couch and I said, 'Have fun.'" He shakes his head. "I am haunted by that moment. I could have been the person who stopped him. He told me *exactly* what he was going to do, and he'd been acting erratic for days—yelling at my mom, trying to beat on me, yapping about bizarre conspiracies—and I had such a gross feeling that day, but I didn't want it to be true, so I ignored it. I dismissed it as a sick joke. There I was, the idiot on the couch who heard his threat and watched him walk out the door with that duffel bag, and I said, 'Have fun.'"

"You . . . you had no way of knowing."

"I'm telling you, I *did* know somewhere. I knew it in my gut. And I didn't do anything."

We sit for a moment in a silence nearly funereal. He sniffs, and all this information swirls around me like a sick merry-go-round of regrets. Maybe he's right, he could have stopped this. Maybe he's the answer I have been looking for all along, and yet I'm left utterly unsatisfied. How is this supposed to help me feel safe in the world? How is this information supposed to help me help Joy?

He hands me a thermos of tea.

"So this whole time," I say, watching the steam rise from the thermos, "the reason you've been so nice to me is because you feel bad that your brother almost murdered my sister and mother. All the nice stuff you've done—picking me up places and taking me out to lunch and being my friend—it's out of guilt."

"No."

"But that's what you said." I put the top on the thermos and return it to him. "You just said that. You can't take it back."

"You became my friend because you wanted to learn about Josh, so is it that different?"

I run my tongue against my teeth, searching for a word to describe this colossal lostness. "It *is* different."

"How?"

"It just *is.*"

"Different the way a mirror image is different. It's flipped, its angles are opposite, but it's fundamentally the same thing."

"It's not the same," I say.

I hear a bird cry, and it occurs to me I am injured somewhere deep.

"I have real feelings for you," he says. "That go beyond what my brother did to your sister."

"Sure."

"Please don't do this."

"Look, you don't have to pretend you give a shit about

me now," I tell him, looking away, far away, at a violet mountaintop I'll never reach. "You did your charity work by befriending me. We can move on."

"Are you going to tell me you don't feel anything real for me? That it was all about Josh this whole time? That I was your research project and nothing else?"

"Of course not."

"Well, obviously it goes both ways. I have feelings for you," he reiterates. "Real feelings." He seems to catch himself. "I know you're seeing someone."

"I lied about that, and you know I was lying."

He stares at his hands on his knees, folded, so polite. "Is it weird I *hoped* you were lying?"

"Were *you* lying?"

"I was sort of seeing a girl online, but it's over now."

Somehow that stings—that an element of his story was true, and mine was a pathetic lie.

"This is all wrong," I tell him, standing up.

"Betty," he says softly. "It's *not*. Please don't hate me, after everything I told you."

"I don't hate you," I say, but I can't meet his eyes. "But I don't want to pretend like everything's okay anymore. I think we made a mistake becoming friends. This was all a mistake."

"It hurts to hear you say that."

"Honestly, it's best this way. Forget me. I'll forget you. I'll forget your brother and you forget what he did to my sister and mom, and let's just move forward."

"How?"

"Please just take me home!" I nearly scream.

"Of course," he says, so quickly it almost hurts, standing up and heading down the trail. "Anything you want."

I watch him walk ahead of me and follow, numb. There's a fork in the road, and I consider going down the one that heads into darkness, away from him. We pass a laughing couple, an arguing family, a contemplative dog walker. My heart beats steady and too loud in my veins, begging to be heard. *I don't know,* it seems to say. *I don't know, I don't know, I don't fucking know.*

"This is really it?" he asks. "This is how it ends?"

"Rip off the Band-Aid," I say, thinking of my mother.

I'm glad I'm following Michael, because where we've been and where we're going, they are all unclear. As I watch the back of him, so simultaneously familiar and yet the outline of a tall stranger—because he is a stranger, still, I get the privilege of certain intimacy, yet hardly know him—I want him so badly. I want to pull in step with him, put my arm in his, but I can't. Because I don't know how to bridge a gap so wide it includes the death, or near death, of our loved ones. *I don't know, I don't know, I don't know.* The pathetic stutter of my heart, which, I remind myself, is nothing but a muscle with an obnoxious, lifelong twitch.

THIRTY-NINE

I haven't felt such nauseated sadness since Adrian broke it off with me a year ago. The sun had set but still left some light behind. It was spring, and it was drizzling; the white buds were new and dewy on the violet tree branches. We were there to see a Kurosawa film at the Pacific Film Archive, in line waiting to buy tickets. I hooked my arm in theirs. The way they sidestepped to unhook, I knew something bad was coming.

"Hey," they said. "Can we talk a minute before the movie starts?"

Oh no, I thought. But my mouth went ahead and said, "Sure."

Adrian and I left our place in line and walked around the block to the front of the building, a shiny silver spaceship-looking behemoth with a screen flashing stills from upcoming films. Adrian looked down at me, put their hand on my shoulder.

"I found out I got into University of Washington today," they said.

"Wow, congratulations!"

"Thank you. But that means . . . I'm going soon. And I can't give you the kind of focus you deserve." They smiled. "You are so wonderful and beautiful and funky and sweet and perfect. I hope we can stay friends."

So many flattering adjectives had never felt so painful. I nodded, forcing a smile on my lips. I didn't betray the clenching in my chest. "Of course we will. I get it, completely," I said instead. "Now's not the time for a long-term thing."

What this humiliating memory I'd since buried has to do with my conversation with Michael today, I cannot figure out. People leave, people aren't what they say they are, people never care for you for the right reasons or in the correct amounts. These are lessons my father taught me years ago, lessons I guess I have to learn again and again. I think about talking to Joy about it, but Joy is drunk in her room. I assume so, anyway, because she's having some dramatic conversation on the phone about Lexy not loving her enough, and then she plays her bass guitar for a long time, singing about how the man in black never loved her. If it were yesterday, I would have texted Michael with these lyrics and laughed. It's not yesterday, though, nor will it ever be again.

I text Antonio and ask what he's doing tonight. It's been a while since I've reached out to him. Ever since I moved to a different corner of the office, we haven't talked as much. Antonio tells me he's doing nothing, just eating cheese puffs and working on a poem while watching trashy TV.

So cultured. How's the banker?

He's not a banker anymore. You know how he
was all incommunicado? Turns out he quit his
job, bought a yacht, and moved to San Diego.

!!!!

Yeah, it's been a week.

What a prick.

Actually I think he had a nervous breakdown.

Long story. I still hold out hope. Am I bananas??

We had a thing. Like an actual thing.

I get it.

(Because I do.)

Antonio and I decide to meet up at the Starry Plough
for open mic night. I get cute in a maxi dress, denim jacket,
and scarf. Two braids in my hair, red lipstick. I look good,
I think, as I look in the mirror. I recall, with a throb, how
close Michael's lips got to mine. How betrayed I feel by him.
I don't even know why I'm hurting, when I was just as rot-
ten to him as he was to me. He opened up to me and showed
me his guilt, his ultimate fear, his ugliness, and I stomped
away from him feeling rejected. Nothing that has happened
between me and Michael Lee makes any semblance of sense.

"Bye," I say to Joy on the way out, popping my head in
her doorway. "Going to an open mic night."

She's sitting, phone in her hand, sour look on her face—a
face full of makeup, a fully dressed person you would never

guess cannot/will not leave the house. "Have fun."

"You sure you don't want to come?"

"Will you ever stop?" she asks.

"No."

"Just *go* already," she says angrily.

I notice her eye makeup, smudged beyond the usual smudging. "Have you been crying?"

"Not your business."

"Have you been drinking?"

"What are you, my new mom? You want to adopt me?"

"No, but I'm probably going to have to once Mom moves."

"Fuck you," she says, her eyes welling up.

"Joy, I'm sorry—"

She gets up, pushes me out, and closes the door.

"Joy—"

A moment of silence, then Iron Maiden begins blasting so loud, there's no use. I feel bad, but feeling bad has become a strange new normal. I head out the door because I'm going to be late.

Seeing Antonio out front of the Starry Plough, in his polka-dot tie and red suspenders, is a breath of fresh air. I run up to him and hug him extra long. I close my eyes and inhale his cologne. We stand outside, next to the colorful mural of pub people, and catch up. I try to tell him about what happened with Michael to the best of my ability, but I can't even really explain it. Once I articulate it, it seems so convoluted.

"Wait, so . . . like . . . basically, you both wanted to get to know each other because of the shooting?" he asks.

"Kind of," I say.

"And that makes you . . . mad?" He puts a hand up. "I'm honestly trying to understand this, BB."

"It's just—it wasn't real, you know?"

"But was it real for you?"

"Yes," I say after a minute. "I didn't mean for it to be, but it was."

"Why can't the same be true for him?"

"He friended me because he felt sorry for me. Do you know how much that sucks?"

"I feel for him," Antonio says after a moment. "He's been through a *lot*. Can you imagine carrying that kind of guilt around all the time? Feeling like you could have stopped something, and you didn't?"

The day of the I Glam shooting, I could have been in the building. I could have gone in with my sister and mother. I could have observed the scene, as I do so well, and spotted a boy coming in who didn't look quite like he belonged, who had a duffel bag, who opened the duffel bag and took out a weapon. I could have yelled at my mom and sister, ran out before he began shooting. I could have pulled the fire alarm. I could have dialed 911 on my phone. I could have looked Joshua Lee in the eyes and yelled the right combination of words to make him understand he was about to do something he could never take back, that he was going to rob a stranger named Shandra Pensky of her life that had only just begun, that this was not the way to be remembered. I too could have stopped Joshua Lee.

"I can imagine," I say.

We go inside. The place is packed, but we find a little corner table to sip our lemonades. We watch a white-haired woman freestyle about gardening tools over a beat emanating from a child's Casio keyboard; a trio of kazoo players; an opera singer named Billy Bob Bilby; then the announcer says Antonio's name, and to my complete shock, Antonio raises his eyebrows at me and runs up onstage. He didn't tell me he was going to read a poem! I stand up and immediately start filming him on my phone as he grabs the mic. The crowd gets quiet for him.

"This is a poem about a love that was worth every moment of hurt," he begins. "I just wrote it tonight. It doesn't have a title.

> "*We were too late. All of us*
> *Too late for the stranger's salvation,*
> *Too late for the Transbay bus.*
> *We were tunnel-bound, a people-sea,*
> *And the air swelled with emergency.*
> *The whispers, collected, clouds thick with words*
> *Like 'suicide,' like 'jumped,' flapping frantically as*
> *trapped birds.*

There were hundreds of worried, unfamiliar eyes
And you.
And I.

Death and love give no second chances.
I met you under morbid circumstances
But you, stranger, took my side and whispered,
'Want a ride?'
Never too somber for a double entendre,
I obliged.

I thought of the man who made us late
Who made the world wait
For his spent life, who turned
A crowd into a congregation that night.
As we escaped, held hands on rainy streets,
Contemplating the death of a man we'd never meet,
Our lips met on our first accidental date.
It seemed that man was always with us,
His ghost a gust of wind that settled
into every conversation. We wondered
Where he was, somewhere now forever,
and marveled that his death
brought us together.
When we stopped laughing, the silence
Held whispers of a distant train.
You left, a mess;

What a mess you left.
I wipe my cheeks, and blame the rain."

I applaud so fervently, my hands hurt. When Antonio comes back to the table, I hug him long and tell him what an incredible poet and human he is. We sit and catch a couple other acts—a bearded man and his banjo, a student with hilarious limericks about cats. After our lemonades are done, we go outside and walk around the neighborhood. Our breath makes little clouds in the sharp February air.

"That poem, Antonio . . . I loved it," I say. "I can't believe you sit there all casually talented and then jump up there and read a poem like that. That you just wrote *tonight*. Who are you?!"

"Sometimes it feels good to get it out, you know?"

"It was about when you first met the banker?"

"Yeah."

"I know you two met because of a subway delay. . . . I didn't realize someone had died."

"Right? How *didn't* I know the relationship was doomed?"

"That's deep."

"You should write a poem, BB. We should start a club."

I smile. "Maybe I'll try."

We hug and part ways at Adeline and Woolsey, where someone has spray-painted in red on the sidewalk the words *the personal is political.* As I head home, I think about Antonio's poem, about how sad it was that man killed himself—who was he? What was inside him, what tortured him, what did he leave behind? I want to know every story, every secret, and can't, and that there is life's greatest tragedy. And yet, despite all we can't know and all we can't control—despite strangers who kill on purpose or who die on purpose—sometimes the worst situations can bring people together. Perhaps they can even serve a new and beautiful purpose. I wonder if Antonio is sorry because things didn't end up well with the banker, but I think I already know the answer.

As I head toward my house, I spot a fire truck parked ahead, swirling lights of a police car. Curious, I quicken my steps. It's on my block. Parked in front of my house. Oh, Lord. I begin to run. More than run. I fly home and get a sick feeling in the pit of my stomach, flashbacks to the I Glam shooting. It is my house. My front door is open, our front window is smashed, and our landlord is downstairs talking to a police officer. A thousand possibilities flicker through my mind, all too horrible to entertain. I bound up the stairs.

"Excuse me," I tell a police officer standing in the doorway. "I live here. What's going on? Where's my sister?"

"You live here? What's your name?"

"Elizabeth Lavelle. Where's my sister?"

"She's in there," he says. "Talking to my partner. I want you to know she's fine. Everyone's fine."

"What happened? Can I see her?"

"In just a minute. Come in and talk to me a second."

We sit on the couch. Our place looks so tiny with him in

it. The lights are all on, there's glass all over the wooden floor and a trail of blood.

I gasp. "What the hell happened? Is this Joy's blood?"

"It's the intruder's blood," he says. "We'll help clean that up in a moment."

"The *intruder*?"

"They broke in here, probably a smash-and-grab. Doesn't appear they took anything. Your sister startled them and they took off on foot."

"Took off where? You didn't catch them?!"

"Not yet. We're looking. Your sister said you have a video surveillance system, so we'll review footage of that as soon as we can get the password. Do you know the password and account info?"

"My mom does. She's in DC," I say. "Who is the intruder?"

"We're not certain yet. We have officers securing the premises."

"I have to go see my sister," I say.

I get up and go to Joy's room, where she sits on the bed next to another police officer. She's crying, and possibly drunk. I don't know anymore.

"Betty," she says. "Some fuckwad broke into our house."

"I know," I say, coming and hugging her. "Did you see him?"

"No, I heard him and I came out and screamed, and he jumped back out the window. It was dark. I couldn't see any-thing."

I am shaking. I hold my sister, who is also shaking. I curse my mother. This is all my mother's fault, being her loud, obnoxious, opinionated self and making us all targets, and then daring to *leave* us here alone so she can go be her loud, obnoxious, opinionated self in Washington, DC. I should probably be feeling other feelings, but I am seething.

I tell the police about Albert Smith, and they write the information down with interest, along with my mom's contact info so she can get them access to the video footage. Joy is stunned into silence listening to the information. She says nothing, opens her orange bottle, swallows a pill. After they leave, Joy is insistent the man is coming back.

"He targeted us," she says. "In our own home. That's what all this fucking alarm, video-doorbell shit has been about. Nothing is safe. Nowhere is safe. What if he comes back? Crawls through the window?"

"I won't let that happen," I tell her. "Joy, I will not let anything happen to you."

Our landlord comes upstairs and nails two-by-fours to where the window was, grumbling to himself the whole time. Joy takes another pill and passes out. Meanwhile, I'm wide awake. I get a butcher knife from the kitchen and slip it under my bed. I don't know how I'll ever fall asleep. I'm so angry, so very angry; I call my mother and leave a dozen messages, knowing she's flying back tonight and is likely on a plane. I contemplate calling Michael, but that seems inappropriate for multiple reasons, including the fact it is now almost two in the morning.

But if it's almost two in the morning here, it's almost eleven in the morning in Spain.

Though I rarely ever bother to call it, Namaste House lives in my phone right after Molly. Calling Namaste House and reaching my actual father enjoys a success rate about on par with winning the lottery. I reach Sequoia, good old Sequoia, and ask for Señor Paz (my father goes by the name "Father Peace" in Spanish at Namaste House and it makes me wince every time I have to say this), tell her it's a family emergency. In some sort of miracle, Sequoia understands me and tells me to please hold, and then it's me and the hold music, tinkling waterfalls and wind chimes, and it's honestly so soothing I sit on the floor of my room and almost fall asleep. But then I stand to wake myself up again, eyeing each vintage model poster on my wall, spaces perfectly apart, screaming with color. Why? What did they ever mean to me? Right now they're windows on a skyscraper full of dolls. As the hold music continues and my heart sinks and I realize my father isn't coming, he has failed me yet again, I begin to cry. I tear each and every magazine page down with a bandage-on-flesh rip until there is a small flammable mountain on my floor, glossy pages with faces looking up at me, gorgeous and meaningless.

"Lizzy?" my father's voice says, and I clamp a hand over my mouth momentarily in disbelief. "Lizzy? Family emergency?"

"Daddy," I say, taking a deep breath to get ahold of myself. "Daddy, you picked up."

"Of course I picked up. What's happening?"

"Someone broke into our house," I say. "The cops were here—it was terrifying."

"But who? Are you okay?"

"I'm fine, Joy's fine. I don't know who did it yet, we're waiting for the police to investigate, but I'm so scared. I have a knife under my bed."

I hear him breathe in and out. "Please don't do anything crazy. You know knives, guns, they make it more likely you'll get hurt. Negative energy attracts negative energy."

"I don't know what to do!" I almost yell.

"Well," he says, clearly at a loss. "Well, what about your mother? Where's your mother?"

"She's in DC, Dad. She's leaving us. She has this new job, she's this famous activist now, she has a purpose, and she's *leaving* us. Oh, and she has all these psycho gun-nut people after her. So that's probably who this person was—he was probably this guy who's been threatening her with letters. Threatening me and Joy too."

"This is . . . this is the first I've heard of any of this. I'm experiencing some really intense vibrations."

"Yeah, me too," I say. "My vibes are really intense right now, what with being threatened by some online lunatic and our windows being broken in by an intruder no one found whose blood is splattered on my living room floor, and a sister who is experiencing a slow-burn nervous breakdown next door, and a mother who is leaving us to move to Washington, DC, to become a martyr for abolition of the Second Amendment, and I don't have a paying job and I live in the most expensive area in the country. I have really intense vibes, Dad."

"That does sound intense," he says. "Have you tried meditating?"

"Gah." I flop on my bed. I expected fatherly nonsense, but this is truly beyond.

"I wish I could help you," he says.

"You can," I tell him, closing my eyes, which are now watering. "You can, Dad. Just go get on a plane and come out here and help us. Joy is a *mess*. You could come out here and help her—you know what that would mean to her? To have you walk through that door and surprise her, and tell her you crossed a sea for her? Do you know what that would mean to me?"

"I know," he says, so quietly.

"Mom has always been here for us," I go on. "Day in, day out. She sacrificed *everything* to be here for us. She did it all with a stellar attitude, like she *wanted* it this way. But what about you? What have *you* done? When have you ever been there? Hell, when have you ever even remembered to call on my actual birthday, or sent a gift that meant something to one of us? Despite your tattoo, you've *never* been here, even in the tritest ways. Step up. Drug yourself, I don't care; get an emotional support animal; pray to Buddha; cleanse your chakra;

figure out a way to board a plane and come *help us*."

My plea lands into a stillness between us. In the static nothing-said part of the conversation, I'm reminded that there is more than an ocean separating us right now; there is space itself between us. I imagine our voices ricocheting off the lonely pocked silver surfaces of moons and the marbled fire of planets. I am aware, in the silence, of how far we are, and how unlikely the reunion I want so bad is that it leaves a taste on my tongue.

"I wish I could," he says.

In the smallness, the tightness of his voice, I sense his fear, his anxiety. It's not a part of him I ever get to glimpse. It's as much a privilege as it is a disappointment.

"Thanks for taking my call," I say. "Have a good day out there in the Spanish sunshine."

"Lizzy," he says.

"Please call me Betty," I say. "It's my name."

I hang up and hold the phone to my thudding, brick-heavy heart. I close my eyes and am surprised there are no tears. Joy is sobbing through the wall; when I get up and knock on her door, she just tells me to go to sleep, she's fine. She's going to be fine. She keeps repeating the word *fine*, and I'm reminded of my mother when she was at her worst. Joy is anything but fine.

I'm so worried about her.

I go online and scroll through the news: a beached whale washed up ashore on the California coast; an earthquake shook an island in Southeast Asia; another man killed his girlfriend; another shooting, this one at a sports game. On social media, Zoe shares a link for a young writers essay contest from a local book festival where her mom works. The deadline is tomorrow. The topic is *Responsibility*. Which could mean anything under the blinding sun. But I see that prompt and everything opens up; all these ideas braid themselves and become intertwined with one another. And in the same way sometimes I know the right retort in a conversation, or the right copy to sell a sophisticated dress, I know exactly what responsibility looks like and how I would write it down.

And so, dear reader, I write it down.

FORTY

My mother comes home in crisis mode. She calls me from the airport, letting me know the glass people are coming to fix the window, and she reviewed the footage from our front porch and forwarded it to the police. She said it was a young man, one the police officers recognized from other break-ins in the neighborhood, and it was looking like it had nothing to do with the threats she received. But Mom assured me she's still planning on filing a restraining order against Albert Smith, once her private detective can track him down. She's also paying for services online that scrub her data from white pages listings.

"I'm so sorry," she keeps saying, standing in my doorway with her luggage.

"I'm glad it was random and we weren't targeted." I'm still in bed and my eyes are still closed because the sun has barely come up. "Thanks for letting me know."

She leaves the room to unpack, and I scroll my phone with bleary eyes. The essay contest thanks me for my submission.

Did that really happen? Did I actually do that last night—write a whole essay out of nothing and have the audacity to send it to a contest? I don't even want to reread what I wrote. I'm sure it's awful. A sense of shame with a dash of alarm piques me and I push it from my mind.

Joy doesn't leave her bed all day. I come in, offering to make her some food, watch something with her, do facials.

"No thank you," she says.

I would have felt much better if she'd told me to fuck off. This politeness is not Joy. It's as if she broke last night.

There are no texts from Michael on my phone. Not today, not the next day, not the whole next week. At first I had planned to text him, but then, as the days wore on, it seemed that the gap had widened. The more I thought about our conversation (though *thought* is too weak a word, more like *obsessed over*), the more I came to the conclusion that I have deep, real feelings for Michael, and that is dangerous, because we don't like each other for the right reasons, and our friendship is a flaming tire fire. Once it's been a week without a text from him, I take my composition book out and throw it in the recycling bin.

Joy is not well. I had thought Joy was not well before, but now that I see this new stage she's in, it's apparent how functional she was, comparably. She has not changed out of her bathrobe or brushed her hair in a week. She ordered and installed bars on her windows. She did this herself, with a power drill she ordered online. She also has a dead bolt she installed in her bedroom. My mother is angry.

"We don't own this house!" she says. "We can't install things like this."

"I don't care what anyone thinks, Mother," Joy says from behind the door. "The world can go to hell. You included."

Mom stands in the hallway, a peaceful look on her face, her eyes closed. Her face begins twitching. She's fighting tears. I take her elbow and guide her into her room, and we sit on her bed.

"I don't know what to do," Mom says. "I don't know what to do with her. I made an appointment to take her to the doctor, to adjust her medication, and she won't go; I made an appointment for her to go see a guidance counselor to figure out what classes to sign up for, she never showed; I found her a list of jobs to apply for, and nothing."

"She can't leave the house."

"She *won't* leave the house. There's a difference."

"I think she really can't, Mom."

"I don't know what to do," Mom says, shaking her head. I catch a glimpse of us in her full-length mirror. She's still in her work outfit, and I'm in mine. Two women in blazers with hair half up. "I accepted the position this week, but I can't take this DC job. I can't. How can I?"

"Joy could come with you."

"I don't see how I'm going to get a girl who can't leave her bedroom to move three thousand miles away."

I've been hesitant to say this out loud, because I don't want to jinx myself, but I say it anyway. "Well, I have an interview Friday for a copywriting position."

She bounces up and down excitedly. "At Retrofit?"

"Yeah."

"Bets, that's so exciting!"

"If I get the job—big *if*, I'm sure I won't—I could take over the lease here or I could get me and Joy our own place."

My mom shakes her head. "This isn't fair to you. You shouldn't have to worry about your sister."

"It's not fair to you either."

"No, but she's my child."

"She's not a child anymore."

"She's not well enough to care for herself either."

"She won't be like this forever," I insist. I'm not sure if I say it more for me or for my mother.

Mom's eyes begin to water. "I don't want to leave you two."

"I know," I say, hugging her. "But you have to take this job. It's what you want and what you deserve, and someday I hope that I can care about something as passionately as you do. I need you to do this so I can tell myself someday I can do this too."

We hold each other for a long time. She pulls away and wipes her eyes. "Sometimes I look back on those years when you two were younger; when you and Joy wore your hair in pigtails and brought rainbow lunchboxes to school and pretended you were fairies. At the time, I kept telling myself, 'It's hard now, them being so little and so dependent on you, but it'll get easier soon. They'll get older, more mature, it'll get easier.' But I wish I could go back and shake myself and say, 'It doesn't get easier, it just gets different.' And now I wish I could have one of those days again—one of those long days with loud little girls who need their noses wiped, their shoes tied, who loved me so entirely and trusted that I can keep them safe."

I'm not sure what to say, so I just squeeze her hand.

"I'm proud of you," she tells me. "You've become such a levelheaded, bighearted person. You've taken such good care of your sister while my head has been elsewhere. I'm excited for your job interview Friday."

"Thanks, Mom," I say.

When I think about it, I too wish I could have one long day of childhood back. I wish I could even have one long day from last year back, when Joy had herself together, when I thought Adrian might be a perfect fit for me, when working at Retrofit and building a fashion career from there seemed like an exciting trajectory. I wonder what it must feel like to lose someone entirely. How this brand of looking-backward hurt must be exponentially painful to Michael and his mother, to Shandra Pensky's family, to people whose losses are massive.

Friday morning, I put extra time into choosing my outfit for the interview. Mom left early to go drop off some tax forms at her accountant's office. Before I leave for BART, I knock on Joy's door. I have to beg her to get up and unlock the dead bolt. She looks pale, too thin in her robe, there are circles under her bloodshot eyes. Her room has a sour smell to it, and the bars on her windows make long lines across her dim-lit room. She has a row of orange prescription containers lined up next to her bed. She recently got prescribed a sleeping pill, along with another antianxiety medication, delivered in a plastic bag in the mail. I have to wonder what she's on right now, how much she takes, how well she's being monitored.

"This doesn't feel safe," I say to Joy, pointing to the lock.

"Actually, it does. That's the entire point." She looks at my outfit. "You look cute."

"Thanks, going to an interview for that job."

She doesn't ask me what job. "Good luck," she says flatly.

"Joy, are you okay?"

Her face is expressionless, her eyes half-closed.

"I'm worried about you," I tell her.

"I hate that people have to spend energy worrying about me," she says. "I've become such a black hole."

"No, you haven't."

"Lexy doesn't even answer my texts anymore," she says. "He says I'm too much drama."

Joy does have a tendency to go on long texting rants and demand responses right away, so I'm not that surprised. But still. "Lexy is a selfish asshole."

"I don't want to be a black hole anymore," she says.

I look at my phone, both wanting to be here for her and also aware that I'm going to be late if I don't run to BART.

"See?" she says. "Even now, I'm black-holing you. Sucking your time when you're clearly busier with more important shit."

"I have to get to work is all," I tell her. "Maybe I can bring dinner home? Pizza?"

"Don't bother," she says. "I don't need your pity pizza."

She closes the door, clicks the lock.

"Joy," I say. "I'm sorry, I have to go. Are you going to be okay?"

She doesn't respond.

I roll my eyes and sigh. "You *are* too much drama," I whisper.

At Retrofit, Antonio is in the coffee room, dressed in a magenta tie and a dapper vest, his hair slicked back.

"You look hella cute," he tells me. "Are you interviewing for the copywriter position today?"

"I am," I tell him. "Wait, are you?"

"Watch out, bitch," he whispers menacingly. Then he laughs. "Kidding."

"So you are or you aren't?"

"I am."

"Do you know who else is applying?"

"Some external people. You and I are the only internal applicants," he says.

Internal applicants always have the edge here. We stand looking at each other. I don't know why I thought he wouldn't apply for the position. He's been here longer, and he deserves it more. Just because Tammy encouraged me to apply doesn't mean anything.

"I hope you get it," I tell him.

And I mean it. Even though the thought of me not getting the job unleashes panic (*What will I do? What job would I get instead? Am I going to have to wait tables, or become one of those annoying people who asks people to donate to World Wildlife Fund on street corners?*), I also don't want to get a job someone else deserves more than me. I would rather the world be fair than the world be mine.

"Why are you so sweet? I want to hate you and get competitive, but I can't because you're a fashionable little angel," he says.

I reach out and hug him.

"HR no-no," he says into my hair.

I laugh.

When Tammy comes out of her office and says, "Antonio, you ready?" I smile at him from over my cubicle wall and say, "Good luck!"

Even if he gets the job, it's okay. There are more chances, more positions will open up. Having a friend achieve what you want is like winning yourself, in a way. But I'm still going to give this interview my all today, because it's my only shot.

My phone buzzes on my desk and I look at it. It's four texts from Joy. Joy's texts always come in bursts like that. She's probably still pissed off from our interaction earlier, or she has some nonsense she wants to share about a show she's watching. I almost don't look at it. But then it buzzes again.

> Good luck today, and every day.
> I want to let you know you're not just my sister, you're my best friend.
> My only friend.
> I'll always love you, Sissy.

When we were little—and I mean *little*, knee-high and nearly wordless—Joy couldn't say my four-syllable full name and called me Sissy instead. It's something true and a part of us and yet so buried with time that it took me a moment to place its significance. It must have been ten years since we even spoke of it. As I stare at that word on my screen, it seems less a term of endearment and more an alarm ringing. Like Joy has degenerated fully into something primal and tiny, a person unformed, unable to survive on her own. I want to concentrate on my interview that is happening now in fifteen minutes, ten minutes, five . . . but that message has disturbed me. That message has triggered thoughts in me I can't repeat, gory thoughts of my sister self-destructing in our apartment.

Are you drunk? I text back, to no response.

Antonio walks out of Tammy's office.

"Betty?" Tammy says. "You ready?"

"Yeah," I say, standing. At the last minute, I pick up my

phone and put it in my pocket. Damn Joy. Distracting me at this moment when I finally have a shot at something.

Tammy's got a corner office with views of city hall and downtown Oakland, with its half-finished skyscrapers, its rainbow grid of houses, its braids of car-sparkling freeways. I sit in a chair opposite her desk. She has pictures of her children, two boys; I think of Michael and Joshua. I think of the pictures still up in their apartment, of Brandi always carrying that little boy around with her even though he's dead and gone and worse, a murderer.

"I am *so* jazzed you applied for this job," Tammy says, opening her laptop. "You know how impressed we've all been with you. We've actually never had an intern get so much copy accepted for publication, so you should be mega proud of your work here."

"Thanks," I say.

I check my phone discreetly as Tammy types something. Nothing. No response from Joy.

"Now, this job is really similar to what you've already been doing, so I'm going to skip a few of these questions that are aimed more at outside hires. Let's start with a fun one. What are your long-term goals?"

"My long-term goals," I say, trying to buy myself time to think of a proper response.

Months ago, I would have said becoming editor at a fashion magazine was my end goal. But I don't know anymore. I stare out the window, at an airplane flying by. Why hasn't Joy responded to me? The thought keeps nagging. *Sissy.* That's what snagged my attention and won't let go. Something's not right. I remember Michael's story. *Have fun!* he said as his brother headed out the door with a duffel bag full of semiautomatic weapons. And he carries that around with him, all day, every day. Smiling through the hurt and the guilt.

"You okay over there?" Tammy asks.

"Yeah," I say. "Um . . . my long-term goals are to be a fashion editor. Someone who can write eloquently about style."

I sound as stupid and distracted as I am. *Sissy.* My sister. *No, fashion. Focus. What was I saying?*

Being a sister is growing a sixth sense. I knew my sister's troubles, the dark rumblings beneath her daily state, before anyone else. I could predict sisterly earthquakes. Before she got grounded for sneaking out with Lex in high school, before she turned the cold shoulder on homework in seventh grade, before she fell into sleepwalking spells after my father left us, I felt her unease nameless as a twin might. I looked in her smile, in her twinkleless eyes, and knew without consciousness something was unquiet in her. Something was wrong. Very wrong. I know this now, miles away, from a few messages from her that appeared on my screen.

This was not a text; this was a goodbye.

"I'm really sorry," I tell Tammy, getting up. I check my phone once more: nothing. I know I can't sit here and concentrate on this copywriting job when my gut is afraid my sister is at home self-destructing. Loving people means you have a special sense when something's wrong. With love comes responsibility. I wrote about this the other night in that essay. I should know. "I have a family emergency."

"Right now?" Tammy asks, alarmed.

"Yeah. I know, terrible timing. I have to run." I get up and head to the door. "Antonio deserves this job—you should give it to him."

"We can reschedule," Tammy says, getting up and following me. "Do you need to take a sick day? Are you sure you're okay?"

"I'm not," I say, and leave her office. Antonio looks up at me, surprised, as I grab my purse and head out of the office. Downstairs, I text Joy.

Please respond. I'm worried.

I mean it, just text me one letter, something.

I'm leaving work, missing that interview.

I grab a Lyft and take it home. I chew my lip. Out the window, women in business suits wait on street corners, people blab into their phones, a man rides a scooter with a boom box on his shoulder blasting classical music. Lights change, trees sway, people drive their cars, biting their lips, too. What are their worries? Who have they lost? Who are they afraid of losing?

I get home and run up the stairs. The brand-new window shines a perfect reflection of myself with my worried expression as I grab my keys and open the front door. The living room is dark, quiet, clean. In this moment, such a combination seems ominous. My sister's things permanently hang near the door, along with a windbreaker my mother hardly ever wears.

"Joy?" I shout.

I go to her door and pound on it. There's no response. The silence settles into a panic in me and I try to open it, shouting her name. But the stupid dead bolt. The door won't budge.

"Joy, please, this isn't funny," I yell. "Joy, wake up! Wake up!"

I begin kicking the door. When that doesn't work, I go to the kitchen and get the bottom of the blender, a heavy piece of metal, and run back to Joy's door and start hurling it, over and over, toward the middle of the door. I scream as my finger gets hit and begins to bleed, but I don't stop. The door begins snowing to the floor in pieces, wood chips and white paint flying. I think, *This is madness. What if Joy left the house? What if she went to the doctor? What if she's sleeping?* But I know, inside. This is why I break a hole in her door, because I know, and I'm not willing to run the risk of ignoring myself the way Michael ignored Joshua.

Soon there is a hole in the door wide enough for me to look through. I can see my sister, slumped on the floor.

"Joy!" I scream.

I reach through the hole and slide the dead bolt, swinging the door open. I run to my sister's shape on the carpet.

She's lying there, facedown. I pull her up, lay her head on my lap. I think she's still breathing. It's hard to tell. There's some vomit on the front of her shirt. I slap her face gently with my hands.

"Hey, Joy, hey," I say.

She doesn't respond. She's pale. I think she's dying. I begin to cry.

"Joy, what did you do?" I ask. "You can't do this, you can't. Please wake up. Please, just wake up."

On her bed, I see a trio of orange pill bottles. I reach and shake them, hear no sounds.

"Joy," I sob, petting her cheek.

I call 911 and say, in one sentence, "My sister overdosed on some prescription medication and I need you to send an ambulance right now." The woman on the phone tells me to turn Joy on her side in case she vomits again while unconscious. I keep crying and talking to her as I wait.

"Joy," I tell her, through tears. "It wasn't all bad. It's been a shitty few months, but it wasn't always like this. You have your whole life ahead of you. You need to finish your album! You need to finish school! You can't just leave me and Mom like this. You can't. It's not allowed."

I hold her head and put my head down near her lips, uncertain if she's still breathing. She feels chilly. Oh my God, oh my God. I slap her face—nothing. I start frantically looking up how to do CPR on my phone, when the doorbell rings and I get up to run and let the paramedics inside.

"I can't tell if she's breathing," I yell at them as they come in. "Help her, please. Hurry!"

They ask me where she is and swarm her room. Her room looks smaller with these uniformed people inside, her body looks so much smaller there under them. They take her pulse and one of them flips Joy back on her back. They try to wake her up and she doesn't answer. They ask me how many pills she took and when, and if she was drinking, and I tell them I don't know. Sometime in the last two hours, since I left for work. I point to the empty pill bottles on her bed. The EMTs murmur to themselves, then radio in, and in this confusion, I hear terms like *unresponsive* and *respiratory depression* and all I can do is cry and shake my head and look at my sister there, my still sister, my big sister who is suddenly so small. Someone asks me to move aside so they can roll a gurney in. I watch this happen from the doorway, my hand over my mouth, my hand utterly smashing my mouth, so surreal, the thought *Joy is dead* there in my brain, a horrible three words I never thought to think before in my life.

"What's happening?" I ask.

"She's breathing," one of the EMTs says to me. "But she's unresponsive."

"Is she going to die?"

"We're getting her in an ambulance. You can ride with her."

I follow them out the door. My landlord stands downstairs with a *what the hell is going on* look on his face. First the cops came, now the EMTs came; we are clearly tenants in constant crisis.

"I don't have time to explain," I yell.

As they open the back doors of the ambulance, Joy's eyes squint open. She looks bewildered, but unafraid, a curious half smile on her face.

"Joy!" I scream, rushing to her side. "Joy!"

"Fucking where are we?" she says, slurred. "Namaste House?"

She closes her eyes. She falls asleep again. She doesn't look well, especially as they put the oxygen mask on her and give her fluids in an IV on the bumpy ambulance ride. But I hold on to that hope that she's still there. She's still herself in there. She's not lost, not yet.

FORTY-ONE

In the hospital, everything is clean, eggshell white, and the TV is stuck on local news. *LOCAL DOG PUTS CAR IN REVERSE AND DRIVES IN CIRCLES FOR AN HOUR*, says the chyron. Endless footage of police officers standing helpless as a dog drives around in circles. *Fuck you*, I think. My sister almost died, and this is the news? What a stupid world we live in. I tell my mom this and she looks up at the news in a daze.

"I'd rather have stupid news than bad news." She goes back to studying her phone, writing things down on a pad on her lap. "This article I'm reading says there's been mixed success with something called flumazenil to reverse benzodiazepine overdose. And that occasionally they do administer activated charcoal to absorb during overdoses, but I'm not sure that's an option considering the blood tests show alcohol and SSRIs in her system."

"Mom, put the phone down," I say. "Just let the doctors do their job."

"I have to help her," she says insistently. "This is my fault.

It's my job to help her and I didn't. I have to make this right."

"It's not your fault."

"Some of it is," she says, looking at me, her mascara a blur around her eyes.

I hug her and tell her she's wrong, even though I get the sentiment.

Aren't we all responsible for each other? Aren't we the only safeguards between danger and our loved ones? Isn't there something we could do that could have changed where we are, each person's action a pebble thrown in a vast pool of water that ripples outward for miles? And yet we can't live in a constant shock of regret for all we didn't do or couldn't have done, or else we become paralyzed. How do we find the balance? These questions—questions I wrote about only days ago in that essay—echo in my mind today as I hold my mother, as I wait for news of my sister at the same hospital on the same floor from the same doctors who treated her for shock only six months ago now.

In a few minutes, the doctor tells us Joy's condition has stabilized. My mother begins taking out her phone and asking about various antidotes she read about online and the doctor says, "Ms. Lavelle, kindly stop googling." My mother reluctantly returns her phone back to her purse and listens. He tells us he's given Joy an IV and she's awake now, although still sleepy and confused. He says she'll be kept overnight and then transferred to the psychiatric ward in the morning.

I utter a sigh of relief. The sun shines in my soul again—Joy is alive, awake. And I know going to a psychiatric ward isn't a dance party, but she's going to get help.

"She's going to be okay?" Mom asks. "No—no brain injury, no respiratory problems? I was reading online that some people can go into a coma."

The doctor shakes his head. "She's going to be okay."

"See, Mom?" I murmur. "Stop googling."

"She got brought in just in time," the doctor goes on. "If it had been much later, who knows? But she'll survive this. And with some treatment, hopefully, she'll be herself again."

Such a strange term, when you think about it—to "be herself" again. As if Joy hasn't been here this whole time. As if an imposter took over her body. Such terminology is false, of course. We are always ourselves, even at our most difficult. But I get the saying, because that is how it feels. That is how I miss my sister so constantly, even when she's inches away.

I still miss her today.

There she sits, in her hospital bed, in her hospital gown with her leather jacket on backward, though one sleeve only—the other naked arm has an IV in it. She looks nearly as pale as the white sheets she's on.

"Hi. I'm sorry" is all she says when we come over to her, Mom on one side of the hospital bed, me on the other. This hospital room is on the fifteenth floor, and the view stretches over Mosswood Park, lords over the boulevards twinkling with cars; the view reaches all the way back to the bay, the bridges, the green hills, the campanile on Berkeley campus. "I'm really sorry."

Her voice is hoarse and still a little slurry, like someone who had a couple too many.

"Honestly I still don't remember a lot. I just know the doctor seemed very disappointed in my behavior and worried for my well-being. So I know I did something really stupid."

"You took all your benzodiazepines, your antidepressants, and drank alcohol," Mom says.

"Yeah, and my sleeping pills. Don't forget my sleeping pills. They told me. I know. I'm sorry." Her eyes fill up, but don't spill over. "Could have been worse, though. I do know I was running low on my meds."

"Do you remember doing it?" I ask.

She thinks for a moment. "Vaguely. Pieces."

"Why, Joy?" Mom asks. "Why did you do this? You've never even talked about doing something like this before."

"Because I'm an impulsive asshole. You really have to ask?" Joy says. "Look at me. Look at what a fucking loser I am. I can't leave the house, I have no friends, I have no ambition, Betty's going to end up inheriting me like a disabled charity case when you move. Even *Lexy* won't talk to me. You know what a deadbeat you have to be for Lexy to not put up with your shit?"

Joy isn't crying. She seems angry, genuinely angry. There's something refreshing about this—she's been in this weird, self-medicated state of agoraphobic bliss for so long, I forgot what a knife of a girl she was.

"Maybe you're not what you thought you were," I say.

"Meaning?" she asks.

"Well, at least you left the house," I say. "So there's that."

Joy looks at the window. "Yeah, what a triumph."

"We're going to get you help," Mom tells her. "I've already been researching options. They have a couple substance abuse groups that meet here on weeknights. Plus an anxiety group I was thinking that might be worth checking out. And I know this is going to sound hokey, but would you be open to seeing a life coach?"

"Mom," Joy says, closing her eyes. "Do you have to be so . . . Mom all the time?"

"What? The life coach, is that what you're resisting?" Mom asks.

"I'm just tired," Joy says. "Can we not think about tomorrow anymore today? Tomorrow's exactly what I wanted to escape."

"Sure, I'll email you a few options that you can look through when you're up to it," Mom says. "I'm going to go call work and tell them I won't be coming in tomorrow. They wanted me to come in this weekend to catch up on some projects."

"You don't have to miss work for this," Joy says. "I don't want you getting in trouble."

"What are they going to do, fire me?" Mom asks. "I

already put in my notice. No, I'm staying home to be with you tomorrow, Joy."

"Always with tomorrow," Joy mutters.

Mom goes out of the hospital room, phone in hand. It's early evening. People from my office have only recently come home, are likely eating their dinners. The darkness out the window is new. So much happened in the last six hours, I feel like my hair should be gray.

"Do you remember waking up outside our house after the EMTs came?" I ask Joy.

"No. I remember nothing between taking the pills and waking up here."

"You asked if we were at Namaste House."

She snorts. "I probably thought I'd died and gone to hell."

"Seriously. Why did you ask that?"

"Who knows? I was on a lot of drugs. I still am on a lot of drugs. I feel fucking *buzzed* right now."

She sounds buzzed, too. But she's much more lucid than I expected when I came into this room. Apparently it takes a lot to suck the Joy out of Joy.

"Were you the one who found me?" she asks.

"Yeah."

"How'd that even happen?"

"You texted me. You were being oddly nice. You called me Sissy."

"Sissy," she says dreamily, staring into the air, and I know what she's seeing. She's seeing us with lighter, curlier hair, and littler bodies and unscratched souls and bright eyes and futures infinite.

"I left work and came home and knocked a hole in your door to undo your stupid dead bolt."

She gasps. "No."

"Yes."

"And what was I like?"

"You were lying on the ground with barf on your shirt, looking like you were dead." My lips trembles. "It was the worst moment of my life. It was like how it was after the I Glam shooting, that sick gross feeling that I had lost you and nothing would ever go back to the way it was."

"You think things can go back to the way they were?" she asks.

"Well, no." I put my hand on her sleeve with the leather jacket over it. "But it can definitely get better than this."

"How do you know?"

"Because it *must*," I say.

She puts her hand on my hand. I look at our hands there, her chipped black nails and her hand with the IV drip. There seems to be nothing more exquisite in the whole world than my sister right now, exactly as she is, still existing, still herself in all her fierceness and flaws, perfect in her imperfection.

"Sissy," she says, smiling and shaking her head. Her smile melts as she thinks deeply, expressionless, focused on nothing. "Thanks for saving my life, I guess."

"You guess?"

"I just have to get better, and then I know I'll mean it." She looks at me, a tear making a run for it down her cheek. Joy flicks it off like an annoyance. "I've been having a really hard time."

"I know you have," I say, hugging her. "I know."

We spend a little more time there, until Joy gets tired and goes to sleep. Mom and I take a Lyft home, and in the car, I text Michael for the first time since our crushing conversation during our walk in the majestic redwoods. What even was said? Whatever did it matter? I have a hard time remembering now, in the daze of today. But I do know one thing, and I text it to him.

Hi Michael. I want to say thank you. You played a part in saving my sister's life today.

I shouldn't be surprised that he doesn't respond, after how I treated him.

FORTY-TWO

Joy is released from the psychiatric ward in downtown Berkeley on the first day of spring, a day where the sun is evaporating puddles and the cherry trees are in bloom. Yesterday's rain seems to make for a brighter, crisper today. The parked cars take on a special shine, the grass sparkles, the world is still wet and saturated with color. When I come to meet her, she's got her sunglasses and leather jacket on. She's sitting on the front steps of the building of the psychiatric hospital, a plain white building with rows of identical windows.

"Isn't it a gorgeous day?" I ask.

"I hate the sun," she says.

"Right back to your old goth self."

"There's a reason I was prone to agoraphobia."

"Intense trauma?"

"Well, yes. But also I'm part vampire."

We walk up to Shattuck and pass a fabric store, an acupuncture clinic. There are tents set up across the street, where homeless people have created a village. Joy's gaze lingers on it while we wait for the light to change.

"I have to figure out what to do with my life," she says.

"Have you thought about it?"

She has been in there three weeks, weaning off her anti-anxiety meds and onto a new antidepressant and attending substance abuse meetings. Every time I went to visit her, I was shocked by how happy she seemed in there, how well she was taking to the treatments. She played with the therapy dogs, participated in knitting therapy, and meditated every morning, proudly telling people her dad is a guru. She was excited to join a local twelve-step program for her drinking and abuse of prescription medication. But she didn't talk about her future yet, and I didn't ask her about it. Mom asked her enough times for the both of us, even creating a goals journal for Joy that she promptly filled with lyrics to metal songs about poisonous snake-women and dragonslayers.

"A bit," she says. "Thinking I'll go back to school next fall. Study psychology, maybe. You've heard this story before, right? Girl goes nuts, girl decides she'd make a great psychologist. It's the American dream, really."

"Truly."

"In the meantime, I don't know, maybe I'll see if Lexy will let me roadie for Electric Wheelchair."

"That sounds like a terrible idea."

"But I'd like to travel or something, and at least that

would be free. And then you don't have to worry about finding a place for both of us."

We've got until May first to move out. Mom's flying to DC at the end of March, in just two weeks. Everything's changing too fast.

"Joy, you don't have to feel like you're a burden. You're not."

"I know. But it's hard to explain. I locked myself up for so long, now the lion's out of the zoo and I'm hungry to get the fuck out of here."

There are so many reasons why I don't want her roadie-ing (is that even a word?) for Lex. One, he's a jerk. Two, he parties constantly and Joy will fall right back into her bad habits. Three, how is that progress? Moving amps and selling T-shirts for your ex's band? But I know how Joy is. I've got to be gentle with my suggestions or else she'll reject them entirely.

I don't know what's going to happen to me and have started to panic myself. Retrofit gave Antonio the job, which he definitely deserved, but he told me he heard they might be opening up another copywriting position soon, so I've been holding on to hope that I might get another shot at that one.

Our apartment is in disarray. Chunks of it are missing, ghostly dust-free squares where chairs once sat or pictures once hung; my mother's entire room is nothing but a bed now. She's packed up her whole life and sent it to DC in boxes. She offered to stay so many times now, but Joy and I refuse to entertain the idea. The closer to her exit date we get, the more panicked checklists and emails with resources we get. Mom starts sending me job listings. She mocks up résumés for us. On the night before she flies to DC to move into her new apartment, a studio in a brick building where you can apparently see the Capitol Building from her balcony, she gives us her engagement ring and tells us to pawn it if we need to.

"Mom, we are not selling your engagement ring," Joy says. "Times are not that desperate."

"Sell it," Mom says. "It means nothing to me."

"This is weird, Mom," I agree, and give the jewelry box back to my mother.

We're sitting at a Creole restaurant a few blocks from our apartment, a place with New Orleans flair, mannequin heads with Mardi Gras beads, so much kitschy framed art hung on a glossy orange wall. It's a place we've eaten so many times, and I have to constantly stop myself from feeling a deep loss about my mother's relocation. I can't let on how scared I am of her going and of me confronting adulthood, because otherwise she'll stay. And my mother is so alive right now, as she shows us pictures of her new place, of her new office, of DC covered in snow, of monuments and museums and everything she's so excited to explore. She seems younger than I've ever known her, nervous, eyes bright with what's to come.

"Fine," Mom says. "I'll hold on to it. And if you need the money, you call me, and I'll sell it and wire it to you."

We eat quietly. What a miracle this moment is, how long

it's been since the three of us have gone out to eat in public together. I cherish it, trying to take a picture in my mind.

"I'm proud of how far you've come, Joy," I tell her.

"Don't be so fucking condescending," Joy says.

"Joy," Mom says, annoyed. "Do you have to be so *mean*?"

I smile. "It's good to have you back," I tell my sister.

"Gross, stop it."

"Oh!" Mom says, dropping her fork. "I forgot to tell you both—that private detective I hired? He finally found Al Smith."

"Are you still getting letters from that sick dude?" Joy asks.

"I'm not, actually. I got an email a month ago, it barely made sense. And now that the detective tracked him down, I might know why." Mom wipes her mouth with a napkin. "Al Smith is ninety-four years old and he lives in a nursing home in Nevada."

"The guy threatening you is . . . ninety-four years old?" I ask.

Joy makes a *pffft* sound.

"Yeah," Mom says. "So I don't think you have to worry about him."

"*That* is how he's spending his retirement?" I ask. "Sending threatening letters to activists?"

"Fox News is a helluva drug," Mom says. She reaches out and squeezes my hand. "That warms my heart that you called me an activist."

"Well, it's what you are," I say, surprised by how touched she seems. Is this really the first time I've used the word?

On our way out, Mom goes and asks the woman in the large sweater with a cat's face something while Joy and I wait in the doorway.

"They're hiring!" Mom says loudly, walking toward us. Everyone in the restaurant turns around, but she doesn't even notice. "You can bring your résumés in, she says!"

"Actually, I'll never be coming here again," Joy says to me. "Thanks, Mom."

We take a long walk home. We talk about all the businesses that have sprung up in the neighborhood—a yoga place with wide windows, a new soul food restaurant, a closet-sized coffee shop—and all the places that have been here since we moved into this neighborhood after my dad left. The corner store with a tattered awning, the laundromat with rows of dryers spinning rainbow apparel, the antique store with its fainting couches and Tiffany-style lamps. We pass our elementary school and Mom stands outside the chain-link fence, looking at it like she's watching a movie in her head. We're all watching movies in our heads, it seems, all the time. We're in two places at once—the past and the present. Some of us are even in the future. Our ability to live in simultaneous realities all at once is what makes us human.

I wake up the next week to a house more than half-empty, motherless, feeling a world of quiet pain and fear of what's to come. That fear propels me out into the world with a folder full of résumés. I don't drop one off at the Creole restaurant, but I drop it off at the soul food place and the closet-sized coffee shop, I drop it off at the grocery store, I go up to Telegraph Avenue and drop it off at the weed club and the drugstore and the tattoo shop and the vintage store and the sock shop and the bookstore and then stand, with only a few left, looking up at Amoeba Records, my heart beating wildly. I pass the man in the knitted hat selling knitted hats, and the man burning incense selling incense, push open the glass doors, go inside.

It's colorful in here, posters on every inch of the store, media stacked and shelved everywhere, stickers covering the surface of the front counter. Yet all I notice in this sea of visual and aural noise is the profile of the tall brown-haired guy standing behind one of the cash registers. He doesn't notice me as I walk up to the counter, at least not at first. He's staring into the air, no smile on his face, so serious-looking. His eyes are so wide when they're not crinkled up with cheer. He turns and notices me and flinches, he physically *flinches* at the sight of me, and that hurts, even though I deserve it; especially because I deserve it.

"Hi," I say.

"Wow," he says after a moment. "Hi."

"I'm sorry," I say.

"Are you?" he asks flatly.

"Yes," I say, my eyes filling with tears. I'm ashamed of my emotion and I stare at my oxford shoes for a moment to collect myself.

"Me too," he says when I look up again.

"Really?"

"Yeah. But when you're me, sorry is basically a constant state of being. A chronic illness."

"It shouldn't be."

"What are you doing here?" he asks.

"I'm looking for a job," I say, showing him my stack of resumes. "You hiring?"

"I can give your résumé to Max," he says. "Why would you want a shitty job like this? Don't you want to work in fashion?"

"My mom's moving to DC and I need to get a job and an apartment in a month. Desperate times."

"Your mom's moving?" he asks. "What about your sister?"

"I don't even know. Long story. How's your mom?"

"Even longer story. Sorry, I have to help this person," he says, gesturing to a woman waiting with a stack of records.

"Sure," I say. "I was just stopping by to say hi. Hope you have a good one."

I turn to go, and he yells, "Elizabeth!" so I turn back again.

"You want to stick around for . . ." He looks at his phone. "Twenty minutes? I'm off then."

"Sure," I say, smiling, feeling like he just handed me the world.

He smiles back that enormous, glowing grin.

In that moment, it hits me how much I missed him.

FORTY-THREE

It turns out that Michael never even got my text. His phone got shut off for a week because his mother didn't pay the bill; she went on what he describes as a "bender to end all benders" and ended up hospitalized for dehydration due to drinking nothing but liquor for days, then was admitted for substance abuse treatment. We compare notes and are astounded that she was in the same facility Joy was in, at the same time.

"You and I are star-crossed in the absolutely most twisted ways," Michael says.

"What the actual hell?" I ask.

"Not the figurative hell?"

"No. The *actual* hell."

I text Joy to ask. Oh yeah, Brandi, lady with the spiky hair and awesome makeup? Total badass, she responds. I played ping-pong with her.

Our hot cocoas billow steam up in the air like smoke. We sit on a bench in Sproul Plaza at UC Berkeley, blocks away from Amoeba. Sproul Plaza was a place where, a lifetime ago, the famous Free Speech Movement happened—a massive student protest in the 1960s my mom has made us go to many boring museum exhibits for in the past. I've never cared before, but tonight I sit here on the quiet, streetlamp-lit campus with its strange trees opening up to the moon like gnarled hands and realize that this peace we have now, it was something that couldn't exist without the fights and the movements before us. We owe the quiet we enjoy to strangers with loud voices.

Anyway, I show him the text I sent, and I explain the story. I tell Michael that if he and I hadn't had that conversation, if Michael hadn't told me about what guilt he carried for letting Joshua go against his own gut feeling, then I never would have followed mine. Joy would be dead.

"If Josh hadn't shot up I Glam, your sister probably never would have tried to kill herself in the first place," he says. "So in a way, I was responsible for her even being in that terrible situation to begin with."

"Michael, stop. You have to *stop*," I say. "Stop carrying this around with you. Enough. You're a good person. The best person I know. You have to find a way to forgive yourself, to see that life can go on despite what happened and what you didn't do."

"When I'm with you," he says, looking at me, "I feel that way. You're . . . the silver lining."

"Same," I say softly.

The night is cold, too cold for a California April. But it gives me a reason to sit closer to him.

FORTY-FOUR

It's common knowledge that life can change in a matter of moments—a shooting, a break-in, a nervous breakdown, a political revolution. But it isn't only tragedies and tumult that strike suddenly. Great joy and fortune can explode like blossoms in springtime. In a single day, I get two pieces of good news that fill me with relief, and then shock. First, I am straight-up offered another copywriter position that opened up, based on my performance at Retrofit. Hallelujah! I don't even have to interview for it. And before I even pick my jaw up off the floor, I get an email saying I won the young writers essay contest. My essay has been published online. I go home from my workday to this news, notifications all over the place, tagged on social media by various strangers, congratulations from all sorts of people. Zoe sends me an all-caps message saying YOU ARE AMAZING JUST LIKE YOUR MAMA!!!! And Adrian sends me a message saying Dang, that was deep. There's a voicemail from my mother, weeping that she's so proud of me, that the essay was so profound. I'm flooded with a mix of disbelief and horror.

Holy shit, I think. I don't even remember what I wrote at this point! It feels like so long ago now. I just wrote it and sent it, never looked back. Now I'm too terrified to read the link everyone is passing around, afraid I'll be embarrassed of my pontification.

Thanks! I text, I comment.

Even my father calls to try to tell me how proud he is of me. My father. He read my essay. My mother sent it to him. I cannot believe my mother reached out to my father for anything less than a complete emergency, and I tell this to my sister, who is in her room at seven p.m., lying in bed.

"Good for you," she says, muffled by the blanket mountain she's buried in. "I'm happy for you."

I come sit next to her.

"What?" she asks.

I begin gently, although the alarm in me is ringing loudly. I realize that I haven't seen my sister leave the house in several days, maybe even since my mom was still here a week ago. I've been so distracted by trying to find a job, researching places we might be able to live, catching up with Michael again. "Have you just been lying in bed all day?"

"I'm not going to try to kill myself, okay?"

"Comforting. But also, are you going to start living at some point?"

"I don't know," she says, closing her eyes.

I sniff the air. Is that alcohol? No, she wouldn't. She just started a twelve-step program. I peek under her bed and am stunned to pull out a half-drunk bottle of whiskey.

"What the fuck, Joy?" I ask.

"Get out of my room, snoop," she says, sitting up and yelling. "You're not my mom!"

"Oh my God," I say. "After everything? Really?"

She pulls the bottle out of my hand and I consider wrestling her to the floor for it, but don't. Instead, I stand up and look down at the sight of her, in her pajamas, clutching the bottle. I thought everything was going to be okay for her after how well she seemed after her hospitalization, but it occurs to me there is no quick fix here. And that sucks the wind out of me.

I go to my room and sit for a moment, staring at the blank wall where once there were vintage pictures of models. Behind that wall, my sister is probably drinking that bottle. And I don't have the power to stop her. Yes, you can throw pebbles into waters and watch them ripple, but I suppose those waters have to be still. Throw a pebble in a raging river and, well, it does shit. I feel like my essay's thesis, the thing that got me so many congratulations, is nonsense. We do have responsibility over people we love, but sometimes that responsibility isn't enough. The personal is political, and everything we do and don't do matters and plays into the bigger picture, but people are also deeply flawed, hurt things, and mostly lacking in self-awareness. I feel so hopeless, I could cry.

Then I get an idea.

The essay contest came with a cash prize of an unbelievable

thousand dollars, a monetary miracle, which they sent me via PayPal. Of course, I had planned on putting it aside for future rent money, since I will be homeless in three weeks if I don't figure something out. But instead, I go online and I look up flights to Barcelona. I pick the cheapest day available and buy a one-way ticket in Joy's name. After I shower, eat, and check on Joy, who is passed out in her bed but still breathing just fine, I pour her whiskey down the drain and call Namaste House. Sequoia answers and tells me my father is currently at a juice bar doing his morning cleanse.

"Sequoia, I need you to give my dad a message," I tell her. "My sister, Joy, is going to be arriving at Namaste House in four days. She needs to be taken care of, okay? My dad needs to take care of her. She needs . . . cleansing, and yoga and meditation and all that sh—*stuff*. He said we could visit whenever."

"Darling, of course," Sequoia says. "Of course, I'll speak this to your father."

I hang up having no idea if Sequoia understood or wrote down a word I said. But then the next morning, my dad calls, ecstatic at the news. He's crying. He's actually crying when I tell him Joy will be coming. He wishes I were coming too, but I explain this new position is starting and I only had enough for one ticket and I will come someday, I swear. I go tell Joy, who is still in her bed under her mountain of blankets, and she, too, cries, though not at all ecstatically.

"What the fuck, you asshole?" Joy asks. "You're sending

me to Namaste House? I fall off the wagon for one goddamn night, and I'm banished to hippie hell?"

"You wanted to travel," I remind her.

"I hate you," she says, through tears. "I'm not going."

Her words sting bad, though I've weathered hundreds of *I hate you*s in childhood. I was trying to do the right thing. I spent my prize money on a nonrefundable ticket as a last-ditch effort to get my sister on the right track. What an utter waste and an impulsive, dumb idea on my part.

My dad calls her soon after that, though, and after a few hours, Joy comes into my room, where I'm going through my clothes to give things away. Her face is puffy, her eyes pink.

"Fine," she says. "I'll go. Sorry I said I hate you."

"You're going?" I ask, shocked.

"I talked to Daddy and he was so excited . . . who knows, maybe it'll be good for me. I don't know what I'm doing."

"I'm so glad. I mean, glad that you're going."

"He sent me some pictures of the grounds. They were pretty. I don't know. He said they're right near some crazy castles and cathedrals too."

"You're going to have a great time," I say. "And you can always come home."

"Yeah, you'll spring for a return ticket if I need it, huh? With all that dough you're making?"

"There's always Mom's engagement ring," I remind her.

"True." She sniffs. "You're going through your stuff? You have a place?"

"My friend said I could stay with him until I find one."

"Oh, your 'friend.'"

"He really is my friend. He's my best friend."

"Lexy was my best friend."

"No, he wasn't."

"You're right; you're my best friend," she says, and comes over and hugs me and cries on my shoulder. I'm not used to Joy's tears, or her sweet words. It takes me a moment to hug her back and be certain she's not being sarcastic or something.

"Sisters are more than best friends," I tell her. "Best friends can leave or drift away or break up with you or go to college, but a sister can't ever stop being a sister."

"You should write Hallmark cards," she says, pulling back and wiping her eyes. "Ever thought of that?"

"Way to wreck the moment," I tell her.

"It's my way," she says, getting up. "Well, shit, I guess I'd better go pack up my life and figure out what the hell to do with all my furniture."

Days later, I ride the BART train with Joy to San Francisco International Airport and hug her goodbye on the station platform, watching her walk away with her suitcase covered in skull duct tape and not look back. On the way home, even though the train is filled, and awash with artificial light, I can't help but feel my loneliness. My ties are gone now. My mother, my sister, my father all thousands of miles away; my best friend, my ex are states removed and nothing but words on a screen that periodically pass through my life. But as I pass through the tunnel, going underground, beneath the bay, surrounded by mud and rocketing through the earth back to Oakland like a miracle, it hits me, I am also free now in a way I have never been free before; these strangers who surround me, that glitz and grit of lights and streets out the window, this is *my* city now.

This is my life, beginning.

FORTY-FIVE

Two days into my copywriting job at Retrofit, I get an email from my mom introducing me to a friend she knows through MAGS who runs a nonprofit who read my essay and wants to talk to me about a job. I write the woman, Bhavani, and she asks me to come into their office in Oakland, a block from Retrofit. I do during a long lunch break. This office is in a similar deco building, but a completely different atmosphere; there are classrooms set up with high school students dissecting hip-hop lyrics and having passionate discussions about news articles. It's an afterschool writing program for underprivileged youth.

I sit on Bhavani's yellow couch next to a potted palm in her private office. We talk about politics, and about my essay in particular, and about what happened at I Glam. She tells me her favorite part of my essay was about how everyone focuses on different angles—some on gun safety, some on misogyny, some on social media and online radicalization, some on racism, some on mental illness. How we act like

323

they're all competing, but they're not, and we have to address all of them holistically. But more so, we have to try to understand the *person*, and to understand the person, we have to understand the people closest to us—not just the ones who are shooting up shopping malls.

Thank you, I say, not telling her I still haven't reread my essay.

And then, in one sentence, she offers me a job as a communications assistant at her organization. I try to tell her I'm not qualified, and she refuses to hear it. It's entry level. She knows my mother. I have extensive writing experience through Retrofit.

It only takes the uttering of a single word to change the trajectory of life completely.

"Yes," I tell her.

That night, I return to my essay that changed everything, and finally, I am brave enough to reread my own words:

The world changes us, yes, it begins, but more importantly, the opposite is true.

FORTY-SIX

I crash on Michael's couch for a few days while his mother transitions to her new halfway house. He cooks for me. He lets me pick which channels to watch on TV. He introduces me to a coworker named Abby with a room available in Berkeley, near campus. She lives in another Victorian split into units, a Black Lives Matter sign in the window, garden beds on the front lawn. Abby lets us into a living room busy with bicycles, boxes of records, hanging plants.

"This is my friend Elizabeth, the activist I was telling you about," Michael says as I shake her hand.

"Activist"? Since when? What makes me an activist? My new job? What I wrote? I could correct him, but instead I smile and shake Abby's hand. She's very pretty, dark eyebrows, purple hair, a beaming moon face.

"I've heard a lot about you," she says. "Michael won't shut up about how rad you are."

Michael raises his eyebrows. "True story."

She shows me the room in the back—small, with scuffed wood floors, but there's a window with a lemon tree outside it. It's so close, I could open the window and pick a piece of fruit. I can imagine myself here: where my bed would go, new magazine pictures on the walls.

"I like it," I say.

"Cool. Can you move in next week?" Abby asks me.

"Yes," I tell her.

I Venmo her the deposit. And like that, with the click of a button, I have a home.

Outside, on the sidewalk, I squeal with celebratory excitement. My own place. Mine! I reach up and hug Michael so hard, he almost falls. He grins wide and gazes down at me. I love the way his curls are growing out around his face. I love his sideburns and the inexplicable shade of his stare. I hold on to him like I never want to let him go, and in that moment, I realize I don't have to. Gently, he puts his arms around me too. The ash trees whisper with wind behind us. We're still for a moment, just taking each other in at this short distance, mere inches away.

"When I look at you, Betty," he says, "I forget every regret I ever had."

I tilt my head, close my eyes, and follow the magnet of my heart. When we kiss—when his warm lips finally meet mine and become one everlasting gorgeous song, when the release of pent-up desire floods my nerves—it seems the universe is only wide enough for the two of us. Everything else disappears. There is no such thing as danger, as disaster. I am sheltered. I am secure.

For what is love, anyway, if not the beautiful illusion of safety?

ACKNOWLEDGMENTS

It's misleading to only have my name credited on the cover of this book, because it wouldn't exist if it weren't for the following people:

Claire Anderson-Wheeler, the agent with infinite patience, kindness, and bright ideas.

Kristen Pettit, the superstar editor who elevates my work with her brilliance and insight.

Clare Vaughn, Laura Harshberger, Marinda Valenti, and all the other magicians at HarperTeen who transformed a bunch of words in a document into a cohesive story in a beautiful book.

Cover designers Corina Lupp and Alison Klapthor, and artist Ricky Linn, for creating the absolutely stunning cover.

All the librarians, booksellers, and reviewers whose passion for literature makes this all worthwhile.

My friends, who have always supported me and my writing.

My family, quite simply my favorite human beings on this planet.

Jamie, Roxie, and Zora: my heart.

And you, dear reader.